"If you have no interest in becoming a countess, why have you asked me to consider marrying you?"

He was standing closer to her now than he'd done since they'd both been children. Close enough for her to see those blue flecks in his eyes, which prevented them from looking as though they were chiseled from ice.

This close, she'd swear she could see a spark of interest, rather than cold indifference. This close, she could even, almost, imagine she could feel warmth emanating from his body.

Author Note

Some of you will already have met the Earl of Ashenden in my earlier books—in the library of his club, where he was having a delightful conversation with Mr. Morgan about the insect life found in India. And recall how that conversation was so rudely interrupted by Lord Havelock, bursting in and demanding help finding a bride in a hurry.

The Earl of Ashenden, being a man of science, suggested they draw up a list of what qualities said bride needed to have, and was very firm about his own intention to, one day, select a wife primarily for her intelligence.

"I would hate to think," he'd said, giving Havelock a particularly penetrating look, "that I had curtailed my own freedom only to produce a brood of idiots."

Naturally, I could not allow him to settle for such a wife. Instead, I decided to give him a heroine who would turn his ordered existence upside down!

If, after reading his story as told within these pages, you would like to know why Lord Chepstow was trying to brush off an imaginary stain when recounting his proposal to Honeysuckle, you can read about it in "Governess to Christmas Bride," which appears in the anthology *Gift-Wrapped Governess*.

And if you want to discover what measures Lord Havelock took to ensure Mary married him, you can read about their courtship and the early days of their marriage in *Lord Havelock's List*.

ANNIE BURROWS

The Debutante's Daring Proposal

Recycling programs
for this product may
not exist in your area.

ISBN-13: 978-0-373-29932-4

The Debutante's Daring Proposal

Copyright © 2017 by Annie Burrows

Printed in U.S.A.

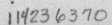
www.Harlequin.com

114236370

Annie Burrows has been writing Regency romances for Harlequin since 2007. Her books have charmed readers worldwide, having been translated into nineteen different languages, and some have gone on to win the coveted Reviewers' Choice award from CataRomance. For more information, or to contact the author, please visit annie-burrows.co.uk, or you can find her on Facebook at Facebook.com/annieburrowsuk.

Books by Annie Burrows

Harlequin Historical Romance

Regency Bachelors

Gift-Wrapped Governess
"Governess to Christmas Bride"
Lord Havelock's List
The Debutante's Daring Proposal

Brides of Waterloo

A Mistress for Major Bartlett

Stand-Alone Novels

Captain Corcoran's Hoyden Bride
An Escapade and an Engagement
Never Trust a Rake
Reforming the Viscount
Portrait of a Scandal
The Captain's Christmas Bride
In Bed with the Duke
Once Upon a Regency Christmas
"Cinderella's Perfect Christmas"

Harlequin Historical *Undone!* ebooks

Notorious Lord, Compromised Miss
His Wicked Christmas Wager

Visit the Author Profile page
at Harlequin.com for more titles.

"...to the one I love..."

Chapter One

Meet me at our place.
G.

The Earl of Ashenden crumpled the note in his long slender fingers, his nostrils flaring with distaste.

Meet me at our place, indeed.

No signature. No polite salutation. After all these years of silence, just five words and her initial.

She hadn't even bothered to state a time. Not that there was any need. If they were to meet, it would be when they'd always met, at first light, before anyone else was about.

If they were to meet? Good God, the woman had only to crook her finger and he was actually contemplating trotting along to see what it was she wanted.

He flung the note into the fire, braced his arm on the mantel and watched with satisfaction as the flames devoured her summons.

Did she really think he'd respond to a missive like that? After she'd turned her back on him when he'd needed her the most? Tossed aside their friendship without a second thought? And then greeted his return to

England with an indifference that hadn't wavered in all the years since?

And yet...

He braced one booted foot on the fender stool. If he didn't go, he'd always wonder what could have made her break through that wall of silence and reach out to him.

Which was probably why her note had been so brief. He ground his teeth. She knew him too well. Knew that its cryptic nature would rouse his curiosity to such a pitch that he'd find it hard to rest until he'd discovered exactly what lay behind it.

He wouldn't put it past her to presume that he'd feel guilty, too, if he ignored her note. Because she'd remember the promise he'd made: if ever she needed help, he would give it. Not that she'd actually stated she was in need of help. No, she'd been too cunning for that. She'd merely teased him with five words that could imply anything.

Edmund bent to take the poker from the stand and slashed it through the charred sheet of paper, scattering its ashes across the hot coals until there were no visible remnants.

But it didn't make him feel any better. On the contrary, it only reminded him that ash was all that was left of a friendship that had burned so brightly for him, he'd believed he'd be able to warm himself at it his whole life.

He stared into the flames, remembering. How she used to pull faces at him over the top of the pew, from her side of church, once the dullness of the sermon had put most of the adults in the congregation to sleep. How she'd walked three paces behind his mother, mimicking the way she stalked down the aisle with her nose in the air.

How she'd rubbed her ear the day Blundell had clouted her for trespassing on to the Ashenden estate, but refused to leave until she'd found her dog, which had wriggled through a boundary hedge in pursuit of a rabbit. How she'd then charmed the gruff gamekeeper into letting her join in his fishing lesson. And subsequently returned the next day. And the one after. How she'd dared him to climb every tree on the estate. Demanded he teach her to fence and box and—

A reluctant smile tugged at his lips as he recalled her fury at the way his gangly arms always kept him out of reach of her fists. The wild way she'd swing at him after every time he got in a blow—until she'd learned to keep up her guard. After that, though she'd *still* never been able to land a punch on him, he'd not been able to break through her defence.

His smile faded. He turned his back on the fire. The uncomfortable truth was that the only good memories he had, from his childhood, centred on Georgiana. She hadn't just been his best friend. She'd been his only friend. His mother hadn't wanted him mixing with children from the village. Nor had she thought him strong enough to send away to school. And his father hadn't cared enough to intervene. He very rarely visited Fontenay Court and when he did, he'd seldom done more than cast a jaded eye over his only surviving child, and perhaps taken a pinch of snuff, before 'toddling off' back to London, or the races, or whatever house party would provide him with the most 'sport'.

Edmund went to the desk, sat down and laced his fingers together on the blotter as his memories carried him back to the winter he'd almost died. Or so his mother had always maintained. She'd kept him not only indoors, but in bed for what had felt like months on end.

Even when spring sunshine had started to lengthen the days, he hadn't been permitted out of that room. She'd come to inspect him every morning, wrung her hands and then, like as not, launched into one of her diatribes against his father.

'You'd think he'd care that his heir is wasting away—but, no! Too lazy even to bother to reply to any of my letters, let alone actually tear himself away from his latest lover.'

A shuddering breath escaped him. His father hadn't cared enough to visit him, even when his mother had written to inform him his only son and heir was at death's door. But he couldn't say that his mother's obsession with keeping him alive at all costs stemmed from maternal love. She just couldn't bear the thought of having to *do her duty* by a man she'd come to heartily detest. She'd blurted out that little gem whilst in the throes of yet another rant about his father's failings, apparently forgetting that her audience was a product of doing that very distasteful duty.

Nobody had cared about him, not really *him*, rather what he represented.

Except Georgiana.

She'd been the only one to care enough to flout his mother's embargo on visitors. And she'd done it by climbing up the drainpipe at the corner of the house and inching along the crumbling brickwork to his window.

The very last time she'd managed to get in to see him, she'd done it with half-a-dozen jam jars strung round her neck. Jars that had been full of the butterflies she'd spent all day collecting. For him.

'I wanted to bring you something to cheer you up,' she'd said with that impish grin of hers as he'd hauled her in over the windowsill. 'It's such a lovely day and it must be rotten being stuck indoors when all the world's bursting into life out there.'

She had certainly been bursting with life. There had been bits of twigs and moss caught in the cap of black curls that crowned her head. Her nose had been sunburnt, her arms and legs scratched from briars and mottled where nettles had stung her.

'I know how interested you are in all sorts of bugs,' she said, her dark eyes turning serious. 'So I thought of bringing you some beetles to add to your collection. Only then I thought I'd be bound to bring the wrong ones. Ones you'd already got, like as not. But then I thought these would be better. And anyway, they're more cheerful, aren't they?' And then she'd grabbed his hand and drawn him over to his bed.

That was probably the moment he'd fallen in love with her, he reflected gloomily. Because he'd been convinced she was the only person in the world who not only cared about him, but really understood him, too.

'Close the bed hangings,' she'd said as she clambered up and unhooked the jam-jar strings from her neck. And he'd obeyed her command, meek as a lamb. He'd have done anything she asked of him, back then. Anything.

'I'm going to perform an experiment,' she'd said. And then tilted her head to one side, the way she did that put him in mind of a cheeky little robin. 'No, actually, it isn't an experiment. You're the one who does experiments. And anyway, I'm not trying to prove anything. It's…more of a sort of show for you.' And then she'd shaken out the jars. And the gloom of his closed-up bed was transformed into something utterly magical as dozens and dozens of butterflies had fluttered up into the air, their wings flashing copper, and blue and white and orange.

He sighed and bowed his head against the memories. He owed it to that girl to see what she wanted of him. Even though she no longer existed except in his memory. Even though he heartily disliked the woman she'd become, that didn't detract from the fact that he'd made her a promise. That very day. While she'd still held his heart in her rather grubby little fist.

'If you ever need anything, Georgie,' he'd vowed from the depths of his sixteen-year-old heart, 'you know you have only to ask, don't you? Oh, I know there isn't much I can do for you now, but one day I'll be the Earl of Ashenden and then I'll be powerful. And whatever you need, I'll be able to get it for you.'

She'd laughed. Making his cheeks heat, though at least it had been too gloomy within the tent of his bed for her to notice.

'Just be my friend, Edmund, that's all I need.'

'I will, I will…' he'd breathed. 'Always.'

He stood up abruptly and, grim-faced, strode to the door.

He was the Earl of Ashenden now, he reminded himself. Going to their meeting place, in response to her request, did not mean he'd become a weak and green youth again, an idiot who'd do anything in return for one of her sunny smiles. He'd long since grown immune to women's wiles. So he had nothing to fear from going to meet her. On the contrary. She was the one who needed to beware. If she wanted him to help her, she was going to have to answer a few questions first.

He paused, his hand on the doorknob. Frowned. Actually, interrogating her over something that had taken place ten years earlier would be an admission that he cared. That he still hurt.

And he didn't.

He was over her.

Completely.

He was only going to meet her because of the sweet memories he cherished of the girl she'd once been. And because of the vow he'd made.

It was a matter of honour. She was finally calling in the debt he owed her and, once he'd done whatever it was she was about to ask of him, they'd be quits.

And he'd be free of her.

Where was he? Georgiana paced along the bank of the trout stream, the train of her salmon-pink velvet riding habit looped over one arm, swishing at the dried-up reeds with her riding crop in frustration. Four days since she'd smuggled her note into the pile of his letters waiting for collection from the receiving office in Bartlesham. And every day since, she'd been here, at their stream, at first light.

He *must* have read it by now.

Which meant she had her answer. He wasn't coming.

She didn't know why she'd ever thought he might. She was such an idiot. When was she ever going to accept that Stepmama was right? Men like the Earl of Ashenden didn't make friends with people of her class. Let alone women of her class. He'd tolerated her when he'd been a boy, that was all, because he hadn't had any other playmates.

She sank down on to the log, their log, where they'd spent so many hours fishing and talking. At least, he'd fished, she reflected glumly, and she'd talked. She'd chattered, actually, like a little magpie while he'd listened, or pretended to listen, with his eyes fixed firmly on the fishing line. She leaned her chin on her fist, gazing unseeingly at the gravel bed beneath the rippling water that made this part of the stream such a good spot for trout. Had he been bored by her mindless chatter? Irritated? She hadn't thought so, but then it was so hard to know what he'd been thinking. Because he'd never said.

Except that last day they'd had together, when he'd promised her that when they grew up, and he became the Earl, he'd still be her friend.

She lifted her head to look at the pollarded willows on the opposite bank, to fix them in her memory, since it was becoming clear that memories were all she was going to have to sustain her in future. Later in the year those trees would form a thick screen that would hide this spot from the path that wound round the lake into which this stream fed. There would be a thick carpet of bluebells beneath them and wild irises cheekily pushing up their heads amidst the reeds which were, today, dry and dead, and flattened in places by recent spates of floodwater.

Like her last hope.

She sighed. It wasn't worth waiting for the stable clock to chime the hour, as she'd done every other morning. Or hang on until the last note had faded to nothing, the way she'd clung to a desperate shred of hope that she could trust him, in spite of all evidence to the contrary. He wasn't coming. She was going to have to accept defeat. After all, he'd only been a boy when he'd promised he'd always be her friend. And in the years since he'd clearly thought better of it.

And why shouldn't he have done so? When her own family found her such a disappointment? If they didn't think she was good enough as she was, and were constantly urging her to change, why should he?

So that was that. She'd have to stop clinging to ridiculous dreams that there might still be one person in the world who'd keep faith with her. Hadn't she learned by now that the only thing she could count on was that she couldn't count on *any*one?

She was just getting to her feet when she heard the sound of a dog barking. And in spite of telling herself it still didn't mean Edmund was on his way, she spun round to face the path along which he'd come, if it was him, so swiftly that she almost lost her balance.

She flailed her arms to try to avoid slipping into the water, as her left foot sank deep into the mud on the bank. She muttered a string of extremely unlady-like words as she struggled to extricate her foot from the sucking grip without losing her boot in the process. How typical that having taken such pains with her appearance, whoever it was approaching was about to discover her either standing on one leg with her other, bare foot in the air and her boot in the mud, or more likely flat on her back in the reed bed.

And if it was Edmund, who never had a hair out of place, she'd…she'd…probably throw the muddy boot at him. At least he wouldn't forget her again as easily as he'd done the last time.

But then the boot came free from the mud, with a slow sucking plop, just as the dog burst over the embankment. It came pelting down the slope and circled her ankles, the whole rear end of its body wriggling in greeting.

'Lion?' She bent to stroke the elderly spaniel's ears. If it truly was Lion, then Edmund couldn't be far behind. She straightened up just as a vision of sartorial elegance came sauntering leisurely along the path from the lakeside. His boots shone in the pale spring sunshine, his coat fluttered out behind him as he walked, giving tantalising glimpses of a beautifully cut jacket and snowy white neckcloth. His light brown hair was cropped so severely that not a single lock could venture out from beneath the brim of his hat.

But his eyes were hidden by the way light reflected off the lenses of his spectacles. He'd probably worn them to create a physical barrier between them. As if she needed to be reminded of the immense gulf that separated them nowadays. Because he couldn't possibly need to wear them for any other reason, not when he was walking about his own estate.

Not unless his eyesight had deteriorated an awful lot since they'd last been on speaking terms.

The Earl of Ashenden came to a standstill and swept her with one of those cold, imperious looks designed to put the lower orders in their place. A look designed to impel her to drop a curtsy and beg his pardon, and go back to where she belonged. A look that made her acutely aware of her windswept hair, her mud-caked boot and the fact that her gloves had worn so thin in parts they were almost in holes.

A look that made her wish she really was holding a muddy boot in one of her hands, so that she could throw it at him and knock that horrid, supercilious, unfeeling, inhuman look off his face. She was just picturing a boot-shaped stain splattering the front of his expensively tailored coat when Lion wheezed and flopped down at her feet.

'I cannot believe you made poor old Lion walk all the way up here,' she said, since she didn't have any other missile to hand.

'I did not,' he replied. 'We came in the carriage as far as the alder copse.'

'You came in a carriage?' Now it was her turn to look at him with scorn. What kind of man took a carriage out to drive a mere mile, especially when he had a stable full of perfectly splendid hunters?

As though she'd spoken those thoughts aloud, his head reared back. 'I thought Lion would be pleased to see you,' he said, with just a touch of emphasis on the spaniel's name, which conveyed the implication that the dog was the only one who regarded this meeting as a treat. 'It is too far for him to walk, at his age. Also, he enjoys riding beside me in an open carriage.'

As if to prove his master right, Lion chose that moment to roll on to his back to invite her to rub his tummy. She bent and did so, using the moment to hide her face, which she could feel heating after his rebuke. She couldn't really believe that his attitude could still hurt so much. Not after all the times he'd pretended he couldn't even see her, when she'd been standing practically under his nose. She really ought to be immune to his disdain by now.

'Did you have something in particular to ask me,' he asked in a bored tone, 'or should I take my dog and return to Fontenay Court?'

'You know very well I have something of great importance to ask you,' she retorted, finally reaching the end of her tether as she straightened up, 'or I wouldn't have sent you that note.'

'And are you going to tell me what it is any time soon?' He pulled his watch from his waistcoat pocket and looked down at it. 'Only, I have a great many pressing matters to attend to.'

She sucked in a deep breath. 'I do beg your pardon, my lord,' she said, dipping into the best curtsy she could manage with a dog squirming round her ankles and her riding habit still looped over one arm. 'Thank you so much for sparing me a few minutes of your valuable time,' she added, through gritted teeth.

'Not at all.' He made one of those graceful, languid gestures with his hand that indicated *noblesse oblige*. 'Though I should, of course, appreciate it if you would make it quick.'

Make it quick? Make it quick! Four days she'd been waiting for him to show up, four days he'd kept her in an agony of suspense, and now he was here, he was making it clear he wanted the meeting to be as brief as possible so he could get back to where he belonged. In his stuffy house, with his stuffy servants and his stuffy lifestyle.

Just once, she'd like to shake him out of that horrid, contemptuous, self-satisfied attitude of his towards the rest of the world. And make him experience a genuine, human emotion. No matter what.

'Very well.' She'd say what she'd come to say, without preamble. Which would at least give her the pleasure of shocking him almost as much as if she really were to throw her boot at him.

'If you must know, I want you to marry me.'

Chapter Two

The Earl of Ashenden took a silk handkerchief from his pocket, removed his spectacles and began to polish the lenses.

The way he'd always done when he was trying to think about exactly what to say before saying it. If she wasn't trying so hard to convince him she could act the part of a grand lady, she would have done a little victory dance. Because she'd succeeded into shocking him into silence. Edmund Fontenay. The man who was never at a loss for a clever remark.

'While I am flattered by your proposal,' he said, replacing his spectacles on his nose, 'I must confess to being a touch surprised.'

Hah! He didn't need to confess any such thing. Not to her. Not when she knew exactly what the whole spectacles removing and wiping and replacing routine was all about. She'd stumped him. 'Would you mind very much explaining why you have suddenly developed this interest in becoming…' he paused, his gaze growing even colder than it normally did whenever it turned in her direction these days '…the Countess of Ashenden?'

She sucked in a sharp breath at the low blow. 'I have

no interest in becoming the Countess of Ashenden. It isn't like that!'

'No?' He raised one eyebrow as if to say he didn't believe her, but would very graciously give her the chance to explain.

'No. Because I know full well I'm the very last person qualified to hold such a position.' At least, that's what his mother would say. And what Stepmama *had* said. Countless times. That it would be useless to *set her cap* at him—even if she'd been the kind of girl to indulge in that sort of behaviour—since the next Countess of Ashenden would have a position in the county, and the country, for which Georgiana simply didn't have the training. Let alone the disposition.

'In fact, I would much rather you weren't an earl at all, but just…my neighbour.' But unfortunately he *was* an earl. And he hadn't been her neighbour for some years. He came back to Bartlesham as rarely as possible. His interests lay in London, with the new, clever friends he'd made. Her real neighbours had begun to wonder if he was going to turn out just like his father, who'd only ever returned to his ancestral seat to turn his nose up at it. 'Oh, what's the use? I might have known this was a waste of time.'

'You might,' he said.

'Well, we cannot all be as clever as you,' she retorted. 'Some of us still do stupid things, hoping that people won't let them down. You might as well say it—some of us never learn, do we?'

'Some of us,' he replied, slowly advancing, 'would be more inclined to assist a…neighbour in distress if that neighbour would explain themselves clearly, without flinging emotional accusations left, right and centre. If, for example, you have no interest in becoming a countess, why have you asked me to consider marrying you?'

He was standing closer to her now than he'd done since they'd both been children. Close enough for her to see those blue flecks in his eyes, which prevented them from looking as though they were chiselled from ice. This close, she'd swear she could see a spark of interest, rather than cold indifference. This close, she could even, almost, imagine she could feel warmth emanating from his body.

She got the most inappropriate urge to reach out and tap him on the shoulder, to tag him and then run off into the trees. Only of course, he wouldn't set off in pursuit nowadays. He'd just frown in a puzzled manner, or look down his aristocratic nose at her antics, and shake his head in reproof. The way Papa had started to do whenever she did anything that Stepmama declared was unladylike.

Just then Lion yawned, making her look down. Which shattered the wistful longing for them to be able to return to the carefree days when they'd been playmates. Smashing the illusion that he'd just looked at her the way he'd looked at her then. As though she mattered.

When the painful truth was she'd never mattered to him at all. Well, she'd never mattered to *any*body.

Still, it did look as though she'd succeeded in rousing his curiosity.

She peeped up at him warily from beneath her lashes. He was studying her, his head tilted slightly to one side, the way he so often used to look at a puzzle of some sort. Her heart sped up. And filled with…not hope, exactly. But a lightening of her despair. And she wondered whether it would be worth explaining why she'd considered making the outrageous proposal, after all.

'Look, you know my father died last year—' she began.

He flinched. 'Yes. I did mean to offer my condolences, but—'

She made a slashing motion with her hand. It was far too late for that now. And she couldn't bear to talk of it. It was bad enough that she'd turned out to be such a disappointment to the bluff, genial man she'd adored. That his final words to her had been an admonition to try and be more like Sukey, her stepsister.

'I don't wish to go over old ground,' she said, proud that a slight hitch in her voice was the only thing betraying how very much Edmund's absence, his silence, last year, had added to her grief. Which had been foolish of her, considering they hadn't spoken to each other for several years. Why had she thought a bereavement would have made a difference to the way he dealt with her?

'The point is,' she continued, 'that now we are out of mourning, Stepmama has decreed we go up to London, so that Sukey and I can find husbands.'

'And?'

The impatience bordering on irritation he managed to inject into the single word cut her like a rapier thrust.

'And I don't want to go! I don't want to have to parade around before a lot of men who will eye me up like some prize heifer at market.' She bit back the painful admission that she could just imagine what they'd say of her, all those smart London beaux. They'd sneer at her, no doubt, and scoff and turn their noses up at her. She couldn't imagine any decent man actually liking her enough to propose marriage. Not when she'd been such a disappointment to her family that they'd spent years trying to turn her into something she wasn't.

'I don't want to have to accept an offer from some horrible man—' who'd probably be deranged; well, he'd have to be to want to marry someone who struggled so hard to behave the way a lady should '—who will probably take me heaven knows where…'

The Hebridean Isles, like as not. Where there would be nobody to talk to. Because nobody lived there. Which was why the wild and hairy Scot would have gone to London to find a bride. Because there simply weren't any women in those far-flung isles. And that would be the only reason she'd look like a good choice—because he wouldn't know any better.

'You may meet some man who is not horrible,' he replied in a flat voice that cut right through her deepest, wildest imaginings. 'That is the whole purpose of the Season, I believe? To meet someone congenial?'

She took a deep breath. Counted to five. 'Whoever they are, they will take me somewhere…' Somewhere remote, so that nobody could criticise him for his poor choice. Or populated with odd people who wouldn't notice her own failings because they were practically savages themselves.

But because her fears about her future would sound pathetic when voiced aloud, she finished limply, 'Somewhere else.'

'Then all you have to do is refuse all offers,' he said in a condescending tone, 'return to Bartlesham and live out your days as a spinster.'

Spinster! Ooh, how she hated that word. She much preferred the word virgin. A virgin was pure. Unsullied. A spinster was…a sort of dried-up husk of a person.

'If you had spent any time at all down here since Papa died,' she spat out, 'you could not have just said anything so *fatuous*. Six Chimneys is entailed. And my prig of a cousin who inherited only gave us leave to stay on here for the year of mourning. Once we leave and go up to London, there will be no coming back. It's marry some stranger, or…or…'

Oh, no. Her eyes were prickling. She'd sworn she wouldn't cry. Not in front of Edmund. She turned away. Slashed at the reeds with her riding crop a few times to relieve her feelings. Turned back, her spine stiff.

'Look, I know I'm not much of a catch,' she said in a voice that only quivered just a little bit. 'I'm not an heiress and I don't have a title or anything, but I wouldn't interfere with your life, like some wives would. You could leave me down here once we're married and go back to London. I wouldn't even put your mother's nose out of joint by trying to take over running the house, or trying to outshine her at county affairs, or anything like that.' Well, she couldn't. She wouldn't know how. But neither would she embarrass him by gallivanting all over the countryside like the hoyden she'd used to be. At least she knew better than that, now. 'I'd keep out of everyone's way, I swear!'

He looked her full in the face for the space of what felt like an eternity, though it was impossible to tell what he was thinking. Apart from the fact that it wasn't anything good, since he'd got that flinty look again.

'It is of no use looking up at me,' he said eventually, 'with those big brown eyes of yours, the way Lion does when he's begging for scraps. I am not soft.'

'I know that. Nobody,' she said bitterly, 'knows that better than I.'

'Which only confirms your unsuitability to become my wife. You wouldn't come to London with me, you wouldn't even run the house if I left you down here alone. Just what, exactly, are you offering? What will

I get out of this ridiculous marriage you claim to wish to make?'

'Well…I don't…I mean…' She swallowed. Lifted her chin. Forced herself to say it. 'That is, I don't know if you remember, but you promised me, you did, that when you grew up, you'd do anything to help me if I needed a friend. And I've never needed one more than I do now…'

'When I made that promise I was a boy,' he bit out, his mouth twisted with distaste. 'A callow youth. And I never imagined that you'd expect repayment this way. By demanding I make you my Countess!'

Georgiana sucked in a deep, agonised breath. The… the…brute. Didn't he know what it had cost her to break through all the years of estrangement and write to him, begging him to meet her? Couldn't he see how desperate she must have been to have broken all the rules by proposing to him?

'I'm not demanding anything,' she protested. 'I was just hoping…' She shook her head. That was the trouble with hope. It might raise your spirits for a while, but when someone tore it away, it left a ragged, gaping wound in its place. 'I can see it was foolish to expect you to keep your promise. I might have known you'd find some way to wriggle off the hook.'

His nostrils flared as he sucked in a furious breath.

'Don't you dare accuse *me* of breaking *my* promises Georgie. Or trying to wriggle out of anything—'

'But you just said you wouldn't marry me. That you wouldn't do anything to help me at all.'

He darted forward as she made to turn and leave, seizing her by the upper arm.

'I never said anything of the sort,' he growled. 'It's

just that you didn't offer me the one thing that might make me consider your…offer.'

Her heart kicked at the inside of her chest. There was something about the way he was looking at her that made her feel…weak. And sort of…trembly inside.

'W-what might that be?'

'Heirs,' he said. 'The only reason I will *ever* marry, *any* woman, is to fulfil my duty to provide heirs to take over my responsibilities when I'm gone.'

'But that would mean…' A vision flashed into her brain of how babies were made. It still made her feel ill to think about that day she'd gone into the stables and seen Wilkins lying face down in what had looked like a bundle of rags, with his breeches round his ankles, pounding that bundle of rags into the straw. There had been a pair of female legs spread grotesquely on either side of his hairy bottom, legs, she had discovered a few months later, which had belonged to one of their house-maids. The whole episode left a bad taste in her mouth, especially since, no matter how hard Liza had wept, Stepmama had insisted on turning her off, for being a bad influence on the daughters of the house.

And, by the way Edmund thrust her from him angrily, her disgust over the whole affair showed plainly on her face.

'What, did you think I'd accept a marriage in name only?'

Once again, her face must have given her thoughts away, because he flinched.

'My God, you did, didn't you?' He whirled away from her, his coat fanning out like the wings of a storm behind him. 'What kind of man do you think I am?' He paced back, his eyes glittering angrily. 'You believe all those stupid things your idiot of a father said about me, don't you? That I'm not a real man at all, because I prefer observing living creatures to galloping about the countryside in pursuit of them? That I have ink running through my veins, not hot, red blood?'

'Papa was not an idiot,' she said, since she couldn't deny she had hoped he might have been willing to accept her terms. Which made her an idiot, too.

'And that is the kind of man you wish to marry, is it? A man you don't think is a real man at all?'

'Yes,' she cried. 'That's the only kind of man I could imagine being able to tolerate marrying. A man who'd let me have a marriage in name only.'

He stepped smartly up to her and took her by both shoulders.

'When I marry it won't be in name only. I want heirs. Several, in fact. I am damn well not going to have only one son, then carry on with my life as though he doesn't exist.'

Her heart went out to him. Because she could see exactly why he was saying that. He'd been such a lonely child, of course he wouldn't want to inflict the same fate on his own offspring.

'And my wife will not be willing to let my mother carry on reigning over the county. She'll have to take up the position herself, not try to stay out of everyone's way. She'll have to be strong enough to stand at my side, her sword metaphorically drawn, not cower in the background lest she put anyone's nose out of joint.'

And then he flung her from him as though touching her had contaminated his hands.

'Y-yes, I see,' she stammered. And what she saw was that, yet again, she didn't measure up. Not as a daughter, not as a possible wife, and not as a woman. 'Oh, God,' she whimpered, seeing her last hope slipping through her fingers. 'You are going to make me go through with it, aren't you? I'm going to have to go to London and face the humiliation of—' she broke off before voicing her fears that no man with any sense would want her as a wife.

'*I* am not making you do anything. This has nothing whatsoever to do with me,' he said, making a slashing motion with his hand.

It was as though he'd landed a blow to her very heart. It was the final proof that he'd changed beyond all recognition. Either that, or her memory of him had been very deeply tinged by wishful thinking.

'I might have known you'd take that attitude. Out of sight is out of mind with you, isn't it? You don't care about anything but what is right under your nose.'

A muscle twitched in his jaw. 'You are deliberately twisting my words.'

'No, I'm not. I'm just forcing you to see what you are doing to me! You. Yourself. Because you refuse to help me, some strange man is going to gain rights over my body. He will paw at me and…mount me…and…I will have to…endure it.' Her stomach lurched in revulsion. 'God, how I hate being a woman,' she said, pressing her hand down hard on the centre of the nausea.

'Georgie,' he gasped, clearly shocked by her explicit description of what marriage meant to her. Her outrageous admission that she hated everything about being female. 'Listen to me…'

'No. I don't want to hear any more stupid platitudes. The only thing you could possibly say that I want to hear is that you are going to marry me. Will you? Will you marry me?'

The look on his face said it all. It was a mixture of shock and distaste, and withdrawal.

'No, you won't, will you? Well then, I will stop wasting your precious time,' she said, dashing her hand across her face to swipe away the one tear she hadn't been able to blink back, and bent to pat Lion one last time. Then she turned and stumbled from the riverbank.

He didn't reach out a hand to try and stop her. He didn't call out her name. He just stood there, coldly watching her flee the scene of her humiliation. At least, she assumed the look on his face was cold. She wasn't going to betray any weakness by looking over her shoulder to find out.

'Well, Lion, what do you make of that?'

The exhausted spaniel flopped down on the hearthrug with a sigh and closed his eyes. Even when Edmund nudged him with the toe of his boot, the dog did not react.

'You are not being any help,' said Edmund, gazing down at the almost-comatose dog. 'You are the one person—I mean creature—who knows her as well as I, since you were there for many of our escapades. Have you no useful advice to give me?'

Of course Lion didn't have any advice to give. He was a dog. By heaven, he was actually talking to a dog, instead of sitting down and going over the encounter with Georgiana in a rational fashion.

But how on earth could he possibly go over the encounter in a rational fashion, when it felt as if he'd been beaten about the body all day by a series of highly irrational explosions?

First, the letter had infuriated him, dredging up as it had a whole host of insecurities and hurts he'd deliberately buried beneath years of strenuous denial.

And then there had been his visceral reaction to seeing her again, standing in the place that represented a sort of oasis during his childhood, wearing that figure-hugging, vibrant pink gown that stood out like a beacon against the background of all those dead reeds. His entire body had leaped in response. That was what it had felt like. Almost the same as the feeling he'd had when taking part in those experiments with galvanism. An involuntary reaction in his muscles that had nothing to do with his brain, his intellect.

And then she'd shocked his mind too, with that completely unexpected proposal. But what had been most shocking about it was the fact that, for a moment, he'd actually considered it. Even though he'd assumed she'd only proposed out of ambition to become a countess.

Which had made him twice as angry as he might have been when she'd explained that the reason she wanted him was because, primarily, she didn't think he'd be interested in bedding her. She might as well have spat in his face. Which had, in turn, provoked him into telling her exactly what *he* wanted from marriage. The words had come pouring out of his mouth like a dam bursting, in spite of never having actually sat down and thought it through.

He strode to the sideboard and wrested the top from the decanter.

He couldn't believe, now, that he'd become angry enough to grab her. Grab her! Which meant that he'd been so close to her that when he'd drawn breath, he'd unwittingly filled his nostrils with the scent of her. And had, at the same time, become aware of the warm contours of her shoulders, rising and falling under his palms.

He shook his head as he poured himself a large brandy. If he didn't habitually keep such firm control over himself, he'd have flung her to the ground right there and shown her exactly how normal and healthy his appetites could be.

What man wouldn't react that way to having such a slur cast on his masculinity?

He downed half the drink and slammed the glass back down on the sideboard.

And how on earth had she reached the conclusion that sexual congress was a revolting act that would humiliate her, anyway? Though at least he now could see why she'd wanted the sterile union she'd imagined she'd have with him.

He whirled away from the sideboard and strode to the window. What was he doing, taking brandy at this time of day? Five minutes in her presence and she'd driven him to drink.

And yet...

She'd turned to him. She might have insulted him in the process, but she had practically begged him for help.

He braced his hands on the windowsill and gazed out in the direction of their stream. If only he'd stayed calm and cool and rational, he could have walked away from that encounter feeling like a victor. Instead of which...

An image of her face swam before his eyes. Her face, not as it had been today, all pinched up as she struggled not to cry, her whole body rigid with the effort of sacrificing her pride and begging him to rescue her from being bedded by a Real Man, but alight with laughter as she hung upside down by her legs from a tree.

'I still miss her, Lion,' he whispered, bowing his head in defeat. 'Where did she go? What happened to that girl who wasn't afraid of anything, or anyone, to turn her into the woman she is today?'

And, more importantly, what was he going to do about it?

Chapter Three

Nothing. That was what he was going to do. Not until he was able to think straight. He'd learned at his mother's knee that giving way to an emotional appeal, out of pity, or guilt, or a sense of indebtedness, or…whatever, only resulted in him committing what he'd later regard as an error of judgement.

But in spite of constantly reminding himself that he had far more important matters to think about, Georgiana's outrageous proposal, and, to his mind, his even more disgraceful reaction to it, kept on pushing everything else aside.

They even affected the way he dealt with estate business.

'I do not care what my mother says,' he found himself saying, shocking both himself and his steward by pounding his fist on the desk. '*I* am the Earl of Ashenden. *I* am running this estate and all my other holdings. And if I wish to…to plant the whole of the water meadow with pineapples, she has no right to gainsay it.'

Rowlands's jaw dropped. 'Pineapples, my lord?'

'It was merely a hypothetical example,' Edmund bit out. 'The point is, my word here is law. Or should be.'

'Yes, my lord.'

'Then why do you persist in coming to me to report that work has not been done *because the Countess would not like it*? I do not,' he said, rising to his feet and leaning forward, resting his palms on the desk, 'wish to hear that excuse *ever* again. Do you understand?'

'Yes, my lord,' said Rowlands, twisting the sheaf of papers he held in his hand into a tight screw.

Edmund wiped his hand across his face. Devil take it, he was losing his temper with a subordinate. Shouting at a man who had not the liberty to answer back.

It was because he was tired, that was what it was. He'd fallen asleep with Georgiana on his mind, then been plagued all night by dreams in which he'd watched her being dragged to the altar by a variety of unsavoury-looking characters. Worse still, he was always present during the subsequent wedding night. Time and again, she'd turn her big brown eyes to him as the men had been stripping her naked and pushing her on to the bed, pleading with him to come to her rescue. But he never could. Either his legs had remained stubbornly immobile, no matter how hard he'd struggled to get to her. Or he'd reached out to thrust the shadowy bridegroom away, only to find his hand was pushing at empty air. At which point he would awake, sweating, and roused, and ashamed. Because he couldn't be sure that his motives for getting to Georgiana were completely honourable. Had he been trying to rescue her, or did he simply want to replace the man in her bed?

Self-disgust had him getting up hours before his hapless valet could reasonably have expected a summons, ordering a breakfast which he couldn't manage to eat and then marching down to the boathouse.

He must have rowed upstream for the best part of

an hour. But no matter how hard he pushed himself, he could not achieve the clarity of mind that being out on the open water normally bestowed.

Infuriated to find that he couldn't even escape her out there, he allowed the current to carry him back to the boathouse, and stalked to his study in the hopes that he could bury himself in work. And this was the result.

'I appreciate you are in a most awkward position, Rowlands,' he said as he sat down. 'I am asking you to carry out orders of which she does not approve. I know that she comes here far more often than I and that you have been used to doing her bidding for some considerable time.'

Rowlands flushed. 'We were all that grateful she took up the reins when your father dropped them, my lord,' he pointed out. 'Begging your pardon for saying so.'

'No need to beg my pardon for *that*. She did a sterling job, considering. I am well aware that had it not been for her, I may not have inherited estates that were in such good working order.' And he really ought to feel more grateful to her than he did. 'Nevertheless, she has not studied modern farming methods, the way I have. Nor is it her place to run things now that I have reached my majority.'

'No, my lord,' said Rowland. And took a breath, then closed his mouth.

'Yes, what is it? You may as well tell me, so that we can clear the air once and for all.'

'Well, it's just that with her ladyship being so used to getting her own way, in these parts, it might be helpful to all of us down here if *you* would have a word with her.' His face went beetroot-red.

'Point taken,' said Edmund.

It was for him to tell his mother to cease interfering with his plans. With an effort, he returned to discussing estate business with the poor man who would have to carry out those plans in the face of probably strident opposition from Lady Ashenden. But he could only manage to keep part of his mind on turnips, drainage and potential yields. The other part kept straying back to Georgiana and the way she'd looked in that gown. The wild, almost primitive surge of lust he'd experienced after breathing in her pure, undiluted scent. His insane desire to prove to her, right there on the riverbank, that he was just like any other red-blooded man.

No wonder his sleep had been so disturbed the night before after a scene like that. Especially as she'd told him that she would hold him personally responsible for whatever happened to her in London.

And as the day wore on, and his mind kept straying to Georgiana's proposal, a couple of other things she'd said started to niggle at him. For instance, she'd flung the words, *'Out of sight is out of mind with you, isn't it?'* As though she was accusing him of turning his back on her. Which made no sense. For she was the one who hadn't answered any of the letters he'd written to her. Apart from, ironically, the first. The note he'd thrust into the gap between the stone wall and the gatepost of the main drive, which was where they'd always left messages for each other if they couldn't meet at their place for any reason.

Dr Scholes has persuaded Mother that I need to live in a warmer climate if I'm going to reach adulthood. I am leaving tomorrow. But I will write to you. Please write to me, too.

She'd written back.

I will. I will miss you.

Miss him—hah!

The footman, who'd been about to remove the cloth and bring in the port, flinched. Which alerted Edmund to the fact he must have actually said the word, rather than just thinking it.

Which infuriated him even more. Dammit, he couldn't even sit down to dinner in peace because of her. He hadn't been this unsettled since…since he'd first gone to St Mary's. And waited for letters that never came. Six months it had taken him to accept the fact that she wasn't going to keep her word. That she didn't miss him at all.

He unstoppered the decanter which his footman had placed, warily, at his left hand and poured himself his usual measure. When he thought of the hours he'd spent, walking along the beach, howling his protests into the wind so that nobody would witness his misery, he couldn't help grimacing in distaste.

It had taken a stern talking-to from Dr Scholes to put an end to it.

'It is as well you learn what fickle creatures females are,' the elderly scholar had told him. *'Not that they can help it. They may well mean whatever it was they said at the time they said it, but five minutes later another idea will come into their head and they will forget all about the first one. Or simply change their mind.'*

The explanation had made so much sense it had made him feel like the world's biggest fool. He should already have learned, from the example of his parents, that men and women never said what they really meant, but only what they hoped would get them out of hot water. But it had been Georgie's casually broken promise that had made him vow never to trust another person so much that he became that vulnerable, ever again.

And until he'd gone to the stream in answer to her summons, he had kept that vow.

He got to his feet abruptly, waving permission to the hovering footmen to clear the table. There was no clarity of thought to be found in port. What he needed was a good night's sleep. But he was not likely to get it, not with his head still so full of Georgiana.

So he went to his study, sat down at his desk and out of habit when first considering a complex problem, drew out a fresh sheet of paper and trimmed his pen. But what to write, when it came to Miss Georgiana Wickford?

Why is she angry? he wrote. As though *he'd* betrayed *her*, not the other way round. What could possibly make her think that? He hadn't chosen to leave. To leave her alone. So it couldn't be that. But…

He closed his eyes, and concentrated. And another inconsistency popped up.

If she was so angry with him, why had she asked him to marry her?

It made no sense.

Especially not when she'd told him she'd almost expected him to *wriggle off the hook*.

From where, he wondered indignantly, had she acquired such a low opinion of him? He was a man who kept his word. Why, he'd even gone to the stream, in answer to her summons, because of a promise he'd made when he'd been too young to know any better. Even though she'd broken hers to him.

Angrily, he scratched another question mark. And

put the matter aside. Because all he was doing, by concentrating on Georgiana, was getting even more angry than when he was trying not to think about her at all.

The next day, during the hours when he was supposed to be going over the accounts, his mind wandered to Georgiana's peculiar view of what a London Season would be like. And he got a vivid flash of himself, as a bewildered youth, being put on a coach and shipped off to St Mary's.

He leaned back and twirled his pen between his ink-stained fingers. She was clearly as scared as he'd been back then, about going to what was, to her, a foreign country. He seemed to recall that he'd even had the odd notion that he was being sent into exile, for some crime he hadn't been aware he'd committed.

That same fear might explain why she had acted so irrationally and said so many other things that made no sense. Perhaps all she needed was reassurance. Perhaps he would not feel so guilty about not being able to accede to her ridiculous demand she marry him, if he could explain that, for him, going to the Scilly Isles had turned out to be the best thing that had happened to him. Once he'd stopped bewailing her betrayal, that was. Dr Scholes had encouraged him in all his studies, even going so far as helping him catalogue the incredible variety of moths to be found on the Isles at various times of the year. He'd encouraged him to row, regularly, which had improved his physique to no end. He'd allowed him to mix with the locals, too.

There, that was something he could do. Encourage her to look upon her London Season as an opportunity, rather than a form of torture.

Because he couldn't leave things as they were. His

conscience wouldn't permit it, no matter how often he told it to be silent. It kept reminding him that he'd made a promise. And even though he couldn't keep that promise in the way she thought she wanted him to, he ought to find some other way to prove he was not the sort of man to *wriggle off the hook*.

The next morning, when he was out rowing on the river, he came up with an answer that was so utterly perfect he couldn't imagine why he hadn't suggested it to her at once.

There were men who, for various reasons, did seek out the kind of marriage she'd asked him to contemplate. He couldn't actually foresee that much difficulty in arranging such a match, if she was so sure that was what she wanted.

There. That was something constructive he could do. He could suggest she look, in London, for the kind of man who *did* want a paper marriage. Perhaps even offer to discreetly put out feelers to that end.

And then, once Georgie's future was settled, maybe he'd be able to get a decent night's sleep again.

Later that day, therefore, he sent for his carriage, heaved Lion up on to the seat beside him and set off for Six Chimneys. Lion had been a great help during their last interview. More than once, the old dog had inadvertently diffused the tension building between the two humans.

Besides which, Lion had enjoyed seeing her and she'd enjoyed seeing him.

It was the only thing about her, apparently, that hadn't changed since their childhood—her love of dogs.

As the carriage bowled along the winding lanes that

separated Fontenay Court from Six Chimneys, Edmund wondered what could possibly account for the drastic changes between the girl he'd loved and the woman who…irked him so much. Yes, irked him. Because, although she looked like a grown-up version of the girl who'd captivated him, she had none of the spark. Miss Georgiana Wickford was all…cool detachment and elegant deportment.

The very minute he'd left Bartlesham it was as if she'd turned into someone else.

Was there a connection between the two? He'd never really considered that the one might have been connected to the other, but it was most definitely the case that *a*, he'd left and then *b*, she'd changed. Apparently overnight.

Well, he'd changed, too. He was no longer the wounded adolescent in the throes of what he'd believed was his first and one true love. Even if he had behaved like one down by the stream, by grabbing her and shouting at her, and sending her away in tears.

Today, he was a rational, adult male who was in full control of himself.

And he wasn't going to let her reduce him to…*that* state, again.

He gave the Tudor manor house a keen perusal as Benson drew the carriage up by the front gate. He'd never actually visited before. As a boy, he reflected ruefully as he lifted Lion down and strolled the few steps from the carriage to the front door, he'd rarely left the estate except for church on Sundays. As a man, he'd spent as little time as possible in Bartlesham, and—he paused with one booted foot on the front step—he rarely left the estate then, either. He stayed at Fontenay

Court only long enough to attend to any urgent estate business, then retreated to London.

He raised the knocker and let it drop. After only the briefest pause, the door was opened by a ruddy-faced housemaid who was completely unfamiliar to him.

'If you would please to come this way, your lordship,' she said, bobbing a curtsy, 'Mr Wickford will receive you in the parlour.'

He blinked. For two reasons. Firstly, though he was sure he'd never clapped eyes on the woman before, she clearly knew exactly who he was. Did he spend so little time down here that he no longer knew who inhabited the place? Georgiana had accused him of being ignorant of things he ought to have known.

It was definitely time to remedy that. The next time he came down here, he would devote at least one day to do a little mingling with the locals. Which would not only enable him to keep abreast of local news, but also convince his tenants that he intended to be an effective, efficient landlord.

Secondly, Mr Wickford? Whenever anyone said that name, he immediately thought of Georgiana's father. The rather shabby, sporting-mad squire of Bartlesham, who always seemed to have a pack of dogs tumbling round his feet.

He and Lion followed the maid across the hall and into a small, sunlit room, where a short, fair-haired man, who had a vague look of Georgie's father about his jawline, was standing.

'Good morning, my lord,' he said, sweeping a heap of what looked like curtain material from one of the chairs and wadding it up into a ball. 'It is so good of you to call, to welcome us to the neighbourhood. An

honour,' he blustered, tossing the bundle of fabric behind the sofa. 'Totally unexpected, I do assure you.'

Totally unexpected on Edmund's part, too. Not that
he was going to alienate the fellow by admitting he
hadn't come here to see him at all.

'Oh, sit, please, do sit.' The man he assumed must
be the Mr Wickford the maid had meant indicated the
chair he'd cleared of curtaining. 'At sixes and sevens,'
he said apologetically. 'Not really ready for visitors,
Mrs Wickford would say. But in your case, of course...'
He petered out.

Edmund sank slowly into the proffered chair and
Lion lay down at his feet with a sigh as the facts settled
into order. This man was evidently the cousin of Georgie's father, the one who'd inherited the house and land.
The one who'd given her a year before evicting her.

And Mrs Wickford must be Georgiana's stepmother.

'She will be wishing me at the devil,' he said, with
what he hoped was a sociable smile. 'Calling upon you
all when she must be so very busy planning her removal
to London.'

'Removal to London?' Mr Wickford gaped at him.
'Whatever made you think...? Oh, I have it!' He chuckled. 'You are referring to my cousin's widow, who has
already left for Town. She and the girls moved out as
soon as we moved in.'

They'd left? While he'd been getting his thoughts
in order, they'd left? Before he had a chance to make
amends for the way they'd parted?

Edmund went cold. Georgie had gone off to Town,
believing that he'd completely repudiated her. That he
cared so little about the fears she'd confessed to having
that he'd left her to deal with them alone.

Even though he'd promised she could always consider him her friend.

No, he shook his head.

He wasn't the kind of man who broke his word.

He *hadn't* been trying to wriggle off the hook.

And he couldn't bear to think that Georgie must now believe he was.

Chapter Four

Edmund's first instinct was to get to his feet and set off for London in pursuit. To explain…

What, exactly?

Meanwhile, the young Mr Wickford was sitting down heavily on a pile of curtaining on the chair opposite and spreading his meaty fingers over his knees. 'Yes, Mrs Wickford senior is going to launch her daughter into society, now they're out of mourning. Has great hopes for her.'

'Does she?' said Edmund, as a matter of form, since he was only half-attending. He was far more concerned with imagining how Georgiana must have felt, having this man and his wife turn her out of doors a matter of hours after he'd so brutally turned down her proposal.

'Shouldn't be surprised if she doesn't do very well,' Mr Wickford was saying. 'A taking little thing, is Sukey.'

'Sukey?'

'Ah, should more properly refer to her as Miss Mead, I suppose, but then she's such a friendly sort of girl, it's hard to stand upon form with her. Not a bit like Miss Wickford,' he said with a shake of his head.

'What,' said Edmund, his hackles rising, 'precisely, do you mean by that?'

'Oh, well, you know,' said Mr Wickford, waving his hands.

'No, I am afraid I don't.'

'Of course, you will hardly know her, will you? Well, let us just say that she is a strange, awkward girl. Not that she can help it, I don't suppose, given the way she was brought up. The mother died in childbirth,' said Wickford, which was something Edmund already knew. But the reminder jolted him. Was that why Georgiana didn't want a normal marriage? Could she be afraid of having children? 'Disappointed my cousin immensely,' Wickford was droning on. 'Wanted a boy, d'you see? Well, that's natural enough, ain't it? Trouble is, he went and treated the girl as if she was the boy he wanted, instead of facing facts.'

That was *not* how it had been. Georgie's father had simply allowed her to act exactly as she wished. Well, Edmund amended, he might have encouraged her love of horse-riding and outdoor pursuits by praising her skills. But he had definitely not attempted to mould her preferences beyond that. If she had shown an interest in…say…dolls and dresses, he was pretty sure the man would have bought her bolts of satin and lace back from the market, rather than new riding boots or a crop.

'It was only when she got to the age where she really needed a mother,' said Mr Wickford, leaning forward in a conspiratorial sort of way, and winking, 'that he saw his mistake. Which was why he married again. Needed a woman to knock the rough edges off. Make her behave like a lady. And, of course, providing her with a sister like Sukey, who could set her a shining example of femininity, was an added bonus.'

Was that what people hereabouts thought had happened?

Was that, in fact, what had happened?

But—why would a man who'd allowed Georgie to run wild for so many years suddenly try to change her? If that even was his motive for remarrying.

'And Mrs Wickford is the sort of woman who enjoys knocking the rough edges off, I take it,' said Edmund, feeling his way forward tentatively.

Mr Wickford chuckled. 'Do you know, whenever anyone says Mrs Wickford, I still think they mean my mother. But there's my cousin's widow now, as well as my own wife. Though that is taking some getting used to. Only been married a fortnight.'

'My felicitations,' he responded automatically and without enthusiasm.

Mr Wickford beamed at him. 'Thank you, my lord. I do consider myself most fortunate. Couldn't think of marriage at all before I came into this property, let alone to a woman like Sylvia Dean. Took some persuading, none the less…'

'Indeed?' He leaned back and raised one eyebrow, inviting further confidences. Not that he had the slightest interest in this fellow. But he'd already learned far more about what had gone wrong in Georgiana's life in five minutes with the loquacious fool, than he'd done in ten years.

'Oh, yes,' said Mr Wickford, smiling fatuously. 'Courting her took up pretty near all my time. If it wasn't for Mrs Wickford senior being so willing to stay on here and keep the place running smoothly, I'm not at all sure I'd have taken the trick.'

Edmund didn't think he'd reacted, but he was not all that surprised when Lion emitted a low growl. The man had admitted that permitting Georgiana and her stepmother to remain in what was, after all, their own home had not been an act of compassion at all. Instead, it had been very much to his advantage. And as soon as their usefulness had come to an end, he had promptly evicted them. In Georgiana's case, from the only home she'd ever known. He glanced round the room as Wickford continued to enthuse about his new bride, noting, everywhere, traces of her heritage. Her father might very well have chosen the hunting prints on the walls and most of the furniture looked as though it had been handed down through several generations.

At which point, he saw another reason for the distress which had prompted her to run to him with her outrageous proposal. Not only was she being forced into taking a step which she found abhorrent, she was also losing everything she'd ever called her own. He must have seemed like her last chance to salvage something—a sort of metaphorical clinging to the wreckage of her life in the faint hope of finding a refuge that was at least familiar, if not what she really wanted.

But instead of being man enough to listen to her, really listen with a view to understanding, he'd rubbed salt into what he could now see were very deep and grievous wounds by getting angry with her. Shouting at her. Rebuffing her.

She hadn't deserved such treatment. Even though she'd hurt him in the past, she'd been scarcely more than a child at the time. The worst she'd been guilty of was thoughtlessness. She had not deliberately set out to hurt him, he would swear to it.

His antagonism for her promptly abated. And as it

did so, he could scarcely credit that he'd carried it into his adult life, or nursed it with such devotion. To repay her, as an adult, by standing back and watching her suffer, or even adding to her woes, was out of all proportion to the initial offence.

Sickened at himself, he got to his feet.

'You will excuse me,' he said, as a chill swept up his spine and lodged in the region of his stomach. 'I cannot stay longer.'

'What? Oh, dear,' said Mr Wickford, leaping to his feet as well. 'Mrs Wickford will be desolate to have missed you. The moment she saw your carriage stop at the foot of our drive she ran upstairs to make herself presentable. I'm sure she won't be but a minute longer...'

'What a pity,' he replied mendaciously. He had no wish to meet the cuckoo who'd thrust the true chicks out of this nest. 'I have urgent business which takes me back to London tomorrow,' he added truthfully. Because he had to see Georgiana again. Apologise. Tell her he meant to make it up to her, somehow. And London was where she had gone. 'So I have much to accomplish today.'

Mr Wickford wrung his hands, swallowing and looking nervously in the direction of the stairs as Edmund made his way to the front door. But he didn't care. He didn't even wait for the man, or his maid, to open it for him. He just needed to get away from here, so that he could think things through.

Georgiana's past was looking very different from the way he'd imagined it. He wouldn't have believed that her father, a man who'd always laughed at her antics, had married a woman specifically to *knock her into shape*. Or worse, brought another girl into the house to show her how she ought to behave. She must have been devastated.

He frowned as he stalked down the path, Lion lumbering at his heels. Surely, she would have needed to write to him more than ever? But it had been from his mother that he'd learned of her widowed father's remarriage. His mother, who, in spite of all her flaws, *had* written faithfully. Back then, it had been one more sin to lay at Georgie's door. But now...

She must have been crushed. And since he had no longer been there, she would not have had anybody to turn to. Because, now he came to consider it, not only was she his only friend, but she spent so much time with him that she hadn't had any other friends either.

So why hadn't she?

And why hadn't she run to him, on the few occasions he'd returned to Bartlesham, instead of flouncing out of the shop when he'd walked in, her purchases abandoned?

It had puzzled him from the moment he'd returned, still hurt by her decision not to write to him, but determined to make the best of things, and at least attempt to treat her with courtesy. But then, on his first Sunday in Bartlesham, she'd refused to return his greeting when he'd been magnanimous enough to accord her a nod across the aisle of St. Bartholomew's. And stalked out with her nose in the air when the tedious service had at length ground to its conclusion.

And so he'd washed his hands of her. He'd really and truly left her behind when he'd gone up to university.

And then, as he was lifting a wheezing Lion into the carriage, he recalled her accusation, that out of sight meant out of mind, for him. As if she was the one who hadn't received any letters.

Good Lord…could it be…if the stepmother had seen it as her duty to *knock Georgie into shape*—in other words, to turn her into the proper young lady she appeared to be nowadays—then she would not have approved of them corresponding. Single females were not, strictly speaking, supposed to write to single men to whom they were not related.

Yes, that would explain why he hadn't received any letters from her, in spite of her promise to write.

But…he shook his head. It didn't explain why she'd been so angry with him when he'd returned for a visit, briefly, before going up to Oxford.

Unless…

What must she have felt, when he'd given up writing to her? Had she felt as betrayed as he had, when he hadn't heard at all?

She might have done.

It was certainly the first hypothesis to explain her behaviour over the past ten years that made any kind of sense.

He sat bolt upright as a *frisson* of insight flickered in the depths of his brain.

The stepmother.

Could she have been the one to fill Georgiana's head with the kind of stories that resulted in her now regarding the act of conceiving children as nasty and brutish?

Who else could it possibly have been?

Georgiana definitely hadn't known anything about that side of life when he'd left Bartlesham. And he couldn't imagine her father describing marital relations to her in such a way that…actually, not in any way at all. It wasn't within a father's remit to educate his daughters about that sort of thing.

But…he blinked, taking in his surroundings for the

first time since he'd left Six Chimneys and saw that he was almost halfway home.

'Dear God, what a fool,' he groaned. He'd been in such a hurry to get away from Georgiana's repulsive cousin that he hadn't ascertained where exactly, in London, she was staying. And there was no way he was going to turn back now and ask him.

'But, Mama,' said Sukey, holding a length of blue ribbon up to the side of her face, 'don't you think this would bring out the colour of my eyes?'

As if to emphasise her point, Sukey widened those cornflower-blue eyes in appeal. The pleading expression would have melted the hearts of any of the young men of Bartlesham—indeed, Georgiana had witnessed its devastating effectiveness on many occasions. Unfortunately for her, Stepmama not only had the same kind of blue eyes, but had also been the one to teach Sukey how to wield them.

'The blue ribbon may be very flattering,' said Stepmama distractedly, merely glancing up from her perusal of the latest box to arrive from the modistes, 'but tonight you will be wearing white. All white. That's what proper young ladies of the *ton* wear for their first Season, and as we are finally going to attend a *ton* event I won't have either of you doing anything to set tongues wagging.'

She'd certainly worked hard enough to get them this far. For the past two weeks they'd toadied to people Stepmama said were essential to their chances of being accepted in society. They'd invited those same matrons to their rented house and plied them with tea and sandwiches, while Stepmama had extolled Sukey's prettiness, and Georgie's pedigree, in the hopes of getting invitations in return.

All to no avail.

Until she'd discovered that some girls who lived two streets over, and one across, who they kept on bumping into at the shops, or crossing the square, had a connection to a viscount. And then, all of a sudden, Stepmama declared they were Sukey's best friends and would never go shopping without inviting them along. And since they were as keen as Sukey to shop, and pore over the fashion magazines, and all the other rigmarole to do with the snaring of husbands, they'd grown inexorably more intertwined.

Resulting in tonight's invitation to Durant House. Home of said viscount.

Where Sukey was hoping to captivate a man with a title and lots of money.

Whereas she… Georgiana tugged at the bodice of the gown she was wearing with utter mortification. And plucked up the courage to voice a protest.

'If we are not to set tongues wagging on our first appearance at a *ton*nish event, don't you think I ought to wear something a bit more…modest?'

'There is nothing immodest about your gown, Georgiana,' said Stepmama. 'I have told you before, ladies do reveal a little more of their shoulders and bosom in the evening than they would do by day. I have seen girls much younger than you showing a lot more of themselves than that,' she said, indicating the upper curves of Georgiana's bosom which were thrusting proudly from the closely clinging bodice.

'Yes, but Sukey is dressed far more demurely…' she began, plucking at her bodice again. Only to have Stepmama step up, slap her hands away and ruthlessly tug it back into place.

'Sukey is *pretty*,' she said. 'Men already take notice of her.'

'Oh, Mama!' Sukey dropped her ribbon on to the dressing table. 'Georgiana is pretty, too. In her own way. I mean, that is, there are sure to be *some* men who prefer larger girls, with thick black hair and brown eyes,' she said staunchly, in the face of all evidence to the contrary.

For not one of the youths of Bartlesham, or any of the nearest towns, had ever shown the slightest bit of interest in her. Even though Stepmama had taught her to behave like a lady, the manners and the clothes were all only a thin layer of top dressing. No matter how hard she tried, she was always going to look big and clumsy in comparison to her dainty little stepsister and rouse entirely different feelings from the males of the population.

Stepmama sighed. 'Men who prefer larger girls will want to get a glimpse of her best assets, then, won't they? I wouldn't have thought I'd need to remind you, Sukey, that all women have to make the best of what God has given them, if we are to survive in this harsh world.' She waved her hand at the wads of tissue paper, lidless boxes, gloves and shoes littering every flat surface of the dressing room the two girls shared.

And Georgiana's protests died on her lips. She knew, deep down, that Stepmama was doing what she saw as her best. It was just…well, she hadn't wanted to come to London in the first place. And, as she'd feared, it was proving to be like living in a desert.

There were no fields, no woods, no streams. Nowhere suitable to gallop, except a stingy little formal bit of parkland. Not that ladies were permitted to gallop even there.

Not that she could, anyway, not now Stepmama had sold Whitesocks. Her lower lip wobbled. Whitesocks had been Papa's last gift to her. The last horse in the stables over which they had any legal rights. According to Stepmama, it made far more sense to sell the animal they couldn't afford to stable in London anyway and put the money towards meeting the expenses they wouldn't be able to escape.

Georgiana had hoped, right up until the last minute that something would happen to prevent the sale. That she'd be able to keep that one last link to Papa—but, no. Even her last-ditch appeal to Edmund had come to nothing. Not that he'd heard the whole story.

Which was, she'd eventually decided, her own fault.

She should have kept a cool head and explained her reasons for asking him for help in a rational manner. That's what she should have done. Perhaps even presented him with a written statement, in which she'd listed all the points she wished to make in alphabetical order, which he could have taken away and considered at his leisure. At least he would have treated that kind of appeal with respect. And then he might have been a bit more amenable to making some kind of deal.

She might, at the very least, have persuaded him to buy Whitesocks so that she would have known he would have a good home.

Instead, she'd spent the time waiting for him brooding over past hurts and present problems, so that by the time he arrived she'd been ready to explode. And had done so. Acted in a way that was practically guaranteed to alienate him.

If it was even possible to alienate someone who'd

become a stranger. A cold, unapproachable stranger who merely happened to look a bit like the boy who'd been her favourite person in all the world. A stranger who had never once attempted to renew their friendship, as adults. Who had, on the contrary, occasionally even cut her in the street.

She pulled out a handkerchief and blew her nose.

'Oh, please don't cry, Georgiana,' said Sukey, rushing to her side to give her a hug. 'Mama, could we not let her tuck a fichu into the neckline, or something?'

Georgiana slipped her arm round Sukey's waist, and returned her hug. Dear Sukey. She was so sweet-natured. Every time Georgiana was upset, over anything at all, Sukey would shed sympathetic tears. Indeed, she'd been more upset over the frequent beatings Georgiana had received when Stepmama first took her place as Papa's bride than Georgiana had herself. She'd come and sit at her bedside, and hold her hand, and plead with her to just try and be good, because she couldn't bear to think of her being beaten so very often. Until in the end, it felt as if every time she misbehaved, it was Sukey who got punished.

Between the pair of them, these two women had crushed her desire to rebel against all the rules and regulations that governed the behaviour of young ladies. Besides, what had been the point of carrying on the way she'd done before Papa remarried? Edmund had gone, so there was nobody to box or fence or fish with. The local boys might have stopped teasing and tormenting her for being different to the other girls, once she'd knocked a couple of the biggest of them down, but that didn't mean they would allow her into their ranks. At that time, Sukey had been the only person who appeared to want to spend time with her. In fact, Sukey had followed her round like a little puppy, declaring that she'd always wished for a sister.

'A fichu? And have her look like a dowd? Absolutely not! If we are going to find a husband for Georgiana, we are going to have to make men look at her.'

'But,' Georgiana said, plucking up all her courage, 'I don't really want to find a husband.'

'Oh, heavens, not this again,' said Stepmama wearily. 'Respectable women have to marry, unless they have family who will take them in and care for them, that's all there is to it.'

'I know, but—'

Stepmama held up her hand to silence her. 'I promised your father I would find you a good husband and that is exactly what I will do.'

Georgiana sank on to one of the dressing stools, the impossibility of protesting about her father's last wishes completely silencing her.

'A Corinthian, hopefully. Isn't that what your papa always said? That only a notable Corinthian would do for you? Someone who could match your energy and horsemanship?'

'Yes, Papa did say that,' she admitted glumly. Though what he'd actually meant was that he hoped that was the kind of son-in-law she'd bring home one day. If she couldn't be a boy, the next best thing would be for her to marry someone who was exactly the sort of son he'd always wanted.

And that wasn't the sort of man she wanted to marry, if she had to marry anyone. Men who liked sport, and horses, always smelled of the stable—which invariably put her in mind of that disgusting scene she'd witnessed. Which she could never think of without remembering Liza's tears when she lost her job and home as a result.

And it was all very well Stepmama saying that Liza should not have let him do what they did until they were married, but Wilkins had been doing it as well. In fact, he'd been doing all the work, from the look of things. And not only had he entirely escaped any form of punishment, but he hadn't shown the slightest bit of remorse when Liza had been sent packing, either.

'Besides, you want to have children, don't you? Of course you do,' Stepmama continued ruthlessly, before Georgiana could say a word. 'It is in our nature.'

'Then I must be a most unnatural sort of female.' She sighed, because the way a man got a woman with child had to be the way she'd seen Wilkins treat Liza and it had looked perfectly revolting. She didn't ever want to let any man do…*that* to her. The very thought made her feel sick.

'You will feel differently once you meet the right man,' said Stepmama. 'In fact, I shouldn't be surprised if you met someone tonight who overturns all your silly girlish fears and fancies with one look.'

'I should,' said Georgiana gloomily. 'Because the kind of men who will be attending a *ton*nish event will only want to marry girls with a title, or a dowry. And I don't have either.'

Stepmama froze. 'Georgiana! I thought you understood about the way I have spent what money your papa left for your future. It was his dearest wish to have you presented at court. And had he lived, I am sure he would have arranged things himself.'

Georgiana wasn't convinced. If he'd wanted her presented at court, surely he would have mentioned it? When she was at an age to have a come-out? Instead of only imparting his wishes to his wife, so that the first she'd heard of it was after his death.

'I…I admit, I did not quite foresee how very much it would cost. What with having to hire that woman, instead of…well—' Stepmama shut her mouth with a snap. 'I hadn't budgeted for that. Not to mention the hoops and the feathers, and the jewels to make you both at least look as though you had every right to be there…'

Sukey shot Georgiana a pleading look.

Georgiana, yet again, stifled any resentment she felt and said what she knew was expected of her. 'I know, Stepmama. I know you are doing your best in…trying circumstances…'

'Trying? If only you knew the half. It is bad enough that imbecile cousin of your father's rented us a house out here, in Bloomsbury for heaven's sake, when I specifically requested a fashionable address…'

Stepmama glared round the cluttered little room the two girls were being obliged to share, with loathing. It was almost enough to lift Georgiana's spirits. So much for Stepmama's insistence that men were much better at handling that sort of thing. She'd been obliged to eat her words the moment their carriage, and the wagon containing all their worldly goods, had drawn up outside. For Bloomsbury was not the slightest bit fashionable. Their neighbours were retired admirals and captains of industry, not marquesses and earls. Stepmama might have forgiven the address if the house had been bigger, but upon inspection they'd discovered that although the reception rooms were generously proportioned, the rooms on the upper floor, where they were going to have to sleep, were so small they could have served as cells for monks.

Georgiana hadn't minded that at all. On the contrary, it meant that for the first time since Papa had remarried, she was going to have a bedroom to herself.

There was no alternative. Nobody could squeeze two beds into any of the rooms on the upper floor. Let alone cupboards and dressers and shelves for all the fripperies they were buying.

But Stepmama had been livid. She was banking on Sukey landing a peer of the realm. A peer who would be so smitten by her beauty and charm, and so rich, that he would think nothing of providing for both Georgiana and herself, as long as he could get his ring on Sukey's finger.

But the chances of accomplishing anything so ambitious from an address in Bloomsbury were as slender as their box-like bedrooms.

'Now,' said Stepmama briskly. 'I want no more nonsense from either of you. Sukey, you will be wearing unbroken white, as befits a debutante in her first Season. And, Georgiana, you are old enough to get away with revealing your charms so as to attract gentlemen who prefer someone a little more...' She made a gesture outlining Georgiana's fuller figure. 'More.'

With that, she bustled out of the girls' dressing room to prepare herself for tonight's outing.

There was a moment of silence, during which Sukey touched the blue ribbon with the tip of her finger, wistfully. And Georgiana stared at her own reflection with disquiet.

'Aren't you the least bit excited,' said Sukey, who must have noticed the expression on Georgiana's face, 'about attending our very first *ton* party?'

'No,' she replied bluntly. 'I am dreading it.' Nausea had been swimming in her stomach ever since Edmund had turned her down. She'd known it was a forlorn hope, attempting to breach his walls and enter the citadel which would have provided her with sanctuary.

And sure enough, like so many soldiers in charge of such an endeavour, she'd been cut down before she'd got anywhere near her objective. Brutally.

'Besides…' She turned to concentrate on Sukey and a new worry that had taken up residence of late.

'Oh, Georgiana, not this again!' Sukey pouted.

'I'm sorry, Sukey. I know that you get on like a house on fire with Dotty and Lotty, now. But I still feel horridly guilty for the way Stepmama practically stalked the Pargetters after she learned that some cousin or other of theirs recently had the good fortune to marry a viscount.'

'She did not *stalk* anybody.'

'We never became so friendly until your mama discovered the viscount in their background.'

Sukey giggled. 'I suppose it was a little…'

Ruthless, Georgiana thought, but didn't say. 'And haven't you ever wondered what will happen if the three of you all fall for the same man?'

Sukey shook her head, adopting an expression so very like her mother's that for a moment Georgiana half-expected to get a scold.

'We will all wish each other well and do our best to be the winner. Heavens, Georgiana, don't huntsmen do the same sort of thing in the field? And nobody expects them to fall out over a bit of sporting rivalry.'

Now it was Georgiana's turn to be shocked. 'You regard men as your quarry?'

Sukey giggled again. 'At the moment, yes, why not? It's fun, Georgiana, taking part in this sort of game.'

'It's not a game, though, is it? It is…our life.' Dread at what she was about to face squeezed at her heart, making it hard to breathe.

'Exactly. And we ought to enjoy it to the full.'

'But—'

'Be sensible, Georgiana. All women have to marry—'

'Which is the problem, in a nutshell. If only I were a man, I wouldn't have to rely on a husband.'

Sukey shrieked with laughter. 'I should hope not!'

'Oh, you know what I mean,' said Georgiana, though unbelievably she couldn't help smiling at the way Sukey had deliberately misinterpreted her. That was the thing about Sukey. Even when Georgiana was at her most despondent, her vivacious little stepsister could nearly always manage to raise her spirits. It was how, in some ways, she'd managed to fill the void left by Edmund's defection. Though Edmund, she reflected wistfully, had never been shocked by her behaviour, or puzzled by her opinions.

'If I were a man,' she continued, though she knew it was hopeless to say so, 'I could learn a trade and earn my own living, and run my own household…' In fact, that was what she'd hoped to be able to do with the money her father had left her. Buy a little cottage somewhere and live simply. Just the three of them. Without having any men at all complicating everything.

But Stepmama wouldn't hear of it. She had an ingrained belief that women needed men to take care of them, which nothing could shake. Not even the house in Bloomsbury.

'Georgiana, really! If Mama were to hear you say that…'

'I know. She'd say I wasn't too old for the switch.' Georgiana sighed.

'No, she wouldn't,' said Sukey. 'Because you are too sensible to say anything so silly within her hearing.' She shot her stepsister a knowing look.

Fortunately, Sukey wasn't the kind of girl who told

tales, either. Even so, Georgiana sighed heavily. 'I am sorry, Sukey. I know you are very excited about getting an invitation to such an exclusive party and I have no wish to ruin your evening with my fit of the dismals.'

'You're just nervous, I expect,' said Sukey charitably. 'Heavens, I'm nervous myself. I cannot believe that Mrs Pargetter somehow managed to get our names on her niece's guest list, when everyone knows it's supposed to be just family and close friends. I hear there's going to be at least two viscounts there and heaven alone knows who else besides.' She gave the bunch of blue ribbon one last regretful look, then turned her gaze upon Georgiana.

'I suppose at least if we are both all in white, we shall match.'

'It's very kind of you to say so, Sukey.' It was her way of showing solidarity. 'But nobody looking at us standing side by side could ever mistake us for sisters. Not that there will be much standing side by side. You will get swept away from me on a tide of chatter and giggles as soon as we arrive and will end up at the centre of the liveliest crowd in the room. While I will be looking about for the quietest, most secluded corner in which to hide. I hope the Durants go in for potted palms.'

'Hide? You cannot possibly waste the opportunity Mama has worked so hard to procure for us, hiding away behind a potted palm.'

'It's all very well for you,' Georgiana protested. 'But you aren't going to have every man in the place addressing every single remark to your breasts. Men actually remember what your face looks like—even what colour eyes you have, I shouldn't wonder. But not one of them has ever looked at anything above my neck since

I grew these.' She gestured in despair to the front of her low-cut gown.

Sukey clapped her hand to her mouth to stifle a giggle.

'I am sure that is not true, but anyway, if they do attract a man's notice, that is all to the good, surely?'

'There is nothing good about them. They are too big and too heavy. And, and…downright uncomfortable when I go out riding.'

'Well, only because you will go everywhere at full gallop. I'm sure if you rode in a more decorous manner…'

'Why should I ride in a decorous manner, just because I sprouted these on my thirteenth birthday?'

'Because it is the ladylike thing to do,' said Sukey with a puzzled shake of her head before walking back to the mirror to admire her reflection.

Leaving Georgiana convinced of only one thing. No matter how lovely and feminine and sweet Sukey was, deep down, she held the same convictions as Stepmama. Which was why, in spite of feeling a great deal of affection for her, she had never seen the point in confiding in her.

Not the way she'd been able to confide in Edmund.

But then he'd been the only person, apart from Papa, who'd accepted her as she was.

Until he'd been sent away.

Which had changed everything.

Everything.

Chapter Five

Edmund pushed his way through the cluster of people gathered by the railings of Durant House and gave his name to the burly footman stationed there.

He'd known tonight's event would rouse interest in certain circles, but had not anticipated it creating quite such a stir. He had underestimated the amount of people who had nothing better to do than gossip, obviously. Though Lord and Lady Havelock, the owners of Durant House, had certainly done plenty to create it. Lady Havelock had been a complete unknown before their marriage, which had taken place just before Christmas, while most of the *ton* had been spending the Season on their country estates. And, according to the very few people who'd been on terms to visit since the couple had taken up residence, she had performed an almost miraculous transformation upon one of the gloomiest town houses known to the *haut ton*.

What was more, before this mysterious woman could take up her place in society, her lord had proved equally efficient in his own endeavours at siring an heir. Her appearances in public therefore were few and far between and invitations to Durant House were scarcer than hen's teeth. Which meant that everyone who hadn't seen inside wanted to know how the young Lady Havelock had managed to effect the sort of improvement upon her new home—that those who had been privileged to see it were raving about—without bankrupting her husband in the process.

'You are expected, Lord Ashenden,' said the footman, before stepping aside to allow him to pass.

A smile tugged at Edmund's lips as he mounted the steps to the front door which swung open as if by magic. Georgiana's stepmother must have been cock-a-hoop when she received her invitation to this 'informal gathering of friends and family', especially once she'd seen how many others were *not* being admitted to the select gathering. After tonight, the three Wickford ladies would be invited to all sorts of events hosted by ladies whose determination to discover the latest gossip about the interior of Durant House knew no bounds. They would not even be deterred by their humble origins, if anyone ever bothered delving into their antecedents.

Edmund handed his hat and coat to the footman who'd opened the door to him, and made his way across the wainscoted hall to the staircase that swept up the left wall, via a series of half-landings, to the gallery spanning the next storey. The hall was massive. And could have been imposing, but somehow felt welcoming, in spite of Lord Havelock's forebears scowling down at him from their heavily gilded frames.

That was possibly because he didn't care about the opinion of long-dead nobles. To be frank, he didn't give much for the opinion of living ones either. The only person whose thoughts interested him in the slightest, at this moment, was Georgiana.

She was bound to be angry with him after the way

they'd parted. Though at least this time he knew why she was angry with him and had a perfectly sound explanation to offer. At least, he intended to explain why he hadn't called upon her before she'd left Bartlesham. He was tolerably certain she would understand his need to think things through. And that she'd forgive his earlier offence once he demonstrated his willingness to be her friend once more, if not her husband.

What he was not going to do, however, was offer any explanation as to why he hadn't called upon her now that he was in Town as well.

A flush crept up his neck as he mounted the stairs, brought on by the recollection of the impetuous way he'd stormed out of Six Chimneys before he'd gathered all the information he needed. And then the difficulty he'd had attempting to track her down. By the time he had done so, it was far too late to simply pay her a morning call, since she was bound to have known exactly how long he'd been in residence at Ashenden House. Various newspapers regularly reported his movements, for reasons that remained a mystery to him. It would have looked as though he'd been too busy, or too indifferent to call before.

Besides, he'd reasoned, they wouldn't have been able to converse privately anyway. He could just imagine the scene in her drawing room, with her shooting dagger glances at him, while he would have been unable to explain anything to his satisfaction. Not with her stepmother in earshot. For he was certain the woman could not have known about their meeting by the trout stream. If she'd been brought into Georgiana's life to teach her how to behave, then one of the first things she would have taught her was the impropriety of meeting single gentlemen without a chaperon.

Once he'd come to that conclusion, he had then briefly wondered how Georgiana had managed to engineer the meeting at all. But only briefly. For she had been wearing a riding habit and there had been no sign of a horse. Somewhere close by there must have been a groom who had somehow been persuaded to let her out of his sight for a few minutes.

He shook his head. The stepmother must be completely hen-witted if she thought she could trust Georgiana out of her sight with only a groom to guard her. Didn't she know what a wild, free spirit dwelled in that shapely body?

Which reflection made his heart speed up considerably.

Or perhaps it was simply that he'd just climbed several flights of stairs and would soon be walking into the reception room in which Georgiana must surely be by this time of the evening. He'd deliberately arrived late, telling Lord Havelock that he would 'pop in' on his way back from another engagement. 'It would be best to commence my association in London with Miss Wickford by meeting as if by chance,' he had explained, 'at some event where we have mutual friends.'

'If that's the way you want to play it,' Lord Havelock had said, raising his brows and grinning, blast him.

Edmund's lips tightened. He'd provided Lord Havelock and his friends with a great deal of amusement when they'd discovered what he was about. But he hadn't had much choice. Time had been ticking away and he'd been getting nowhere. Since Edmund hadn't found a trace of Georgiana in the best circles, it made sense to assume her stepmother was making use of whatever connections she did have. Which, upon reflection, were bound to be from a less exalted sphere, into which he did not have the entrée.

Fortunately, there were a few members of his club who did have those connections and, more importantly, upon whose discretion he could depend. Both Lord Chepstow and Lord Havelock had married women from the gentry, and Mr Morgan—though immensely wealthy—had even more humble origins. Besides which, the four of them had put their heads together once before, when Lord Havelock had confessed his need to find a bride in a hurry.

Edmund had advised him to draw up a list of requirements, to help him focus his thoughts, and the other two had added both their own suggestions and practical help in locating Havelock's perfect bride. Yet not a word of that night's work had ever been revealed by any of them. Which said something about their integrity. Many men, having taken part in such an exercise, would have later made a joke of it.

And so Edmund had felt fairly confident about approaching them and sharing something of his dilemma.

'One good turn deserves another,' Havelock had said, as soon as he had broached the fact that he was in need of assistance. 'In what way can I help you?'

'I am attempting to locate a…certain young lady of my acquaintance, who has come to London. But discreetly.'

'I can be discreet,' Havelock had said, affronted.

Edmund had sighed. He had forgotten just how swiftly Havelock's temper could be roused. And by the most innocuous of remarks.

'I am sure you can be,' he had said in a placating manner. 'Now, to the nub of the matter. This young lady does not move in the circles we generally inhabit. Her stepmother is…' He'd paused, briefly. He was loathe to speak ill of any lady, even though his opinion of Mrs Wickford had been getting worse by the day. But he had very nearly blurted out a most unflattering description of her character. 'According to rumour, her father was a grocer in some nondescript town,' he'd said, determined to stick to the facts of the matter, and only the facts. 'Her first husband a mere tailor.'

'The daughter ain't trying to hide from you, is she?' Havelock had leaned back in his chair and folded his arms.

'Nothing of the sort! This…grocer's daughter happened to marry the widowed master of the hunt, from Bartlesham, the village where I spent my boyhood, since my principal seat is located nearby. Now that he's died, they have had to vacate their home, since it was entailed. She has brought her…daughters to London hoping to find wealthy husbands for them both. I simply wish to…to help them, if I can. And to do that, I need to know where they are living and with whom they are mixing.'

'They sloped off without telling you their direction?' Havelock was still frowning.

Edmund had felt his cheeks heat. 'I meant to call on them before they left Bartlesham. I was…distracted by…other matters and left it too late. By the time I went to enquire after them, they'd already left. And I feel it would be remiss of me not to do something for them, behind the scenes, in a…disinterested sort of way, since they are in the way of being neighbours.'

'Sounds like a hum to me,' Havelock had persisted. 'Why don't you just tell us the truth?'

'You are interested in this girl from your village, aren't you?' Unlike Havelock, Morgan appeared pleased that Edmund had inadvertently made it sound as though he was in hot pursuit of some innocent country miss. But then everyone knew he had a sister to marry off this Season, a sister he wished to keep away from anyone with a title, for some reason known only to himself.

Edmund had, he believed, shut his eyes at that point and swallowed convulsively at the choices he was going to have to take—either to let them go on believing they were abetting him in the pursuit of unwilling prey, or to confess that Georgiana's proposal had rattled him so badly he hadn't been able to think clearly for several days. Eventually, he'd come up with an answer that spared him the necessity of doing neither.

'I am not…*interested* in her,' he'd said, a little testily. 'She is totally unsuitable. Apart from her background, she is a complete hoyden, besides being horse-mad and…fickle.'

'Is she intelligent, though?' Havelock had asked with a grin. 'I seem to recall that was the only factor you insisted I should include on my own list of wifely qualities. So that you wouldn't have to…what was it…forfeit your bachelor freedoms only to sire a brood of idiots?'

Morgan had slapped the tabletop at this point and laughed. 'That was *exactly* what he said. I remember now! Which is why so many people seem to think you might be about to make a match of it with Lady Susan Pettifer.'

'Lady Susan? Good God, no! She has a tongue like a—' He'd only just managed to pull himself up before saying something he would have regretted. 'That is,' he temporised, 'I have no intention of marrying *anyone*. For some considerable time. I simply wish to ensure that Georgie has the chance to meet the kind of gentleman *she* might like to marry.'

'Georgie? You call her by her given name?'

'What does she look like?'

The pair of them had been grinning like schoolboys at his discomfiture. But at least he could tell they were both considering helping him. So, instead of getting up and stalking out, he'd swallowed his pride and given them some pertinent details.

'Her name is Georgiana Wickford,' he'd therefore told them. 'She is tall, and…robust, with black hair and brown eyes. Her stepmother is Mrs Wickford and her stepsister is Susan Mead, though she's normally known as Sukey.'

'No—what, Sukey and Georgiana?' Havelock had sat up straight. 'Mary came back from visiting her cousins the other day saying she'd met some girls just up from the country by those very names. I wonder if it could be them…'

It had sounded too good to be true. And yet, after further investigation, Havelock had confirmed that Mrs Wickford had rented a house just off Bloomsbury Square and that her daughter and stepdaughter had already become friends with his wife's cousins who lived nearby.

'Doesn't sound as though they need any help from you finding husbands, though,' he'd said. 'They've been presented at court.'

'Already?' He wondered how Mrs Wickford had managed it. He wondered what it had cost. And why Georgiana had made it sound as though she was about to live in penury for the rest of her life.

'Tell you what,' Havelock had said. 'Why don't I ask Mary if she'll send them invitations to a little card party and supper she's planning?'

'You would really do that?'

'Yes. For I cannot wait to see the woman who's got you so hot under the collar.'

'She does not have me hot under the collar, as you put it,' he'd retorted.

'Ashe, you went pink when we were discussing her. You very nearly raised your voice. That's as near to getting hot under the collar as I've ever seen you.' Havelock had laughed, slapping him on the back.

He certainly felt a little hot under the collar now. Because, in a minute or two, he was going to see her. Would probably have to stick to a topic of conversation suitable for a polite drawing room, when what he really wanted to do was discuss the conclusions he'd reached since their last meeting. And all the questions that had arisen since, about her finances, her ambitions, her motives, her prospects...

He paused in the open doorway of a large reception room, scanning its occupants for a sight of her face. And couldn't help recalling that face as he'd last seen it, streaked with tears. Because he'd made her cry. Which was something else he needed to explain. That he hadn't meant to. Hadn't realised that a few words designed to cut her down to size would have cut her down completely. Had never dreamed anything he'd said could have had any effect upon her at all, come to that.

But it was Lord Havelock he saw first. He was hovering over the back of a sofa upon which his wife was sitting, deep in conversation with Lady Chepstow. Chepstow himself was sitting on the floor, for goodness sake, gazing up at the woman he'd snatched from her employers during a Christmas house party and subsequently married, with a fatuous expression on his face.

'Would you care for some wine, sir?' Yet another smartly dressed footman stepped forward, a tray of glasses held in his hand. Edmund took just one. And congratulated himself on his self-control.

'You will find a cold collation laid out upon the pianoforte, my lord,' said the footman, waving to a second room, visible through a set of double doors which stood open.

'The pianoforte,' he repeated, eyeing the instrument over which a cloth had been draped 'Of course.'

'Her ladyship is quite determined that there is to be no dancing tonight,' said the footman, with just a trace of a smile tugging at his lips. 'Though you will find card tables, should you prefer to play, rather than merely converse with the other guests.'

Edmund would never prefer wasting his time in a trivial game when he could be conversing with someone of interest. However, it was not the footman's fault that he was serving refreshments at the kind of gathering where gentlemen sat on the floor gazing up at their wives and pianos were put into service as tea tables.

So he nodded his acceptance of the boundaries set for the evening's 'entertainment' and stepped fully into the room.

And then he saw her. And something that felt rather like cold rage started burning in his gut. Because she looked…he swallowed. If it had been any other woman, he would have said she looked stunning. Luscious. Her hair was different. She'd had it cut and styled so that wisps curled round her face. But it was her gown that really stunned him. What little there was of it.

Not only did it plunge low at the front, but the tiny little scraps of material masquerading as sleeves did not even cover her shoulders. It made the whole top half of her gown look as though, at any moment, it might slip from her altogether, revealing the figure to which it was clinging so precariously.

To every man in the room.

For a few moments he stood completely still, grappling with the urge to whip off his jacket, march across the room, and fling it round her shoulders. How could she...flaunt herself in that...tawdry excuse for a gown? After saying she couldn't bear the thought of men... pawing her, that the only kind of marriage she could tolerate would be a platonic one, she was standing there with everything on display, practically begging every man in the room to...lean in and grab a handful.

He downed his drink in one go and slammed the empty glass down on the nearest horizontal surface. Hang offering her his coat to cover herself up. He was going to give her a piece of his mind.

Chapter Six

If this was what *ton*nish people called a 'small, informal gathering', then Georgiana shuddered to think what a large one would be like. Since she'd been here, more than fifty couples had wandered in, shaken hands with Lord Havelock, been presented to his wife, taken a glass of wine and ambled out again. They had included a baronet, a viscount and a marquis.

Stepmama had been disappointed in the viscount, since he'd brought a wife with him. But when she'd seen the marquis come in alone and learned he was as yet unmarried, she'd been so excited it was a wonder she hadn't danced a jig on the spot.

Georgiana had cringed at Stepmama's attempts to attract his notice and push him in Sukey's direction, and then winced at Lord Lensborough's distinctly frosty dismissal.

Her one consolation was that Sukey hadn't flung herself at him. Far from it. She'd made a beeline for Mrs Pargetter's daughters, Dotty and Lotty, and stayed glued to them, whether they strolled to the end of the room to select a plate of refreshments, or sat on a sofa to giggle and gossip. Georgiana had no interest in their sort of chatter, and anyway, the sofa on which they'd eventually settled could only just contain the three of them. So she'd made the excuse of needing to visit the retiring room and slipped away from them all.

She'd stayed there as long as she could. It had been so horrid, being in a room full of people who all knew each other, and who had all quickly pegged Stepmama for the kind of woman who would stop at nothing to see her daughters married off.

If only she wouldn't be so...*obvious*.

Eventually, Georgiana knew she could not stay in the retiring room any longer, or Stepmama would be sending someone to find out if she'd fallen ill. She looked warily round the huge reception room before stepping fully back inside, looking for the safest place to go. In her absence, Stepmama had gone to the card tables, where she was currently frowning over what looked like a hand of whist with Mr Pargetter. The poor man had, earlier on, looked as out of place as Georgiana had felt, amidst all the titled, privileged guests. It was good to see he looked much more at ease, now he was playing cards. And being much more useful, to Georgiana's way of thinking, by keeping Stepmama occupied.

She gave a sigh of relief, fixed a smile on her face and sauntered in the general direction of Sukey's sofa. As soon as Stepmama had noticed her, nodded her approval and returned her attention to her hand, Georgiana veered off towards the furthest, quietest corner of the room. She had just turned and leaned back against the wall, when the footman stationed at the door announced the arrival of yet another guest.

'Lord Ashenden!'

For a moment, a wave of such raw fury gripped her that she forgot to breathe. And it wasn't just because of the way he'd rebuffed her proposal. It was all the years and years of rejection that had come before. Which brought on a wave of pain so intense it made her throat close up.

And then she went light-headed.

Then the fear of fainting away and humiliating herself in front of all these sophisticated people, just because Edmund had walked in, got her breathing again. And firming her knees and her spine. And schooling her features into an expression of what she hoped would pass for indifference.

She was only just in time, too. He'd been looking idly round the room, but his cool grey gaze snagged on her in recognition. And then, as if it wasn't enough that he was actually here, his lip curled in distaste as he raked her from head to toe.

He couldn't have hurt her worse if he'd slapped her. Come to think of it, he couldn't have hurt her at all if he'd tried anything like that. She'd have had her guard up and deflected the blow.

A reflection that served to turn the knife in the wound. For he'd been the one to teach her how to defend herself, and, remembering how close they'd been once only made her more painfully aware of how far apart they were now.

Oh, Lord, why did he have to be here tonight, when she was wearing a gown that made her feel like a…a trollop?

Trollop. The accusation rang in her ears. It had been Edmund's housekeeper who'd first used that word to condemn her behaviour, when she'd found her in his sickroom, that day she'd spent collecting all those butterflies to cheer him up. Which had been the last time she'd ever managed to sneak into his house. Nobody else had ever called her that name again, but whenever she'd heard anyone else called a trollop, in connection with some scandalous behaviour, it had felt as though they were raking their nails across her skin.

Now, the way he was looking at her made her wonder if he'd thought it all along.

She gasped.

Was that why he hadn't written to her, even though he'd said he would? Had someone persuaded him, between their exchange of notes and his arrival in the Scilly Isles, that he'd do better to cut the connection? She'd always just thought he'd forgotten all about her once he'd left the country, that he had found more interesting companions, but…it might explain everything. It would certainly explain the way he'd behaved when he'd come home. Instead of going straight to their usual meeting place by the stream, or tucking a note between the loose stones by his gate post to explain why he wasn't coming, he'd completely ignored her.

Stepmama had explained that she shouldn't expect him to recognise her in public, once his father had died, and he'd become the Earl. Besides which, he wasn't a boy any longer, but a man who'd travelled and gained all sorts of experience. She'd taken another, longer look at him then. And seen that this fashionably dressed, sophisticated man would have regarded the letters she'd written to him as the outpourings of a childish idiot.

She'd gone cold inside as she'd finally understood how pathetic she'd been about…so many things. And promptly vowed not to be so pitiful one moment longer. If he didn't want to have anything to do with her, then she would not embarrass him, or herself, by letting anyone suspect she'd been pining for him.

So the next time she'd seen him, the night he'd

strolled into the local assembly in Bartlesham, she'd fixed a smile on her face and stuck close to Sukey and her throng of admirers. And instead of ignoring the left-over ones that Sukey didn't have time to dance with, she'd offered to stand up with them for once. Most of them were so bemused they couldn't think of a polite way to refuse her, so, for that one night, Georgiana had never lacked for a partner.

But it hadn't impressed Edmund. At least, not the way she'd hoped. He'd looked at her exactly the way he was looking at her now. As though she disgusted him.

So she did exactly what she'd done that night as well. She lifted her chin and turned her head away, as though there was something more interesting to look at else-where. Her gaze came to rest on the baronet, who was standing by the piano, piling his plate with food. And slipping every third sandwich into his pocket.

The sight of a guest stealing food was so shocking that it did actually distract her from Edmund. For a mo-ment, anyway. By the time she glanced back at the place where he had been standing, he was no longer there.

Instead, he was striding across the room, looking as though he was thinking of strangling her.

Her heart started banging against her ribs. She didn't know what she'd done to put such a look on his face, but at least he was coming over. Every other time they'd been at the same function he'd made a point of ignor-ing her. Spoken to just about every other person in the place, but accorded her only a chilly nod as he'd stalked past on his way out.

Not that he had any right to look at her like that. In fact, she had far more right to be angry and to be shoot-ing dagger glances at him. If he'd only been more... reasonable, she might not have had to part with Whitesocks, or see Stepmama spend the money that had been left to her by her father on foolish extravagances, or been shoehorned into ridiculous outfits and obliged to put up with the unwelcome attention such gowns attracted from men who ought to have better manners. She might not have had to come to London at all.

By the time he reached her side, she'd curled her hands into fists, she was so angry with him. Every bit as angry as he looked. For a moment or two, neither of them spoke. Instead they just stood there glaring at each other.

'I see you are set on taking London by storm,' he said, giving the edge of her décolletage one scathing glance.

He might have said something vile, but at least he had been the one to weaken and speak first. So it felt as if she had scored the first point.

'I see you have left your manners behind in Bartlesham,' she riposted.

'Touché,' he said, raising his hand to acknowledge the hit. Which made it two to one. 'But if you want me to make a complimentary remark about your appearance, I am afraid you will be waiting a long time.'

She supposed he'd meant to wound her, but since he couldn't possibly hate the gown more than she did, the thrust had gone wide. What was more, now that he'd spoken to her so rudely, she felt perfectly justified in speaking her mind as well.

'I have already learned that waiting for you is a waste of time.'

'I attended you at the trout stream the very day I got your note,' he said, looking a touch uncomfortable. 'And I did call upon you a day or so later, to tell you that...' He shook his head. 'Never mind that now. It must be obvious that by the time I had calmed down, you had already left for London and what might have been said upon that occasion is now completely irrelevant.'

'You called upon me? At Six Chimneys?' That hadn't been what she'd meant about waiting for him. It had been the years while he'd been abroad, during which she'd pined for his company, which she now regarded as so much wasted time. Because she'd always hoped that when he came back, things would have returned to the way they'd been...

Which just went to show how silly she'd been. They'd both been children when he'd gone away. Adults when he returned. Things could never have been the same between them, even if he'd kept his word about staying in touch.

'Yes,' he said looking grim. 'I had the dubious pleasure of meeting your father's cousin, Mr Wickford.'

'Serves you right,' she said, as if she was twelve again. 'Did you also meet Mrs Wickford?'

'No. She was upstairs, attempting to make herself presentable.'

'You had a narrow escape. Though a meeting with Mrs Wickford is exactly what you deserve for—' She pulled herself up short. For a moment, there, she'd started speaking to him as freely as she'd done when they'd been children. As if she hadn't worked so hard to acquire the manners of a lady. As if all the slights and betrayals had never taken place.

But they had. Besides, he was the Earl of Ashenden now, not her playmate. And she was just a penniless country miss, who ought to know her place and respect her betters, and all the rest of the things Stepmama was constantly reminding her of.

'For letting you down,' he finished her sentence for

her, the way he'd always done when her thoughts had become too tangled for her to get them out sensibly. 'For which I apologise. I told you, once, that you might apply to me should you ever find yourself in need of my help—'

She gasped. She'd thought he'd resented making that promise. That he would do anything to wriggle out of it. And yet now that he'd had time to reflect, it seemed he regretted not being able to do the one thing she'd requested. As though keeping his word was still important to him.

Even if she wasn't.

'And the very first time you asked me for anything,' he was continuing, 'I let you down. Not,' he went on hastily, 'that I have any intention of acceding to your ridiculous proposal of marriage.'

'Naturally not.' It had always been a long shot. Her last, desperate attempt to salvage something from the wreckage left in the wake of her father's demise.

But did he have to look so relieved she'd now said as much?

'But there are other ways I could keep my promise to…to be your friend, I am sure. Other ways I can repay the debt I owe you.'

'Debt? What debt?'

'Perhaps you are right. Perhaps it is not that I *owe* you anything.' He paused, frowning slightly, the way he always did when marshalling his arguments. 'Perhaps it is more accurate to say that I am determined not to break my vow.'

She flinched. Just as she'd thought. It wasn't she that mattered, but his own honour.

'Yes, well,' she said, 'it is a little late now.'

'Far from it. There is a great deal I can do, short of actually marrying you.'

Did he have to keep on reminding her that he had no intention of marrying her? He'd made it plain enough already. She wasn't stupid!

'There is nothing you can do now,' she hissed like a kettle coming to the boil, 'that will make anything right. You cannot get back Whitesocks.' She poked him in the chest with her forefinger. 'Or my dowry.' She poked him again. 'Or my home.' He grabbed her hand before she managed to get a third dig into his chest, so that for a moment, anyone looking at them would have thought they were holding hands.

'Your dowry is gone?' Something flickered across his face. 'That is how she could afford the court presentation, I suppose.'

Edmund always had been quick on the uptake. Her father might have despised him for not being keen on what he'd deemed *manly pursuits*, but even he'd conceded Edmund had a mind like a steel trap. So, because he was sure to work it all out for himself eventually, she didn't see any point in trying to conceal anything from him now. 'Stepmama is determined Sukey will marry a viscount, at the very least. Which means we need to be able to dance at *ton* events. Hence the court presentation.'

She wrenched her hand free. 'This entire Season has been planned out with the efficiency of a military campaign.'

His eyes flicked once more across the immense expanse of bosom left on show by her scanty evening gown. 'So,' he said thoughtfully, 'rather than don armour, you have decided to use what weapons you possess.'

'I would say that it is more a case of setting out the wares,' she countered through gritted teeth. 'I feel like a…' She sucked in a sharp breath. She could only think of one horrid, vulgar word to describe how she felt.

'You look magnificent,' he said.

'What? That wasn't what you said when you first came over here.' She searched his face for signs of mockery, but could detect only what looked very much like sympathy.

'I…' He paused, his lips thinning in annoyance. 'I forgot, when I first saw you tonight, that you have little choice in what you wear,' he admitted. 'This is one of the things you were dreading about the Season, wasn't it? Being paraded about like a prize heifer at market.'

Bother him, now he'd made her want to cry. Because he'd remembered what she'd said to him, practically word for word. And believed her, unquestioningly.

But before she could do anything so weak as to break down or as foolish as to fling herself on to his chest, Stepmama rose from the card table and headed in their direction with a martial gleam in her eye. Which made Georgiana lift her chin and stiffen her spine, thank goodness.

Just in the nick of time.

'Lord Ashenden? Why, what a surprise,' Stepmama cooed. 'I had no notion that you were a friend of Lord and Lady Havelock.'

'Why should you?'

Georgiana almost shivered at the chill in his voice. It was as if the Edmund she'd started to become comfortable with again had vanished. In his place stood Lord Ashenden. And she could easily imagine him delivering the kind of remark that had fallen from the lips of Lord Lensborough, earlier. The kind of remark designed to cut down a vulgar interloper and remind her that though she might have wheedled her way inside a house belonging to a member of the Quality, she had absolutely none herself.

Instead, his frosty expression thawed, even though it was only by about half a degree.

'I have a passing acquaintance with Lord and Lady Chepstow, too,' he said. 'Have you met them?'

'Oh, yes, she is a most charming woman,' Stepmama gushed.

'Lady,' he corrected her.

'Yes, that is what I meant, of course.'

'She is also extremely intelligent,' he said, enigmatically. 'She was working as a governess, you know, when Chepstow decided to marry her.'

'Indeed?' For a moment, Stepmama faltered, unsure of where the conversation was headed. Georgiana could barely prevent herself from kicking him. He was deliberately toying with Stepmama. At least Lord Lensborough's derision had been obvious, though delivered with brutal swiftness.

'I heard,' Stepmama was saying, 'that they had known each other almost all their lives, that she attended the same school as his sister.'

'That may be correct,' he acknowledged. 'In any case, I find it admirable that she was using the talents God gave her to make her own way in the world.'

'Oh, yes, most admirable,' said Stepmama with enthusiasm, though she couldn't possibly have any idea what she was being so enthusiastic about.

'Are you hinting,' said Georgiana, taking pity on her stepmother, 'that I would be better to go out and work for my living, than attempt to get a husband, my lord?' Was that what he'd meant about keeping his promise to help her? Since he knew how reluctant she was to marry, was he going to use his influence, and his connections, to help her find paid employment instead?

'Oh, merciful heavens, how can you say anything so absurd?' cried Stepmama, rapping her over the wrist with her fan. Quite hard.

'Is it so absurd?' Edmund tipped his head to one side and stared at Stepmama as if he was giving the matter serious consideration.

'Completely absurd,' tittered Stepmama. 'Why, who on earth would employ Georgiana? In any capacity? She has none of the feminine accomplishments. I suppose, if we could find a school where horse riding was considered important, she could teach the younger girls to ride, but other than that...' She waved her hand dismissively.

Edmund's eyes barely flickered, but they seemed to her to have turned to ice.

'Did you never teach her any of the feminine accomplishments you consider so desirable, madam? I should have thought that was among your primary duties.'

'Oh.' Stepmama looked taken aback at this deliberate, open criticism. 'Well, naturally, I *tried*,' she said, putting on her most martyred expression. 'Only Georgiana is not the slightest bit biddable, you know. Not like my own daughter.'

'Who is the most accomplished female,' he said with deceptive smoothness, 'I am ever likely to meet, I shouldn't wonder.'

There was an edge to his voice that made Georgiana almost urge Stepmama to beware. He clearly hadn't liked the way Stepmama had belittled her, even though he must know she'd only spoken the truth.

'Oh, heavens, yes. My Sukey—'

'Embroiders and paints, and plays the pianoforte?'

'Why, yes, naturally, and—'

'Speaks Italian and French, and sings like a nightingale?'

'Well, no…not the languages, though she does sing beautifully…'

Georgiana was suddenly torn between the equal urges to laugh and to slap him. He was being at his most cutting, and sarcastic in her defence, and Stepmama had no idea he was making fun of her and her pretensions.

'Madam,' he breathed, with complete insincerity, 'I must certainly have an introduction to this paragon.'

'But of course!' Stepmama swelled with triumph. 'Sukey is sitting just over there…'

'I did not mean now,' he said. 'I was just about to leave.'

'Oh, but—' Stepmama began in desperation.

'No, no, really, I have pressing commitments elsewhere. But perhaps…'

'Yes?'

'You will permit me to call upon you?'

'We should be delighted!' Stepmama beamed at him. 'Should we not, Georgiana?' she said pointedly, giving her another tap across her still-stinging wrist with a fan that felt as though its struts were made of oak.

'Delighted,' she said, with a smile. A big, false smile.

'In that case, you must furnish me with your direction, you know.'

Stepmama rattled it off and urged him to repeat it to make sure he wouldn't forget it.

He merely gave her a curt nod. 'I shall not forget,' he said. And stalked off.

'Well,' said Stepmama, using her fan for the purpose for which it was intended, for once. 'What do you think of that?'

'I'm not sure,' said Georgiana, regarding his retreating back with a frown.

'Oh, you are so dense sometimes, Georgiana, I despair of you. It is quite simple. We've been in Town only two weeks and already we can claim visiting rights with two viscounts and an earl. If I don't see my Sukey married to a title before the Season is out then I'll…'

'Eat your fan?'

'Eat my fan? Eat my fan? Why on earth should I do something so absurd? And really, where do you get such vulgar expressions from?' Stepmama wrinkled her nose in distaste. 'Well, never mind that for now. It is all of a piece with the rest of your behaviour. You are never going to get a husband if you will loiter in the retiring room, or the furthest corner of the salon from where the most eligible men are standing, or come out with vulgar expressions like that when someone does finally get into conversation with you.'

She rolled her lips inwards, a sure sign that she had plenty more to say, but was determined to save it for later.

'Which is why I came over here in the first place. I noted a gentleman come in who may be just the thing for you. A cavalry officer, if I know anything about uniforms. Come along, Georgiana,' she said, seizing her by the wrist. 'We need to get him to notice you before either of those Pargetter girls get their talons into him.'

Chapter Seven

Mrs Wickford's drawing room was already crowded by the time Edmund called the next day. He could hear the hubbub of voices the moment a rather jaded-looking butler opened the front door.

The fellow's demeanour underwent a transformation the moment Edmund handed over his card.

'Would you care to step this way, my lord,' he said, making for the stairs.

'No need for you to show me up,' said Edmund. 'I am sure I can find the way.'

The butler winced. 'Indeed, my lord,' he said apologetically. Though whether from insinuating that he might get lost in such a small house, or for the noise emanating from the upper floors which made his guidance unnecessary, it was impossible to tell.

Edmund mounted the single, narrow flight of stairs swiftly and found his way to the drawing room which overlooked the street without the slightest difficulty.

The first person he saw was Mrs Wickford. It was impossible to miss her, since she was presiding over a tea table stationed right beside the door.

'Why, Lord Ashenden,' Georgiana's stepmother

cooed as she lifted the teapot. 'What an unexpected honour. I did not expect you to call upon us this morning.'

'Did you not? When I specifically said I would do so?'

'Ah but, no,' she said shaking her head in what he assumed she intended as a playful manner. 'You only said you would call. You made no mention of which day you might honour us with your presence. And what with you having so many more pressing concerns than us, I really did not expect you to fulfil your generous offer to look in upon your former neighbours quite so soon.'

She pressed a cup of tea into his hand. 'Sukey is just there,' she said, waving in the direction of a sofa containing a gaggle of girls sporting blonde ringlets. 'Do go and make yourself known to her. We are being quite informal this morning, as you see.'

What he saw was a most efficient system of processing callers and sending them in the direction she wished them to go. Which was towards the giggling blondes if they were male, to judge from the assortment of gentlemen hovering round them. The matrons were all sitting on another sofa, sipping tea and watching.

Georgiana, however, was as far away from everyone else as she could possibly get, just like last night. The only difference today was that she was not occupying the far corner on her own. She had the company of a hulking great brute of a man wearing the garish uniform of a cavalry regiment.

Since he intended to call upon this house regularly, he forced himself to smile politely at Mrs Wickford. And then, since he really needed to keep in her good books, he strolled to the sofa on which the blonde girls sat and stood sipping his tea, pretending to pay attention to them prattling on about some nonsense or other, whilst actually listening to the cavalry officer belabouring Georgiana with a detailed account of a hunt in which, naturally, he'd led the field.

When his cup was empty, he set it down, accorded the trio of blondes a nod, then sauntered across to the corner into which, if he wasn't mistaken, the cavalry officer had pinned Georgiana. She was wearing another pale, insubstantial gown which revealed far too much for his liking, in spite of having long sleeves. The cavalry officer appeared to like it, though. In fact, he was enjoying the view down its tightly fitted front so much that he appeared to have forgotten he was holding a cup and saucer in one hand. The saucer was rapidly filling with the liquid from the cup, which was tilting at a steadily increasing angle.

Edmund quirked one eyebrow and shook his head in reproof. Georgiana, who'd been watching him approach, lifted her chin and glared at him over the officer's shoulder. Ah, well. What else was new?

'Good morning, Miss Wickford,' he said softly, making the officer start and spill what remained of the tea that had gathered in his saucer down his scarlet jacket. 'Won't you introduce me to your new friend?'

Georgiana's lips compressed in annoyance. As though to say the man wasn't her friend at all. However, manners obliged her to provide the information he'd requested.

'Lord Ashenden, this is Major Gowan.'

Major Gowan looked torn between reaching for a napkin to mop up the tea trickling down the front of his jacket and sticking out his hand to shake. Edmund solved his dilemma by whisking a handkerchief from his own pocket and extending it to the Major. The action also solved his own dilemma, borne of his extreme reluctance to extend his hand to this man in friendship. Or even common politeness.

'Thank you, my lord,' said the Major, dabbing at the damp blotch. It would probably leave a stain. And tea stains were notoriously difficult to remove, he reflected with satisfaction. 'Dashed awkward, handling such tiny cups, with hands my size.'

'Indeed,' he said coolly, eyeing the man's sausage-like fingers.

'Don't know why women must insist on serving such pap anyway. Would all do much better for a decent glass of brandy.'

'Ale, surely, at this time of the day?' Edmund glanced at Georgiana, who was, at least, shooting her silent daggers at the Major now, rather than at him.

'Ale?' The Major looked outraged. But then he darted a look round the drawing room and pulled a face. 'Oh! Yes, of course. Need to keep one's wits about one when dealing with the fair sex.'

'*Only* when dealing with the fair sex? Dear me,' he said softly. And had the pleasure of seeing Georgiana bite her lower lip, while her eyes lit with amusement. 'Of course, you hold a commission in a cavalry regiment, don't you?'

'Yes, that's right,' said the Major, impervious to the slight he'd made by drawing the inference between belonging to a cavalry regiment and his reluctance to use his wits. 'Was just telling Miss Wickford here about my absolute passion for horseflesh. Something we share, by all accounts, eh, what?'

He'd turned to Georgiana as he made the remark, but since he didn't raise his gaze to the level of her face when he made it, he completely missed the way she rolled her eyes.

'Do you have something in your eye?' Edmund enquired politely.

She glared at him. But only briefly, for the Major ceased his keen observation of her cleavage for a second, to look up in bewilderment.

'In her eye? What? Eh?'

'A mote of dust, perchance?'

'No, it isn't dust,' she snapped. 'That is,' she added more politely, after glancing in her stepmother's direction, 'I have nothing in my eye.'

'Then why were you squinting?' He removed his spectacle case from his pocket, took out his spectacles, hooked the wires over his ears, and leaned closer as though inspecting her eyes. He came close enough to smell her perfume. It was predominantly something herbal. It made him wonder if she'd rinsed her hair with a decoction of rosemary. It was certainly glossy. Like silk.

Just as he was wondering whether her hair would feel as silky as it looked, he noted an increased tension about her shoulders, as though she was flexing one of the muscles in her arm. Or clenching her fist. Or at least thinking about clenching it.

'Your pupils are constricted,' he said. 'As though the light is bothering you.'

'The light?' Major Gowan looked up at the cloudy sky through the window, in disbelief.

'Of course, the light on a day like this would not bother most *men*,' he said, turning his attention to the Major, 'since we spend a great deal of time out of doors. But the *fairer sex*, you know, are confined within doors for such long periods that at this time of the year, when the days begin to grow longer, it can be quite painful for them to expose the delicate membranes of the optical orb to sunlight. Particularly the sort which comes through west-facing windows.'

'Is that so?' Major Gowan regarded him with astonishment.

'Oh, absolutely,' he said with a completely straight face. 'I recommend removal from the area at once, Miss Wickford. Before permanent damage is done. We do not wish the squint to become permanent, do we?'

'Squint?' the Major echoed, looking at Georgiana's beautiful brown eyes in alarm. 'No, certainly don't wish you to acquire a squint.'

'In that case, Miss Wickford, I must insist that you move away from the window at once.'

When she opened her mouth to utter what would probably have been a pithy account of her estimation of the nonsense he'd been spouting, he adopted his most severe expression.

'Allow me,' he said, 'the privilege of a long-standing acquaintance to escort you to another part of the room. A safer environment.' He crooked his arm. She took a deep breath. And narrowed her eyes. It was touch and go, for a moment, whether she would take it or not. He could see part of her still wishing to hit him, or shout at him, or simply flounce away. Any of which would prove fatal to her social standing.

Fortunately, another part of her was looking for an excuse to escape the Major. And it was that part of her that accepted his offer. That placed her hand on his arm and allowed him to steer her to the one remaining sofa without occupants, with meekly downbent head.

The moment she sat down, however, she shot him a challenging look from beneath her lush dark lashes.

'You really are the most complete…'

'I know,' he replied calmly, sitting down beside her. 'But the Major believed every word, which was the main thing.'

'I know, I cannot believe he swallowed such a… plumper!'

'My dear, have you not heard the opinion the infantry hold of the cavalry?' My dear? He'd called her my dear? He would just have to hope she didn't make an issue of it, but just assumed it was the kind of thing he said to every female he chatted with during at-homes. From now on, it might be a good idea to do just that. 'That all the brains in those regiments reside in the four-legged troopers?'

'No. I have not yet held a conversation with anyone from the infantry.'

'I doubt very much that you have held one with a cavalry officer, either,' he said dryly. 'Though really, you could do with learning something about tactics.'

'Tactics?' Her eyes narrowed with suspicion.

'Yes. For example, when choosing one's ground, one should always have a means of…ah, swift retreat. Have you not heard of the expression, fighting with one's back to the wall?'

'I certainly know what it feels like,' she said with feeling.

'Then next time, I trust that you will not retreat into a corner before you have even engaged with the enemy.'

She nodded. 'I shall certainly regard these at-homes more in the light of skirmishes, from now on.'

'And employ a suitably defensive strategy? I may not always be around to come to your rescue.'

'I—' She swallowed back what looked like an indig-

nant retort with a great effort. 'I suppose you wish me
to thank you,' she said through gritted teeth.

'No thanks necessary,' he said with a languid wave
of his hand. 'I am sure you would have come up with
some means of escaping that booby, eventually.'

She darted him a look of surprise.

'You may be green,' he acknowledged, 'but you are
by no means stupid.'

As the words left his mouth, he recalled Havelock's
conjecture, that when he married, his wife would have
to be intelligent.

And Georgiana was intelligent. He took his spectacles case from his pocket. Substituted the word *intelligent* for *quick-witted*. Unhooked his spectacles from
his ears, remembering that he'd never made a joke, no
matter how obscure, that she hadn't understood. Or at
least, understood it *was* a joke. He put his spectacles in
their case. Though she hadn't had the benefit of much
education as a very young girl, and had subsequently
had little more than lessons in etiquette and deportment from what he could gather, she had an enquiring
mind. She used to pepper him with questions, when
she'd been a girl, as though she was hungry for information. About everything.

Just as he'd been.

She'd entered into the spirit of his investigations, too.

He shut his case with a snap, his mind flying back
to her declaration last month that she would never interfere with his interests in London. At the time, he'd
taken offence, assuming she meant exclusively ama-
tory adventures.

But he now wondered if she'd meant something
more. She'd always understood when he became fascinated by a new intellectual pursuit, whether it was

mastering the moves of chess, or attempting to ascertain how many varieties of beetles he could discover within one square mile of Fontenay Court. She hadn't been squeamish about his collection, either, unlike any of the female members of staff about the place. She'd stood, peering over his shoulder when he'd shown her each latest addition he'd made, even expressing interest in where he'd found the specimens.

Not that the collection existed any more. Mrs Bulstrode had thrown it away while he was in St Mary's. 'Cleaned out' was the term the housekeeper had used to describe the pillage of his early scientific endeavours.

He opened his spectacles case again and reached for his pocket, to extract a handkerchief as he reflected that Georgiana would never have regarded his collection as rubbish that wanted removing. Because she had known how many hours he'd put into it and understood what it had meant to him.

Hadn't she?

At one time, he had thought so, but…

He'd loaned his handkerchief to Major Gowan. So he couldn't use polishing his spectacles as an excuse for not speaking while his mind was occupied with the past. Besides, he'd been in the middle of saying something to Georgiana. Who was sitting patiently, waiting for him to finish. Unlike many women, who would have been fidgeting and pouting by now.

'Safety in numbers,' he said, putting his spectacles away and, in so doing, jerking his shoulder in the direction of the sofa on which the blondes were sitting.

She pulled a face. 'The general principle is sound. But I couldn't sit with them for more than ten minutes without starting to wish I could tear out my hair by the roots. All they talk of is clothes and ribbons, and flounces and husbands.'

Now that sounded far more like the Georgie he used to know. The girl who cropped her hair short so she wouldn't have to bother with it much. The girl who was more comfortable in breeches and only wore a skirt over the top, for appearance's sake. Was she still there, then, the girl he'd adored? Hidden somewhere beneath the conventional surface, the way her breeches had been kept hidden under her skirts?

'You would do better to mix with females whose interests you share,' he observed.

'How, exactly,' she said acidly, 'am I supposed to do that?'

He turned his spectacles case over, several times, since it was the only thing he had left to occupy his hands whilst going through the catalogue of the females with whom he was acquainted. Not that it helped. There were too many distractions about him. Giggling girls and braying men, and matrons slurping their tea and sprinkling crumbs on the carpet. And the scent of rosemary, which was for remembrance. Which actually did bring back memories of her compact, warm body pressing up against his as they lay side by side on their stomachs, poring over the pages of Hooke's *Micrographia*.

'I shall make sure you have introductions to some,' he said, getting to his feet. And then taking her hand. 'I shall take my leave,' he said, raising it to his mouth. What the devil? He couldn't kiss her hand. He couldn't think why he'd begun the manoeuvre, as though it was the most natural thing in the world. 'I will call again in…a day or so,' he said, patting her hand, as though it was what he'd meant all along, before restoring it to her.

The moment he got outside, he drew a deep breath.

And his head cleared. He knew exactly who to approach on Georgiana's behalf. It was so obvious he couldn't think why he hadn't told her all about Miss Julia Durant straight away.

There must have been something in the atmosphere in that drawing room that had acted upon his intellect the way fog affected the ability to see. Something that had made him leap to Georgiana's defence quite unnecessarily. Something that had made him forget he didn't have a handkerchief with which to polish his spectacles until he was actually reaching for it. Something that had made him spend so much time dwelling on their shared past that when it was time to leave he'd taken her hand as though it was the most natural thing in the world to kiss it.

Instead of turning left and heading for the hackney stand on the corner of the next street, he turned right, since he'd decided to walk back to Grosvenor Square and give himself time to think. About their past. And his reaction to their separation. And most especially the irrational way he was acting round Georgiana nowadays.

It had to stop. He couldn't respect himself when one moment he was despising her for drawing men into her orbit, the next dashing to her rescue. One moment seething at her for something she'd done when she'd been scarce more than a child, the next wanting to lift her hand to his mouth and kiss it.

Was it all because he kept catching glimpses of the girl she'd once been, peeping out at him through cracks in the veneer of her company manners? Was that why he kept responding in kind? Reverting back to the easy camaraderie they'd shared? It was certainly what had prompted him to think of introducing her to Miss

Durant, Lord Havelock's horse-mad and wilful half-sister, even though he had not named her just now. She would do Georgie the world of good, since she was never the slightest bit apologetic for being exactly who she was.

And nor should Georgie be. She'd been far more appealing as an impulsive, warm-hearted girl than she was now—all stiff and simmering with resentment and suppressed hurt.

If he achieved nothing else, this Season, he would coax that Georgie back to life. And he would start by ensuring she had female companionship of the sort that would nurture the side of her that was being systematically starved.

With a new determination in his bearing, he strode off in the direction of Durant House.

Chapter Eight

Stepmama waited until the last visitor had gone before commencing her interrogation. 'What was he speaking to you about? Lord Ashenden, that is. I don't need to ask what Major Gowan said to you. He has a clear voice. The voice of a man used to command.'

She meant, Georgiana thought, that he was used to bawling orders across a parade ground and hadn't bothered to adapt his tone to what was suitable for a polite drawing room.

'But Lord Ashenden can never be heard above a crowd,' said Stepmama with just a hint of a sneer. 'Besides which he turned his back to me, when he got you on that sofa, just as though he didn't want me to so much as guess what he might be saying.'

He probably hadn't.

'Military tactics, Stepmama,' said Georgiana without the slightest hesitation and almost complete honesty. Because that was, on the surface, what Edmund had been talking about. Anyone overhearing them would not have guessed that he'd been attempting to give her a few pointers on how to handle herself with an unwelcome suitor. If the Major *was* a suitor for her hand.

She shuddered. He'd certainly been keen to tell her all about the estate from which he hailed, the horses his father kept in the stables and the hunting to be had in the area. Was that how a man showed he was interested in a girl as a prospective bride? By talking incessantly about himself?

'I am not surprised to see you shudder. What a strange thing to talk about during an at-home,' said Stepmama, completely misunderstanding Georgiana's reaction. Thankfully. 'Still, he always was a very odd young man by all accounts. Not surprising that he's grown into an eccentric.'

'Eccentric? He is not eccentric. He's—'

'I think he's rather fascinating,' put in Sukey hastily, before Georgiana could get herself into trouble by launching a defiant and heated defence.

Fascinating was a very good word to describe the adult Edmund, actually. Even when she was angry with him, he could make her laugh. Or want to laugh, anyway. She'd had to bite down quite hard to stop herself when he'd spouted all that nonsense about the delicacies of the female eye.

'He was certainly fascinated by *you*, my dear,' said Stepmama to Sukey, happily diverted from the subject. 'I saw the way he was looking at you as he was drinking his tea. He stood there, just gazing down at you, as though he'd never seen anything so lovely.' She leaned forward and gave Sukey's cheeks a loving pat. 'And little wonder. You are exactly to his taste. By all accounts.' She leaned back, flushing. 'Not that we should pay any attention to that sort of thing. All men have their little diversions before they are married. And some of them, particularly those of his rank, have them after, as well.'

Georgiana couldn't think why that statement made

her spirits sink. It wasn't as if she had any matrimonial hopes in that direction. Edmund had rejected her proposal in no uncertain terms. He had only called upon them today, because... She frowned. Actually, she wasn't sure why he'd called. To let her know that he disapproved of her gown and her behaviour? He'd done that, right enough. And then gone on to rescue her and to give her advice as to how to avoid getting backed into corners by idiots like Major Gowan, whilst admitting she didn't need it because she had the sense to avoid such situations now she knew they were likely to occur. He'd also totally confused her last night by saying she looked magnificent, directly after expressing his disapproval of her low-cut bodice, and then, to crown it all, today he'd taken her hand and patted it.

She looked down at it, in bewilderment. It still tingled from his touch. In fact, her whole being had leapt when he'd taken it in his. Probably because it had been the first time he'd touched her in a natural, affectionate sort of way since...since they'd been children. And because, for the entire time they'd been talking, she'd been able to forget that he was an earl and she was a nobody. He'd made her feel like a person again, instead of an... an object of lust, simply by looking directly into her eyes while he'd been speaking to her, without once appearing tempted to let his gaze slide down to her bosom.

Except in disapproval that too much of it was on show.

Which meant he didn't feel the slightest bit attracted to her, as a woman. Not that she wanted him to start acting like a lustful, drooling idiot. And yet...it was perplexingly depressing, all the same.

She'd given too much credit to his declaration she looked magnificent, that's where she'd gone wrong.

He'd probably only said it in an attempt to make her feel better about herself, once he'd remembered what she'd said about disliking being treated like a prize heifer.

She eyed her stepmother with resentment. Trust her to take all the pleasure out of the encounter with Edmund, with just a few choice phrases. For that was what she'd done. Before her remark about the way he'd been looking at Sukey, she'd been basking in what had felt almost like a return to old times. She'd loved the way he'd launched into that nonsense about optical orbs and sunlight from west-facing windows, to tease her for rolling her eyes at the Major. She loved the way he'd wielded his intellect, like a rapier, skewering an opponent who'd been too slow to even notice the attack. Or the defence, rather, because he'd befuddled the Major on her behalf.

Which had been most chivalrous of him. Until now, she'd thought he'd grown into an aloof, and cold, and cutting man. But she'd never heard of him using his intellect against anyone who didn't deserve a set-down. And there was always talk about him. There was talk about all people of his rank. The doings of the *ton* filled columns of print every day. Even though the names were left out, the newspapermen gave sufficient clues to leave nobody in any doubt about who had been doing what with whom.

Perhaps that was what had made it much harder for her to put him out of her mind, than for him to forget about her. She was always hearing snatches of gossip that had reached Bartlesham from London, or Oxford. Not just the gossip about his love life, either. Locals had been vicariously proud of each paper he'd presented to various scientific societies, even though it confirmed the opinion that he was an odd sort of man, to sit up all night catching moths, let alone wasting hours of daylight cataloguing them.

But what was she ever likely to do that would make a newspaper wish to write about it? Nothing.

She might scoff at the Major for being a slowtop, but the truth was she had far more in common with him than with Edmund nowadays.

Though she hated to admit Stepmama could be right about anything, Major Gowan was just the sort of man she ought to consider marrying. He liked living in the country. When he was in London on duty, he was grateful that he could at least spend a great deal of it on horseback, he'd told her. And more to the point, he liked the look of her. Or her bosom, at any rate.

She shuddered again. Was that to be her future? Shackled to a brainless boor who would only ever be interested in her body?

'Now that the visitors have gone, you may run up and get a shawl, Georgiana,' said Stepmama, mistaking her shiver of revulsion at the prospect of having to marry a man like Major Gowan for one of cold.

'Thank you, Stepmama,' she said meekly, relieved to escape the room before the interrogation went any further. For if she had to give her opinion about the first suitor her stepmother had flung in her path, it would have been a struggle to say anything even remotely polite.

She would rather go to work as a...as a...

She came to a dead halt halfway up the stairs. Actually, what sort of work could she get? Not as a governess, Stepmama had been right about that. She had none of the accomplishments young ladies required. Her father hadn't thought that sort of education necessary when she'd been little, and by the time he married

Stepmama it had been considered too late to make a silk purse out of a sow's ear. Stepmama had therefore concentrated on drilling her in correct behaviour.

Her bottom winced at the memory of just how mercilessly she'd drilled that behaviour into her, which got her moving up the stairs again.

What other occupations did indigent females of her station go into? Milliner, seamstress? Out of the question. She couldn't sew a straight seam to save her life and had no eye for fashion whatever. Companion to an elderly lady? She'd go mad.

She could, probably, go on the stage. The one thing Stepmama had succeeded in teaching her was how to pretend to be something she wasn't. She didn't think she'd have any difficulty learning her lines, either. The trouble was, actresses had to put up with lots of men drooling over them on a nightly basis, rather than just one.

A reflection that put paid to any thought of having a career on the stage. She slouched along the hall, went into her room and draped a shawl round her upper body in a purely defensive gesture.

Perhaps next time she met Major Gowan, she'd better try harder to look as though she didn't find him altogether repulsive.

Because so far, he appeared to be her only honourable option.

And at least he'd let her have a horse.

The next day, Mrs Pargetter and her two daughters were, yet again, the first callers to arrive. To Stepmama's delight, they arrived in a carriage with a crest on the door. Sukey spied it from the drawing-room window, where she'd been standing watching the traffic going round the square. Stepmama cast her embroidery aside and joined her at the window, where they both pressed their noses to the pane to see who might emerge.

'It's Dotty and Lotty,' said Sukey, in amazement. 'Oh, and Lady Havelock!'

'Well, that explains the carriage, then,' said Stepmama, hurrying back to her chair and flapping her hands to Sukey and Georgiana to adopt similarly domestic poses.

When the Pargetters tumbled into the room, flushed from climbing the stairs, Stepmama pressed her hands to her bosom in feigned surprise.

'My dear Lady Havelock, how good of you to call. What an unexpected pleasure!'

'I hope you don't mind. I have also brought my husband's half-sister, Miss Julia Durant,' she said rather breathlessly, as a rather spotty girl who didn't look old enough to have emerged from the schoolroom came in behind her.

As soon as everyone had dropped the necessary curtsies, Dotty and Lotty made straight for the sofa on which Sukey was sitting. They were soon busily discussing the gowns they planned to wear for the rout they were all attending that evening.

Mrs Pargetter and Lady Havelock sat on the sofa closest to the fire. Stepmama joined them and immediately launched a barrage of questions. Ever since they'd visited Durant House, all sorts of people had approached Stepmama, wanting to know how Lady Havelock had managed to transform the place from a dreary mausoleum into what they now declared was a showpiece. And now that she had the chance to find out, Stepmama was wasting no time furnishing herself with as much information as she could.

Which left Georgiana to entertain the spotty schoolgirl, who'd wandered across the room to the only remaining sofa and dropped on to it sulkily.

Once Georgiana had made sure all the others had cups of tea and as many biscuits as they wanted, she took refreshments over to Miss Durant. The girl took her cup of tea with a polite enough smile, but when Georgiana made as if to sit next to her, the smile vanished and was replaced by a scowl.

'If you're planning to start talking about frills and furbelows, don't bother,' she growled. 'And I don't want to hear another word about paint or plaster or curtains or upholstery either.'

'I didn't have any topic in mind when I came to sit here,' said Georgiana, promptly deciding that such frank speech deserved a frank answer. 'It is just that, before much longer, there are bound to be some gentlemen callers and I'd rather not give them a chance to think they can sit down next to me.'

Miss Durant's eyes narrowed in suspicion. 'Don't you want to have admirers, then? Isn't that why you've come to London? To find a husband?'

'It is why I've come to London,' she conceded with a sigh. 'Yes.'

'But you don't like the way they will squash you on sofas if they think they can get away with it,' said Miss Durant, demonstrating a quick understanding.

'Good heavens, do they do that to you, too? But you're only…'

'Fifteen, yes, but that doesn't stop them. In fact, it positively encourages some of them, because they think I'm too young and ignorant to see what they're about.'

'Good heavens,' said Georgiana again, too stunned to think of anything more original. 'That's…that's… disgraceful. Are all men such…?'

'Bounders,' said Miss Durant resentfully. 'Yes, they are. All of them except my brother, that is. Gregory is a regular trump.' She half-turned to Georgiana, her face coming alight. 'He even married her,' she said, nodding her head in Lady Havelock's direction, 'to save me from the perfectly ghastly man my stepmother was going to marry. And now I live under his roof all those scabby fortune-hunters will think twice about trying anything with me. Gregory would shoot them dead,' she finished with relish.

'Would he?'

'Oh, yes. He's already fought two duels and is a crack shot.'

'That's all very well, but…'

'I suppose you're going to say I shouldn't be talking about duels and fortune hunters wanting you to elope, and stepfathers wanting to…' She clammed up.

'No. That wasn't what I was going to say at all,' said Georgiana indignantly. 'I was actually just wondering why your brother hasn't taught you to defend yourself, that's all.'

'Defend myself? What do you mean? Shoot a pistol?' Her eyes lit up.

'Oh, ah, yes, I did mean that, but—' She darted a guilty glance in Stepmama's direction. Oh, dear. She hoped this rather bloodthirsty girl wasn't going to go home and tell Lord Havelock that Miss Georgiana Wickford had suggested she take up shooting pistols as a hobby. Stepmama would be livid.

Miss Durant followed the direction of her guilty glance and cocked her head to one side. 'She's the kind of woman who lives by a set of silly rules and regulations, and thinks girls shouldn't step one foot outside them, isn't she?'

'Yes, but how did you…?'

'Oh, I've had dozens of stepmothers just like her,' said the girl scornfully. 'Not a one of them could break me, though.'

Georgiana could instantly see Edmund's hand in this meeting. Only last night he'd said she ought to mix with girls with whom she had something in common. Not only did Julia have an aversion to importunate suitors, but she also had experience of overbearing stepmothers.

What was more, even though part of what she'd just said was clearly an exaggeration, it certainly confirmed a suspicion that was slowly forming in Georgiana's mind. 'You are…what they call…a hellion, aren't you?'

'Yes,' said Miss Durant with pride.

'I…I think I envy you,' said Georgiana, faintly.

Miss Durant's upper lip curled in scorn.

'No, truly,' said Georgiana, with feeling. 'I have only ever succeeded in being a bit of a hoyden.' She'd crumbled under the pressure to behave the way Stepmama decreed. Not because of the beatings, but because of the more subtle pressure exerted by Sukey's distress and Papa's disappointment. Yet Julia was proudly defiant. Here was a girl who would say exactly what she thought, and behave exactly as she pleased, no matter what.

For a moment, her heart lifted. For Edmund was sending her the message that he believed it was perfectly acceptable to be her true self.

Or… Her heart plummeted. Was the message one of censure? Was he telling her that he was disappointed in her for not sticking to her guns, the way Miss Durant had clearly done, no matter how many stepmothers had attempted to 'improve' her?

While she was wondering exactly what message Edmund had been trying to convey, through Miss Durant, the girl in question was laughing at her.

'You?' She scanned the stupid mass of curls clustering round Georgiana's face, the frills and flounces abounding on her fashionable gown and the dainty slippers on her feet.

'Yes, me,' protested Georgiana hotly. 'I might be dressed up like a Christmas goose, fattened for market, but that is only because *she* is determined to get me off her hands.'

'I've had stepmothers like that, too,' said Miss Durant with a twist to her lips. 'Trying to make you into a lady. Strapping you into corsets and swathing you in muslin so flimsy you can hardly go for a decent walk let alone—'

'Climb a tree,' Georgiana finished for her.

They sighed, in unison.

'Do you hate London as much as I do?' Miss Durant asked.

'Probably more. At least nobody is trying to make you get married.'

'No, I shall be spared that for a few years yet,' Miss Durant agreed. 'But in the meantime, what is a girl supposed to do? I mean, it wouldn't be so bad if I could get out for a decent ride, but ladies aren't allowed to go out without a groom—'

'Or have a really good gallop.'

'No. I say, though, does that mean you ride?'

'Well, I would if I could, only…'

Something must have shown on her face as she silently mourned the loss of Whitesocks, because Miss Durant's own puckered in concern.

'What is it? Did they make you leave your favourite hack behind?'

'Worse. He had to be sold. We are—oh, dear, I'm not supposed to admit this…'

'Under the hatches?'

'Oh, no. It's not as bad as that. It's just that Stepmama wants people to believe…that is—' She broke off, aghast at how close she'd come to confiding their financial circumstances to a virtual stranger.

'Well, never mind that,' said Miss Durant brusquely. 'What concerns me is—' Now it was her turn to break off mid-sentence. And her eyes darted about rapidly, just as though she was scanning several options. 'Yes, I have it. The perfect solution to both our difficulties. You see she—' she jerked her head in Lady Havelock's direction '—is always saying I cannot go out riding without a suitable escort. And she cannot ride herself, even if she *wasn't* in a condition I'm not supposed to mention—though I cannot think why, since it's common knowledge she's breeding.' She paused to draw breath. 'And you don't have a horse in Town, so this will really make me look good, too.'

'What will?'

'Why, you will be my suitable escort, of course. I can come round for you first thing, with my spare hack, and a groom, of course.' She pulled a face. 'Cannot shake the fellow off, but I suppose it's probably for the best, the way London beaus carry on if they catch a female on their own.'

'Even in a drawing room,' Georgiana agreed bitterly.

'Exactly. Groom welcome, then. Pistols optional.'

'I haven't got a pistol any longer.' Georgiana sighed, shaking her head. 'Have you?'

Miss Durant grinned. 'No, but I'm going to ask Gregory to buy me one. And to teach me to shoot it. And, oh, I say, we could practise together!'

'I should love that,' said Georgiana wistfully. 'Only—' She darted another guilty glance at her stepmother.

Miss Durant wrinkled her nose. 'I cannot think why some females are so stupid about that sort of thing. Why shouldn't we learn to shoot? It's not as if we are planning to turn to a life of crime, is it?'

'No, but—' Georgiana clapped her hand to her mouth.

'What?'

'I was just imagining lying in wait, behind some bushes, and leaping out upon…someone.'

'One of your dastardly suitors? Or, no, even better,' said Miss Durant, getting into the spirit of things, 'some drunken bucks. Staggering home at dawn from White's, or Boodles. Lawks! Only think of what the newspapers would make of that. Footpads in petticoats.'

'No, no,' Georgiana protested. 'You said we were going out on horseback. We'd have to be h-highwaymen in p-petticoats.'

At which point they both collapsed in giggles.

Which made Lady Havelock rise from her sofa and come across the room.

'I am glad to see you girls getting on so well,' she said. 'What are you two finding so amusing?'

'Miss Wickford was just suggesting…' Miss Durant began with an impish gleam in her eye which made Georgiana hold her breath. 'That is, *I* thought,' Miss Durant continued, 'that she might like to come out riding with me some mornings. She hasn't brought a horse to Town with her. So I could lend her Snowdrop. Oh, do say yes, Mary.'

'Could you possibly spare your stepdaughter some mornings,' said Lady Havelock, turning to Stepmama with a winsome smile, 'to accompany this hoyden for a ride in the park? I am afraid that Julia is finding her stay in Town sadly flat, since I am unable to take her out riding. Lord Havelock and I really would be most terribly grateful if you would say yes.'

Georgiana held her breath. She couldn't see Stepmama refusing Lady Havelock's request that she become intimate with a member of such an exalted family. Not as long as Miss Durant said nothing about the pistol shooting. Which was a very real danger, considering how rash the girl appeared to be about voicing her opinion.

'Georgiana would love that, would you not, my dear? Although…' Stepmama twisted her hands together '…I do not like to sound overprotective, but…and of course I do not mean to sound stuffy, either, but you will provide a groom to attend the girls, won't you?'

'Of course. Gregory—that is, Lord Havelock—is terribly strict about that sort of thing. Julia is an heiress, you see, so we cannot guard her too carefully.'

Stepmama relaxed into a smile of genuine delight. Not only had she just discovered that Julia Durant was an heiress, but her own insistence on having a groom in attendance had clearly done her no harm in Lady Havelock's estimation.

'Well,' she said, as soon the last of their morning callers had gone, 'isn't it a good thing you have your riding habit with you? Even though we couldn't afford to stable a horse in London?'

Georgiana bit back the retort that she no longer had a horse to stable anywhere. And that the only reason she had her riding habit was because they'd had to pack *all* their possessions and remove them from Six Chimneys when her father's cousin had moved in.

She was not going to say, or do, anything that might induce Stepmama to change her mind about permitting her to go out on horseback. Nor give her cause to suspect she might be taking up an activity of which she disapproved so strongly that she'd confiscated the pistols Papa had given her.

She just hoped Miss Durant's brother was as open-minded about it as the girl believed, that was all. Because he sounded too good to be true.

Chapter Nine

Edmund could never understand why so many people he scarcely knew persisted in sending him so many invitations to events they must know wouldn't interest him in the slightest, whenever he came to Town.

Nevertheless, tonight he was glad that Lady Twining had invited him to her daughter's come-out ball. Because Lord Havelock had informed him that his wife had somehow managed to get Georgiana's name on the guest list, too. And although on first hearing this, he'd just been pleased to see that his ploy was working, that Georgiana was, gradually, getting to know females who would encourage her to discover her true self again, as the hours had ticked by he'd found himself increasingly unable to concentrate on his work. Because he couldn't stop wondering what sort of reception she'd get. Just because Lady Havelock had managed to get her name on the guest list, it was no guarantee that people would receive her cordially once she got there. They would be just as likely to take one look at her stepmother, draw their own conclusions and cut her dead.

Society tabbies could be incredibly cruel. Especially those with unmarried daughters who would regard both

Georgiana and Sukey as a threat to their own matrimonial ambitions.

In the end he tossed his pen aside, changed into evening clothes and sent one of his footmen to fetch him a hack, since it was raining too heavily for him to walk.

He need not waste his entire evening, after all. He could just take a look in to see how Georgie was faring and, if it looked as though she was not being well received, he would…

As his footman shut the door of the cab behind him, Edmund wrinkled his nose in distaste. And not entirely because it smelled as though a previous passenger made their living boiling onions. No, it was mostly because he'd realised that if he wanted to make sure Georgiana was enjoying herself, he'd have to go through all the rigmarole of approaching her stepmother, and asking permission to dance, or for the honour of escorting her into supper, or some such foolery. He'd have to spend enough time with all of them to demonstrate that he endorsed their presence in the polite world.

A footman bearing an umbrella opened the door of Edmund's hired hack the moment it drew up. But the unfortunate man received only a baleful glare in return for escorting him up the front steps to the open door. Because light and noise were streaming out in about equal measure, proclaiming that Miss Twining's come-out ball bore all the hallmarks of being what people referred to as 'a squeeze'.

People were queuing up the stairs inside, chattering and laughing and jostling those who were trying to descend. People who'd clearly had enough and were attempting to leave. For a moment Edmund considered turning around and joining them.

But then he remembered the way he'd found Georgiana cowering in a corner at Lady Havelock's gathering, gave a deep sigh, surrendered his hat and coat to yet another footman, and joined the end of the queue.

When he was about two-thirds of the way up the staircase, a mature lady attempting to go down gave an exaggerated start and came to a halt.

'Good heavens! Lord Ashenden?' Lady Tarbrook clapped her hand to her heavily jewelled bosom. 'I never expected to see you here, of all people!'

Several responses sprang to mind. All of them rude. On any other occasion he would have selected one and tossed it carelessly at her feet, hoping she would stumble over it. Because she was one of those gossipy, henwitted matrons with whom conversing was a colossal waste of time. He wouldn't have cared if he offended her. He didn't care what females of her type thought of him, or said about him.

But tonight he didn't have only himself to consider. Georgiana's position in society was far from assured. She couldn't afford to offend any one of these tabbies. Therefore, tonight, for her sake, nor could he.

So he confined himself to merely raising one eyebrow, and saying, in what he hoped was a manner sufficiently off-putting to discourage further conversation, yet not cold enough to leave any lingering hostility, 'Indeed?'

Lady Tarbrook appeared to regard his bland response as an invitation to linger, even though she was preventing the people on the stairs behind her from getting past.

'Yes, I should have thought you would consider this ball far too frivolous a way to spend an evening,' she said archly, ignoring the portly gentleman on the step above her who was noisily clearing his throat.

'You are correct,' he bit out, realising his error too late. There would now be no escape until he'd furnished her with some sort of explanation. 'I would not normally waste my time at such an event. However,' he continued, 'some people who hail from the environs of Fontenay Court, who have recently come up to Town, are attending. And I thought it would be a neighbourly gesture,' he said, feeling a muscle at the corner of his eye give a twitch, 'to take a look in and see how they are faring in the Polite World.'

There, that should send out the message that he approved of the Wickfords. As their life-long neighbour, who was better placed to know what kind of people they were? And what better person to whom to divulge that information than one of the busiest gossips in England?

He gave her a nod of dismissal, and, as the queue surged upwards, climbed the next two stairs.

'Neighbours, you say?'

To his acute annoyance, tossing her that bone had not satisfied Lady Tarbrook. On the contrary, as she fell into step beside him, her eyes alight with curiosity, he saw that all he'd done was whet her appetite.

'Anyone I know?'

'I should not think so.'

'Oh? I would have thought—that is, since your mother is also here tonight I had assumed they must be here under her aegis, since they are such close neighbours of yours.'

'She is here?' *Damn.*

'You did not know?'

'No.' He'd managed to avoid her since coming up to Town, even though they were both currently residing in Ashenden House. It wasn't all that difficult. Ashenden House was enormous and their vastly different habits meant that they scarcely even passed each other in any of the corridors.

'I do not share her tastes,' he said. He spent most of his time in London amidst the intellectual set, whereas she cared for nothing but *ton* parties. Moreover, his secretary always warned him if Lady Ashenden intended to dine at home, when the fellow knew Edmund didn't have a previous engagement, so that he could seek refuge at his club.

'Well, I am sure she will be vastly pleased to see you here tonight,' said Lady Tarbrook, with a knowing smile.

Yes, dammit, she would. His mother made no secret of the fact she believed it was past time he was married. As soon as he'd come down from Oxford she'd started introducing him to nobly born females of whom she approved. At previous *ton* balls, she'd done it in such a way that he never felt he had any choice but to lead the poor chit on to the dance floor. Which was another reason for avoiding events such as this.

Still, forewarned was forearmed.

Though he didn't think his mother would waste much time before attempting to introduce him to somebody, he suspected. As they reached the landing Lady Tarbrook went scuttling off down the corridor which probably, knowing his mother's penchant for games of chance, led to the card rooms.

He permitted Lady Twining to gush over him for a moment or two when he reached the head of the receiving line, however. It gave him an opportunity to scan the ballroom beyond.

He soon spotted Mrs Wickford, amidst the other chaperons, sitting out the dance in progress. She was fanning herself briskly, leaning in close to Lady Havelock as though sharing some confidence, and looking mighty pleased with herself.

Sukey was on the dance floor with a well-heeled baronet, whom he knew by reputation.

But he scarcely gave the couple more than a passing glance. Because he'd also seen Georgiana, dancing with Major Gowan. And she was wearing another scandalously low-cut gown. Major Gowan was making no attempt to disguise his hope that the next energetic move might have her bouncing right out of the confines of her stays. His tongue was practically hanging out, his eyes glued so fixedly to Georgiana's frontage that he was paying no attention to where he was going. And since he was such a large man, it meant that other dancers were obliged to take evasive action.

He stifled the urge to stride across the room and trip the damned rogue up. Though it would give him the greatest pleasure to see the Major stretching his length on the floor, he had no wish to embarrass Georgiana by making her the centre of such a spectacle. There were enough lecherous bucks watching from the sidelines with avid expressions as it was.

Instead, set-faced, he strolled around the perimeter of the room—not looking at the dancers even out of the corner of his eye—and made his bow to Lady Havelock.

'Oh, Ashe,' she said, her face lighting up with pleasure. Or relief? She couldn't possibly be enjoying sitting tête-à-tête with a woman like Mrs Wickford and might well be hoping he'd come to rescue her. 'Thank you so much for putting me in the way of finding a friend for Julia,' she said, nodding her head in the direction of Georgiana. 'She is so much happier now she has someone to talk horses with and to go riding with.'

'Why, Lord Ashenden,' put in Mrs Wickford, her

eyes widening as Lady Havelock revealed his part in bringing the two girls together, 'I never dreamed we had you to thank for our good fortune.'

'No?' Why on earth did she think Lady Havelock had introduced her husband's wealthy half-sister to a family with no connections in Town, unless she'd done so as a favour to a friend? Why else did she think Lady Havelock had arranged for invitations to be sent to an event such as this, come to that?

He took out his pocket watch and gave it a cursory glance. Which was a singularly stupid thing to do. There was no way he could estimate how much time he would have before his mother came to the ballroom to find out what he was doing there. It would depend entirely upon the state of play.

He snapped the case shut and replaced the watch in his waistcoat pocket as the orchestra wailed to a crescendo. The dancers all stopped capering about, bowed to their partners and began to disperse.

The baronet arrived first.

'Thank you so much for the pleasure of that dance,' he said, making a bow which included both the stepmother and Lady Havelock.

Mrs Wickford preened as her daughter sat down. She clearly thought Miss Mead had made her first conquest. Little did she know that Lord Freckleton was not interested in females in the slightest. He only sought out those his family would consider completely ineligible, or the perennial wallflowers who always drooped around the edges of the room, in an attempt to throw dust in their eyes.

'Lord Ashenden,' said Lord Freckleton next, giving him a mocking smile. 'What an unexpected pleasure to see you here.'

Edmund couldn't return the compliment. Lord Freckleton always eyed him with a little too much interest for his peace of mind.

And then the Major returned, with a flush-faced Georgiana on his arm, and Edmund's lack of a smile turned into a decided scowl. At some point the Major must have got so close to her that he'd trodden on her hem because she was trailing half a yard of sparkling, gauzy stuff that clearly belonged with the rest of the flounces and frills adorning the lower quadrant of her gown.

'My thanks for the dance,' the Major said, bowing over her hand with a flourish. 'Haven't enjoyed one so much in ages. A pity you cannot stand up with me again. A great pity.'

'Oh, but you have stood up with my stepdaughter twice already,' Mrs Wickford protested with a false titter. 'Besides, she is promised to Lord Freckleton for the next,' she said with a great deal of satisfaction.

And then several things happened in rapid succession.

First, Georgiana's blush turned a deeper shade of pink as she tugged her hand from the Major's grip.

Which gave Edmund a strong urge to punch the smug, lecherous look off the Major's face. And to upend her stepmother's chair. He also wanted to rip off his coat, drape it round Georgiana's exposed shoulders and take her somewhere safe.

And then, while he was still wrestling himself under control, Lord Freckleton shot the Major a withering glance and stepped forward, obliging the oaf to yield his ground as he extended his arm to Georgiana.

At which point Edmund saw that Lord Freckleton was exactly the sort of man Georgiana thought she wanted to marry. He would definitely leave Georgiana unmolested. Not only that, but Freckleton would probably be so grateful to any woman who would make it look as though he was doing his duty to his family name, whilst making no demands on him in that regard, he would probably be extremely generous. In his own way.

With just a word or two in Freckleton's ear, and a short explanation to Georgiana about what kind of man he was, Edmund could arrange the kind of future she claimed she wanted.

He looked hard at Freckleton's bland face. At his slender shoulders. His neatly manicured nails.

And his whole being revolted. A man like Freckleton might be able to provide Georgiana with what she thought she wanted. He'd leave her alone, right enough, but he would do so because he didn't care about her. He would never stir himself to encourage her to live her life to the full. To strike off the shackles her stepmother had weighted her down with. In fact, he'd probably impose a whole new set of rules so that she could play the part he wanted her to play.

All of this flashed through his mind in less time than it took for Georgiana to lift her hand and place it on Freckleton's sleeve.

Which meant that it never reached its destination. For Edmund intercepted her movement, taking her hand firmly in his and laying it on his own sleeve before she could make such a terrible mistake.

'You won't mind if I cut in, will you, Freckleton?'

Lord Freckleton raised his eyebrows, his eyes dancing with amusement.

'I am not able to spend a great deal of time here tonight,' said Edmund, tucking Georgiana's hand possessively into the very crook of his arm. 'You understand,' he said, and then, without waiting for Freckleton's reply, he tugged her in the direction of the dance floor before anyone could voice any objections.

'What do you think you are doing?' Georgiana asked as he led her inexorably to the bottom of the newest set that was forming.

'I might ask you the same question,' he retorted. Because he was angry. At himself for acting so impulsively, at Freckleton for being Georgiana's answer even though she hadn't yet asked him the question and at the Major for…being the Major. 'You were smiling at him,' he found himself growling, rather than saying anything to the point.

She frowned at him in confusion. 'Who?'

'Gowan,' he snapped. 'While you were dancing.'

'Why should I not have been smiling at him?'

'No reason, if you actually liked him. Which I thought not to be the case.'

'Perhaps,' she said through a grimace that showed all her teeth in the parody of a smile, 'beggars cannot be choosers.'

'What do you mean by that?'

'Well,' she said, dipping a curtsy as the music began, 'do you see any other suitors clustering round me?'

He'd seen Freckleton. He would be a much better match for her, in some respects, than the Major. Not that he was ever going to let her find out, he decided as they formed a square and honoured their partners to the diagonal.

'You have been in Town less than a month,' he said when they next came close enough for him to say anything without the words being heard by the others in the set. She crooked one eyebrow at him as she turned and went back to her place.

'You have plenty of time to meet eligible men,' he said the next time he got the chance.

'You know very well,' she said with a brittle smile, 'that I have no interest in meeting eligible men.'

'So you intend to marry that great lump of beef then, do you? Oh, this is intolerable.' One could not hold a rational conversation whilst dancing and this one went on for another three hours. Or at least, that was what it felt like. The moment it ended, he took Georgiana's hand in a none-too-gentle grip and towed her in the direction of the refreshment room.

'You are supposed to return me to my stepmother,' she hissed up at him.

'After two dances with the Major, and one with me, you are entitled to a drink of lemonade.'

'Well, yes, I would be, if I wanted one,' she pointed out.

'Don't be facetious. You can see I wish to talk to you. And one cannot hold a sensible conversation whilst capering about like a…like a…cricket.'

'What,' she asked as they passed through the doors that led to the refreshment room and took their place in the queue, 'did you wish to talk to me about?'

He scanned the room for signs of either the Major or Freckleton, but there were none. They'd either gone to the card room, or left altogether. Both of which suited Edmund equally well.

'Husbands,' he said grimly. 'I thought you did not wish to get married, but now you are positively encouraging the first man to show a decided interest in you.'

She shrugged her shoulders. Looked at a point somewhere beyond his left ear. 'I have to face facts. I am going to have to marry somebody. And since there doesn't seem to be much difference between one man and the next, I thought I just might as well get it over with as quickly as possible.'

'Georgie, no.' He gasped, his stomach roiling at the thought of those meaty great hands getting hold of what they so clearly wanted to grope. Of those blubbery lips slobbering all over her. Her face, her body...

'No,' he repeated, more decisively. 'It is intolerable to think of you in his keeping.'

'Well, I thought so at first, but then...' she sighed '...upon reflection, I think he might not make a terrible sort of husband.'

'How can you say that?' The queue shuffled forward. And there were couples behind them now, as well as in front.

'Well, he does appear to be a fairly decent sort of man, from what Stepmama has been able to discover. He isn't terribly clever, but then wouldn't that be to my advantage?'

'In what way?'

'Well, I could... That is he'd be easier to...um...manage than a more intelligent man.'

The expression on his face must have clearly conveyed what he thought of that, because her stubborn chin went up and her eyes flashed defiance.

'And at least he would understand my need to go riding. I'm sure he'd let me have as many horses as I wanted.'

'As many as he could afford, you mean, or, to be more precise, his father could afford.'

'I know he doesn't have what you would probably call a great deal of money,' she said defensively, 'but then I'm used to living fairly simply. And he's a second son, too. Told me outright that it meant he could marry to please himself, so long as his bride didn't mind living on his income. Which means he must really like me, mustn't it? I mean, a lot of younger sons go after fortunes and even he must have realised by now I don't have two brass farthings to rub together.'

'That doesn't mean you have to settle for him,' he snarled as they reached the table where footmen were ladling out drinks from a variety of cutglass bowls. Edmund procured a glass of cloudy-looking lemonade for her, then took one from a bowl that most of the gentlemen ahead of him seemed to prefer. It was a rather more propitious shade of amber.

'Have you no higher ambition from a husband than that he would like you tolerably well and would permit you to have a horse?'

She shrugged morosely. 'You know very well that I don't wish to marry at all. The whole notion of...' She shuddered and then took a gulp of her drink, as though to wash away a nasty taste. 'But I don't have the luxury of choice. I have to get married, or face...' She shrugged. 'Well, I don't know what.'

'You have no home to go back to, I do know that, now. But surely your father did not leave you unprovided for?'

'He left it all in Stepmama's hands, saying she was the most capable person he knew of to handle a girl's future. And she firmly believes the best way to invest my inheritance is by launching me into society as lavishly as she can, so that I can find a good husband.'

'To say nothing of her own daughter,' he snarled.

She shrugged again.

'That is preposterous,' he said. 'There must be something else...' But of course, there wasn't. Not for a girl like her. Of good family, but limited education, what could she do but marry well? Now was the time he ought to tell her about men like Freckleton. Men who would agree to a marriage on her terms, because just having her at their side would disguise their true inclinations.

Why on earth had condemning Georgie to such a fate seemed like a good idea, back in Bartlesham?

She was already struggling to be the kind of female her stepmother wanted her to be. Marrying a man who would use her as a sort of smokescreen would mean she'd spend the rest of her life pretending to be someone she was not.

At least Major Gowan appeared to like her enough to actually consider her likes and dislikes. He would attempt to make her as happy as he could, in his bumbling, fumbling way. Except that he wouldn't be able to make her anything but miserable. Because he'd want to bed her.

He drained his glass and set it down on a convenient window ledge with a decisive snap.

'Don't make any hasty decisions,' he said. 'Once you are married, there will be no escaping it. It will be for life.'

'I know that.'

'So you will make no promises to Major Gowan until I have had time to…to…'

'To what, exactly?'

'To find a better solution to your problem.'

'And just how do you propose to do that? If indeed it is any of your business, which actually, I don't think it is.'

'Of course it is. You came to me in the first instance, specifically asking me…' he wavered, amending what he'd been about to say '…for help.'

She glowered at him. 'Yes, and you refused to be

the man to come to my rescue,' she said bitterly. 'In no uncertain terms.'

He winced. 'I was not in a position to make an informed decision, since you left out several pertinent facts,' he said in self-defence.

'Oh, and it would have made you reach a different decision, would it, if I'd succeeded in making you listen to what you didn't want to hear?'

'I...no...I...but I would have handled the encounter differently had I known how very desperate your circumstances are. I could never have imagined your father leaving you so wholly dependent on that woman.'

She made a derisive noise halfway between a snort and a cough.

'I would also have explained,' he said loftily, 'before you left for Town, that there are many ways in which I was prepared to help you, without—'

'Actually going to the lengths of marrying me yourself,' she finished for him bitterly.

'Did your stepmother never teach you it is the height of bad manners to interrupt a man when he is doing his damnedest to explain how he intends to help you get out of a fix?'

'Oh, she taught me all sorts of lessons in manners. Do, pray, continue,' she said with a falsely sweet smile. 'I cannot wait to hear the brilliance of your ideas.'

He clenched his teeth. He did not, actually, have any brilliant ideas. Not a single one, to be perfectly honest. But he had no intention of admitting that.

'You cannot just marry the first man to show an interest in you in case nobody better comes along,' he snapped. 'You need to think it all over, in a rational manner.'

'In a rational manner,' she repeated, with scepticism.

'Yes,' he said firmly. 'For example, it might help if you were to draw up a list of factors which would make living with some man…'

She tilted her head to one side. 'Bearable?'

'I was trying to think of a more positive word, but, yes, in your case, since you have a ridiculous aversion to the whole idea of matrimony, perhaps the word *bearable* would do.'

'You are a fine one to talk,' she said, setting her own empty cup next to his on the windowsill.

'What do you mean by that?'

'Only that it's common knowledge that you are not the marrying kind.'

'Not the marrying kind?' His whole being swelled with outrage. How dare she imply that he was of the same ilk as Lord Freckleton? He had a good mind to drag her into one of the convenient alcoves set aside for the purpose and make violent love to her until she had no doubt about his proclivities.

None whatsoever.

The idea of kissing her into submission…or…no, he could not see Georgie being a submissive partner. She'd either fight him off, or become an enthusiastic participant.

'I'll have you know,' he said indignantly, 'that I bedded my first woman while I was at Oxford. And have had a score of mistresses in my keeping since then.'

Her eyes widened in shock. 'I don't think you are supposed to talk about that sort of thing to…to someone like me.'

'Well, I needed to make it clear.'

'Yes, I suppose…I mean, I dare say a lot of men prefer to keep a string of mistresses rather than tie themselves to just one woman. That was one reason I thought you might not mind, um, giving me a home. As long as you knew I wouldn't demand fidelity, or…'

'What?' Now she was insinuating he was loose in the haft. It was a good job he hadn't been taking a drink at the time because he had a notion he'd have just sprayed it all over the curtains. 'You knew about my mistresses?'

She widened her eyes as though what he'd said was rather stupid. 'Everyone in Bartlesham knows about your mistresses. People gossip about everything you do, since there is so little going on down there. And you have lived such an exciting life…'

'Me? Exciting?'

'Yes. First of all going off to the Scilly Isles, for all those years, which everyone said was as good as going on the Grand Tour for a young gentleman nowadays—'

'It was nothing of the kind! My health—'

'And then you went off to university and created a scandal by getting involved with the daughter of your bedmaker—'

'It wasn't a scandal! Betty was—' He pinched the bridge of his nose. This was making no sense. If she knew he'd been active in that way, for so long, then she couldn't possibly suspect him of being…

No. Of course not. Georgiana was far too innocent to know about that sort of thing. Which brought him neatly to the next point.

'Nobody should have repeated such gossip to you, at that age. Why, you could hardly have been more than…' Actually, she hadn't been that much younger than Betty. Which reflection made him feel rather flushed.

'Oh, they didn't,' she said blithely. 'But I couldn't help overhearing things, sometimes.'

Now it was her turn to blush and look uncomfortable.

The whole situation was deuced awkward. She clearly knew details about his life he wasn't at all comfortable with her knowing.

Though he supposed that was marginally less unpleasant than having her suspect he did not find women attractive at all.

'Well, you shouldn't have! You should not repeat the things you've overheard, either, especially not to me.'

She sighed. 'I beg pardon. I know I'm always blurting out things I shouldn't. It's just—well, it's so hard not to be frank with you, now that we are talking again. I keep forgetting that we aren't…friends any more.'

'Of course we are friends!' He stared at her, feeling almost as shocked as she looked. And then something flared in her eyes. A sort of wistful look. And she leaned a little closer.

But then whatever it was died.

'No,' she said, with a rueful shake of her head. 'Stepmama says that single ladies cannot be friends with single gentlemen. It isn't proper.'

He was about to say that was nonsense, when he recalled that actually, it was true. It wasn't proper. So he clamped his mouth shut.

'And that being so,' she said, 'I think you ought to return me to Stepmama now. Don't you?'

'No, I don't. We still haven't made any progress in defining what sort of man you could tolerate marrying.'

'What, you still think I ought to draw up some sort of list?'

'It couldn't hurt,' he said. 'As a mental exercise, it would certainly help you to get your thoughts in a less chaotic state than they are in at present.'

'My thoughts are not in a chaotic state.'

'They are. Otherwise,' he said, when she drew breath

to object, 'you would not think it a good idea to marry Major Gowan, nor would you be talking to a man about what mistresses he keeps whilst in the same breath implying—'

'Implying what?' She looked up at him in confusion.

He felt a touch confused himself.

He never blurted out what he was thinking—or to be more precise, feeling. *Especially* not what he was feeling. He could normally keep a cool head during any debate, no matter how heated other participants might become.

'Never mind what I thought you were implying,' he ended up saying, since he was definitely not going to explain that *one*, some men did not find women attractive, *two*, he'd thought she'd thought he was one of those men, *three*, he resented her assumption, and so on and so forth. It would take far too long and only end in embarrassment all round.

'It is time I returned you to your stepmother.' He'd lost track of time whilst bickering with Georgie. Any moment now his mother would be hauling some husband-hunting debutante up before him and insisting he dance with her.

'I shall call upon you in a few days,' he said, taking her by the elbow and steering her out of the refreshment room at a brisk pace. 'Which will give you time to set your thoughts down on paper. And then I can see what I can do to match you up with your...ideal man.'

She shot him a look of resentment.

'You do not need to bother.'

'Oh, but I do,' he said firmly. 'If you think I'm going to have a moment's peace, if I stand back and watch you throw yourself away on the likes of Major Gowan, then you are very much mistaken.'

'But, Edmund—'

'But nothing, Georgie. He'd make you miserable.'
And so would Lord Freckleton, albeit in an entirely
different way.

And he didn't want her to be miserable.

He walked her back to her stepmother, was aware
she said something, and he said something back, and
that people were chatting and laughing and somewhere
in the background music was playing. But he was only
half-aware of any of it. Because he was reeling at his last
unspoken thought. He'd meant it, too, with every atom
of his being, without even knowing he felt that way.

And it made no difference what she'd done, or not
done in the past, or even what she thought of him now.

He couldn't bear to think of her being miserable.

Chapter Ten

Of all the high-handed, arrogant, supercilious…men! Georgiana glared at Edmund's back as he sauntered out of the ballroom, his mind already clearly elsewhere. She spent the rest of the evening fuming. By the time she reached their rented house, all she could remember of the ball were the moments she'd spent with him. Being lectured and dragged round and forced to drink lemonade, and lectured again, and then tossed aside as if he'd grown bored with her antics. And all whilst trailing two feet of spangled floss trimming.

Georgiana tore off her ball gown, wincing as one of the pins she'd used to repair the damage scored her ankle, kicked off her slippers and brushed her hair so vigorously that sparks crackled. When Sukey dreamily bade her a goodnight and wafted to her room on a cloud of happy reminiscences, she grunted a brief response, shut her bedroom door with exaggerated patience and then flung herself on to her bed, thumping the pillow for good measure.

He was a beast to speak to her that way!

The worst of it was more than half of what he'd said made perfect sense. Drat him. She *had* been foolish, thinking she might as well accept Major Gowan's proposal—if he ever made one—simply to get the business settled.

But Edmund had no idea what it felt like to have a sword hanging over his head, or the terrible strain of being braced for the moment it finally fell.

Oh, she should have said that to him! Why hadn't she come up with that clever analogy when it might have impressed him?

She buried her face in the pillow and screamed her frustration into it. And then, since she was never going to be able to sleep, the way she felt, she rolled off the bed and went to her window, and sat on the sill with her knees drawn up, looking out at the night sky.

As she watched the last few stars still valiantly twinkling in the face of approaching dawn, it occurred to her that at least he hadn't had things all his own way. Once or twice she'd had the satisfaction of shaking him out of his cool, superior attitude. He'd blustered instead of making his point in a clear, concise fashion.

Her lips curled up, just a touch, as she recalled the moment when he'd halted mid-sentence and then gone off on a completely different tack. It was a small victory, but a victory none the less. And all the more valuable since not many people ever managed to shake his utter certainty in himself, these days.

But then Edmund was so very often right. Even she could concede that it was a good idea to think seriously about what would make a husband tolerable and discovering if any man in London possessed those qualities, before settling for the likes of Major Gowan.

If only he wasn't expecting her to apply reasoning to a problem that stemmed from her emotions. Whenever she bent her mind to the act of getting married, it was her body and her heart that shied away from it. The prospect of letting any man do what she'd seen Wilkins doing to Liza made her feel physically ill.

She hugged her knees, trying to imagine Major Gowan...

Ugh! No. She couldn't bear *that*.

Edmund was right. She couldn't marry a man who would expect that of her. Who would be disappointed, and probably hurt, too, when she responded to his embraces by... She pressed her hand to her stomach.

So what was she to do?

Think—that was what. About what sort of man she might be able to stomach.

Funny, before coming to London, she'd thought only some sort of savage would deign to consider her, but in fact, several perfectly respectable and well-mannered men appeared to find her attractive. Not Edmund, though. She knew, thanks to Bartlesham's gossip mill, that every time he'd taken a mistress, they had been blonde, dainty little creatures.

Not that she cared. She sniffed and lifted her chin. She'd always known she couldn't compete with all those fairy-like beauties he so admired. She had never intended to try. She had just hoped he might have taken pity on her, for the sake of their shared past, and given her a home.

But she hadn't taken into account his need for heirs. His need for legitimate children to carry on his line. And more than that, his need to see them flourish.

Edmund would be a good father. She could see him with two or three sons, and a couple of daughters as well. She could see him taking the whole tribe down to the trout stream, where the boys would sit with their sketch pads, drawing the insects they'd watch running up and down the rushes. While his little girls would wade into the shallow with jars to collect tadpoles.

She'd never felt even the slightest yearning to become a mother, no matter what Stepmama said about it being a natural urge. She still couldn't imagine herself holding a baby. But those children of Edmund's— she sighed. She could all too easily grow fond of them. Partly Edmund and partly… She sucked in a juddering breath and dashed the back of her hand across her somewhat watery nose. They would be like their mother. A woman who was willing and able to give him children. A woman who would be as nobly born and arrogant as his own mother, like as not.

Whereas she…all she wanted…was…

She raised her head and looked blankly round the room. All she'd asked of Edmund was that he give her a roof over her head. That was all she wanted of any man, really. She didn't even care how small that roof might be, as long as she could feel secure in it. But then her eyes came to rest on her narrow single bed and she amended that proviso. She wanted to have a room of her own. Even if it was as small and cramped as this one. Even though there was only room for a bed, with a nightstand on one side and a chair on the other, and a washstand next to the window which had a sill just wide enough for her to sit on, it was her own space. And having her own space into which she could retreat had been the only thing making this visit to London bearable. It would probably be the same in her marriage. Particularly if she ended up with a man whose opinions she couldn't respect.

Or who was too stupid to hold up his end of a conversation.

She didn't want to marry a man with whom she

couldn't converse, she promptly decided. She would end up very lonely.

On the other hand, if she liked and respected her husband too much, it would be harder to bear his disappointment in her when she proved far from enthusiastic in his arms.

Oh, this was impossible! She couldn't face marrying a man she didn't like. She couldn't face marrying a man she liked too well either. There was no way through the dilemma that she could see.

So what was the point of even trying to write a stupid list?

There was only one man she'd ever seriously wanted to marry. And marriage to him was out of the question.

'Have you completely lost your mind?'

Edmund looked up from the pile of correspondence on his desk, currently awaiting his attention, and regarded his mother with resignation.

'Good morning, Mother,' he said with heavy irony. 'I take it your question is rhetorical, since it must be obvious that I am in complete control of all my faculties?'

'Not to me it isn't,' she said, surging forward in a cloud of Brussels lace and indignation.

Beyond her, he could see his secretary wringing his hands as he hopped from one foot to the other. Poppleton had standing instructions not to admit anyone, especially not his mother, to his study while he was working. But nobody could stand in his mother's way when she really got the bit between her teeth.

'Actually, I do have some business I wish to discuss with Lady Ashenden,' he said to Poppleton. 'You may leave us.' Ever since his last visit to Fontenay Court he had known some sort of confrontation was inevitable.

It was unlikely she'd come to discuss the issues upper-most in his mind. Nevertheless, now that she was here and clearly spoiling for a fight, he might as well get it all out in the open.

She turned and shut the door in Poppleton's face with a triumphant flourish, then whirled on him.

'Is it true? That you attended Miss Twining's debut and set tongues wagging by showing marked attention to one female only?'

'Ah.' That aspect of it had never occurred to him.

'So it *is* true! You…you…imbecile! You cannot dance only once, drag your partner into the supper room without consulting her chaperon, engage her in intense conversation in a secluded corner and then leave without so much as paying your respects to the girl in whose honour the ball was being held, without it giving rise to the kind of speculation that simply will not do. Not in relation to that…' She pulled herself up with visible effort. 'With Miss Wickford.' She ejected the name from between her teeth as though spitting out a lump of gristle.

'You could easily nip any gossip in the bud,' he pointed out, 'by reminding people how eccentric I am. You are always complaining of it. Of my lack of…how have you termed it? Social address. Why not put it about that last night was simply another example of it?'

'I have already done so,' she said, sweeping her demi-train impatiently aside as she took the chair facing his desk. 'But while I have always deplored your lack of social address, it has never given me such cause for alarm. Don't you realise that singling out a schem-ing trollop like that Wickford girl is just asking for trouble?'

'Trollop?' He sat back, eyeing his mother coldly. 'Take care, my lady, what you say.'

Her eyes met his. They were equally as cold. And just as determined. 'Or what?'

So, it was going to be like that, was it? This was where he was going to have to draw the battle lines?

So be it.

'Or you are going to find,' he said firmly, 'that I am nowhere near as complaisant as my father. So far I have placed no curb upon your behaviour, irksome though it has often been.'

Her hand curled into her skirts, claw-like. 'How dare you?'

'But I warn you,' he continued as though she had not interrupted, 'that there are lines I shall not permit you to cross.'

She sat up straight, her lips compressing into a bloodless line.

'Permit me! Permit me?' She tossed her head and laughed. 'There is nothing you can do to stop me behaving exactly as I please.'

'You seem to forget who picks up your bills, madam. Who allows you the run of all the properties you currently enjoy—even though, technically, you ought to be living in a far more economical style in the dower house.'

'All I have ever done is take care of your interests,' she gasped, as though he'd struck her. To make sure he got the message that he was an ungrateful brute, she pressed one hand to her bosom, whilst widening her eyes until they watered. 'Somebody has to think of what you owe to your tenants, while you are wasting your time on those stupid books and experiments of yours. And as for last night...' She shook her head, eyeing him up and down as though he was a servant caught with a pocket full of silver teaspoons. 'Do you care nothing for your reputation? What you owe to your family name?'

'I hardly think my reputation is going to be damaged by dancing with a former neighbour of mine. A girl I have known since the cradle.'

'Well, that just goes to show what a fool you are when it comes to women! If only you moved about in society a bit more, you would have so much more experience. And I don't mean the kind you get with your bits of muslin,' she said with a dismissive wave of her hand. 'They are different. But when it comes to a girl like that…' She shook her head. 'For God's sake, Edmund, I didn't go to all that effort to see you fall prey to her wiles in the end.'

All that effort? What could she mean? Though the remark had roused his curiosity, he did his best not to reveal it. In fact, he lowered his eyelids and regarded her steadily, though his mind was racing. He'd already detected an anomaly of some sort regarding his past dealings with Georgie. Was he now about to discover that his mother had played some part in it? She was so angry that she was already being highly indiscreet. Hopefully he could goad her into losing her temper altogether. It wouldn't take much, by the look of her. She always ended up like this if she didn't get her own way. If tears and pleading failed, she worked herself up into a fury. It was one of the reasons his subordinates found it so hard to defy her, even when they knew it would mean disobeying his orders.

But he was made of sterner stuff. And hadn't been scared by one of her tantrums since he'd been a very small boy.

Which made it almost a pleasure to say the very thing most likely to infuriate her.

'Georgiana does not need to employ any wiles,' he said, with what he hoped was a smile she'd take for that of a besotted suitor. 'She is far too beautiful to need to bother. Besides being by far the most interesting conversationalist…'

'Interesting? Interesting! That girl knows nothing about anything except hounds and horses! How can you…lower yourself to that level? But it is all the same with you…men,' she said scornfully. 'You may claim to be intelligent and care for intellectual pursuits, but deep down all any of you can think of is the bedroom.'

He gave her a mockingly innocent smile. 'Is that so? The bedroom? Why, madam, whatever can you mean?'

'Don't give me that innocent act,' she screeched. 'I know all about your proclivities. And hers. Why do you think I let Dr Scholes remove you from Bartlesham in the first place? You were just at the age to start noticing the difference between male and female, and there she was, climbing into your bedroom at all hours of the day and night. Romping in your bed, in her undergarments…'

He frowned. 'Romping?' They had never *romped*. He'd barely started noticing that she was becoming a young lady. And wondering whether she really was as pretty as he thought, or if he liked her looks so much because he liked *her* so much. Every single one of her features had appeared perfect to his inexperienced eyes. Especially her lips. He'd become fascinated by the way they moved when she talked. The way she pressed them together when she was thinking hard. And, yes, he might have wondered, once or twice, what it would be like to kiss her, when they grew up, but that was as far as it had gone.

'Yes, romping! I knew all about it, from the very first. Because Mrs Bulstrode came straight to me and told me the whole, the very day she caught that bold little piece in your bed.' Lady Ashenden clasped her hands so tightly the knuckles went white. 'I knew the only way to save you from getting embroiled in a sordid scandal was to send you away. Somewhere she couldn't reach you. Though, what it cost me—' Her voice hitched. 'You were my boy. My only boy. I knew I'd never have another, not with your father—' She pulled herself up. Gulped. 'And you never came back. Not to me...' Her voice faded away. The sheen of moisture in her eyes welled completely naturally this time. And then to his surprise, her whole posture changed. She looked as though she was actually shrinking.

Until that moment, he'd never thought of her as old. Because her personality was so forceful. Her mannerisms so vibrant.

But beneath all the bravado, and the fashionable clothes, and the jewellery, and the gossip and the brittle laughter, he could now see there lurked a sad and lonely woman who was well past her prime.

He cleared his throat. 'You are telling me that was the reason you sent me away? Because Mrs Bulstrode came to you with some tale about Georgie and I getting up to no good?'

'It was for the best,' she said in a hollow voice. 'By the time you came back, you'd...grown out of the infatuation.'

'Firstly,' he said, 'Georgie and I were never more than friends, in those days.'

His mother snorted. 'She was in your bed, with her dress hitched up to her waist.'

'Because she had just climbed up to my room with a dozen jam jars full of specimens she'd collected for me. Good God, woman, she was only twelve. And completely innocent, most particularly because she'd been brought up more like a boy than a girl. She had no notion that showing her legs was indecent. Her skirts hampered her ability to climb, so she simply hitched them out of the way.'

'Trust you to try to defend her. But don't forget, Mrs Bulstrode heard the pair of you giggling. Behind closed bed curtains. And when she twitched them away, the pair of you were the picture of guilt.'

'Of course we were the picture of guilt. She knew she wasn't supposed to be there. You had forbidden all visitors lest they bring some infection to my room, hadn't you? It was no more than that. Nothing—' he slammed his open palm on the desktop so hard the inkwells rattled '—absolutely nothing improper ever crossed either of our minds.'

'Well, it does not matter now.'

'Doesn't matter? Doesn't matter? Have you no idea how unhappy I was when you sent me into exile?'

For the first six months, he'd been in daily torment, waiting for letters that never came. And when Dr Scholes had given him the explanation about women being fickle creatures, he'd absorbed that lie to the extent that he'd based every interaction, with every person he'd ever met since then, male or female, on the premise that if he was fool enough to believe a word they said, if he trusted them, then they'd let him down.

'Well, I'm sure you were. As was I, to have to do it. But it was worth it, in the end, wasn't it? You came home strong, and well, and free from...' She trailed away at the look of fury he was sure must be blazing from his eyes.

'Sending me away was not all that you did though, was it? It wasn't enough to physically part us, you did your utmost to kill our friendship, by preventing us communicating at all. Somehow you prevented my letters from reaching her, didn't you? You made sure she thought I'd forgotten all about her the minute I left Bartlesham.' He got to his feet. 'And I thought she'd forgotten all about me, too, but now I wonder. Did she write to me? And did you prevent her letters from reaching me?'

She lifted her chin. 'It was for the best.'

He could scarcely believe it. He didn't think he'd ever had a hypothesis proved correct in such short order.

'How did you do it? No, wait...' He stalked to the window, then turned back. 'It would have been remarkably simple.' The man who came up to the house with the letters always handed them to Dr Scholes. 'You ordered Dr Scholes not to permit me any communication from her. What did you tell him, that she was an undesirable connection? A corrupting influence?'

She sat as though turned to stone. But he did not need her to say a word. Dr Scholes had done his work well. He'd known the truth, yet had no scruples about tarnishing Georgiana's image by spouting all that nonsense about women being fickle and forgetting what they'd promised, or changing their minds at the drop of a hat.

'But why, that is what I cannot understand.'

And why had he trusted Dr Scholes, a man he barely knew, a man employed by his mother, rather than in Georgie? When she'd been the only person to have cared about him without having some ulterior motive? Why hadn't he searched for another reason to explain why he hadn't heard from her?

And why, when he'd finally returned to Bartlesham, hadn't he simply gone to see her and demanded an explanation? He steadied himself by resting the tips of his fingers on the desk before speaking again.

'How could you have…destroyed the one friendship I had? What, pray, do you have against her? Why did you feel it was necessary to take such…steps?'

'Mrs Bulstrode found the pair of you in bed together. Isn't that enough?'

'No. I have already explained it was perfectly innocent. So, apart from a mistaken belief she was some kind of…sexual adventuress as a child—' his voice dripped with disdain '—what other reason do you have for finding her so unpalatable as a daughter-in-law?'

Her eyes widened in horror. 'You cannot mean you actually do propose to marry that…that…'

He couldn't help himself. She'd put him through so much misery. Set events in motion that had warped his view of all females. Made him believe that Georgie had betrayed him. And probably made her hate him in return. Though he'd had no thoughts of marrying at all, he couldn't help taunting his mother with the prospect that the only daughter-in-law she was likely to get was the very one she'd worked so hard to exclude.

'Miss Georgiana Wickford,' he therefore said, 'is from a perfectly respectable family. She is a sensible woman with whom I can converse, without feeling one moment's tedium. And, moreover, she is as healthy as a horse. Since you profess to be so anxious for me to ensure the succession, I should have thought you would be glad I am looking at a woman who is bound to produce healthy offspring.'

'You cannot mean that,' she said faintly, reaching into her reticule for her vinaigrette. 'Not…after all I have done…the sacrifices I have made…I won't have it,' she whimpered. 'I won't be supplanted by that… great…ungainly…'

'Be careful what you say about Georgiana, madam,' he said coldly. 'To anyone. Because if I discover,' he said, leaning towards her across the desk, 'that you have done anything, or said anything, to tarnish her reputation, I will make you regret it.'

'Oh, but you *are* just like your father,' she said, as though it was the deepest insult she could fling at him.

'No, madam, you will find that I am not,' he said coldly. Not in any respect. 'I take duty to my tenants very seriously, for one thing. And as for marriage,' he continued, warming to the subject, 'when I do decide to tie the knot, I will not settle for a dynastic union which has been arranged for me, which I subsequently make no effort to sustain. I will choose my own bride, because she is a woman I can regard as a partner and a friend. A woman I can respect and admire. A woman who will complement and complete me.'

His mother reeled back as though he'd struck her. Though he could not tell whether it was because he'd described the very antithesis of her union with his father, or because she believed he'd been listing reasons for marrying Georgiana in particular.

Because she didn't give him the benefit of her opinion for once, before turning and flouncing out of the room.

Chapter Eleven

For the whole of the next week, Georgiana made sure she stayed out of secluded corners, smiled at every man who asked her to dance and tried not to object whenever her cleavage got more attention than she did.

After all, it wasn't as if her eyes were behaving much better. Instead of giving every partner her wholehearted attention, the way Sukey did, Georgiana's gaze roamed freely over the other guests attending whatever ball, or rout, or breakfast she happened to be at. Especially if it was the slightest bit *ton*nish. Even though she knew Edmund didn't make a habit of going to such things, he *had* turned up at Miss Twining's debut and he *had* danced with her.

But evidently he had no intention of giving anyone a chance to gossip about them again. Which was a good thing, she decided gloomily one afternoon as she sat in the drawing room, listening to the rain lashing the windowpanes. She hadn't liked the way Lady Tarbrook, for example, had looked at her the next evening, at the Fairweathers' musicale. Or the way she'd nudged the fat woman sitting next to her and started whispering behind her fan. She knew they'd been speculating about her relationship with Edmund, because that kind of whispering had started the moment he'd left the Twinings' ball.

And because Stepmama had confirmed it on their way home.

'It isn't that you have done anything wrong,' she'd hastened to assure Georgiana, when she'd been on the verge of defending herself. 'It is just that Lord Ashenden's behaviour was so very unusual for him. It was bound to cause speculation. Now that I've explained our long-standing connection, all you need do is continue to behave properly and the talk will die down. As long as he doesn't make a habit of monopolising you and ignoring every other eligible female in the room,' she'd said irritably, 'you should be able to brush through without a hint of blame attaching to you.'

Which implied that people might blame her for Edmund's behaviour if she did put a foot wrong anywhere else.

Which conclusion absolutely infuriated her. Why did people always blame the woman when there was any sort of scandal? She would wager that nine times out of ten it was the man's fault.

Her mood today wasn't improved by the fact that Stepmama was making them all sit here pretending to do needlework just in case somebody called. Which wasn't likely. What kind of idiot would venture out in such foul weather?

Just then, as if to mock her assumptions about the intelligence of Town dwellers, there came a knock on the door. And a murmur of male voices in the hallway. And the sound of a light tread upon the stairs.

Then in walked Edmund.

'Mrs Wickford,' he said, 'Miss Wickford, Miss Mead.' He bowed to each in turn. 'I was just passing on my way to Bullock's Museum and it occurred to me that you might care to accompany me.'

'Oh! Lord Ashenden,' said Stepmama, mangling the needlework in her lap. 'You have taken us all by surprise. Indeed, I am sure I don't know why you have even come up here and walked in upon us this way when Wiggins is supposed to announce visitors.'

Edmund frowned. 'Your butler is not here to announce me because I did not care to kick my heels in the hall while he disposed of my coat and hat. I have an intense dislike of loitering about, wasting my time.'

And didn't she know it. Georgiana couldn't help recalling the way he'd pulled his watch out and practically tapped his foot while waiting for her to explain her situation to him, that day down by the trout stream. It wouldn't surprise her to see him do something similar now.

'Oh, I see,' said Stepmama, with something of the air of a landed trout. 'I meant no disrespect to you, my lord. Indeed it was on that account that I…I mean…we would not wish you to feel…that is, of course you are most welcome, whenever you wish to pay us a visit. And if you prefer informality over—'

'Kicking my heels in the hall,' Edmund put in helpfully as she floundered to a halt, gulping. 'I do, most emphatically.'

'Well, then,' said Stepmama, attempting a smile even as she was drawing in a much-needed breath. 'That's good. And so, here you are.'

'Yes. Here I am,' said Edmund. 'With an invitation to take the young ladies on an outing that they should find both educational and improving.'

Since Edmund was standing looking down at Stepmama and Sukey was sitting on her favourite sofa which put her out of his eye line, he didn't see the look of horror that flashed across her face at the prospect of spending the afternoon being educated and improved.

'The *young* ladies,' said Stepmama with barely concealed relief, at the same time as Sukey made a valiant effort to school her features into an expression of dutiful gratitude. 'How very kind of you to think of them. I am sure they are most grateful to be offered such a treat,' said Stepmama, ruthlessly ignoring Sukey's initial reaction. 'We have been so dull here today.'

'All your beaus have deserted you? I cannot believe it,' he said gravely.

'I dare say the rain is keeping them at home,' said Georgiana.

'I shouldn't be a bit surprised,' he said, turning to her. 'However, a little bit of weather has never prevented me from doing exactly as I please. Nor will I permit it to spoil your own enjoyment of the outing. Your charges will both be completely protected from the elements, I do assure you,' he said, returning his attention to Stepmama.

'Oh, do I take it to mean you mean to convey them to the museum in your carriage?'

Sukey brightened up at once. The prospect of being driven through the streets in a carriage with a crest on the door clearly more than made up for the fact that the destination was to be somewhere she would rather not go.

'Not my own carriage, no,' said Edmund, causing Sukey's face to fall. 'I do not habitually use a carriage when in Town. I prefer to walk wherever I am going, or hire a hack should the weather be inclement.

'However, I have procured Lady Ashenden's barouche, for the occasion.'

'Lady Ashenden's barouche,' repeated Stepmama, one hand rising to her neck, even as Sukey made a moue of frustration.

'Yes. It is, even now, waiting at the foot of your front steps,' said Edmund with a slight emphasis on the word waiting.

Which was enough of a hint to spur Stepmama into action.

'Yes, run along upstairs, girls, and get your coats and bonnets on, do,' she said, making a shooing motion with her hands. 'His lordship does not like to be kept waiting.'

'Are you not coming with us, Mama?'

'No, my dear,' she answered Sukey with a complaisant smile. 'I am sure I have no need to chaperon you when you will be escorted by none other than his lordship.' She shot him a sickly smile. 'And each other,' she added, sternly. Although she had her sights set on a title for Sukey, she had no wish for her daughter to go off alone with anyone, no matter how high ranking they might be, and acquire a reputation for being fast . It would be fatal to her chances of marrying well.

Georgiana and Sukey rose to their feet, dropped dutiful curtsies and made their way to the door at a decorous pace to prove they were young ladies of good breeding, rather than obeying the order literally.

Edmund bowed, then went to take a seat on a chair opposite Stepmama.

'While we are alone,' he said, as the girls were shutting the door gently behind them, 'I feel I ought to drop a word of warning in your ear. Concerning Lord Freckleton.'

Sukey and Georgiana froze.

And then pressed their ears to the door.

'What about him?' came the slightly muffled response.

'It is merely that I do not think you should place too much significance in any attentions he may pay either of your charges.'

'Oh?' In spite of the door, Georgiana could clearly hear the affront in Stepmama's reply.

'It is not the fault of your girls,' put in Edmund soothingly. 'The fault is entirely his.'

'What do you mean by that?'

'Just that he is not the type to ever, willingly, make an offer of marriage to any female. His preferences lie in another direction entirely.'

'Really?'

At the very same moment Stepmama let out the shocked response, Sukey clapped her hand over her mouth to stifle a giggle. And then she began to back away, towards the stairs that led up to their bedrooms, her eyes alight with mirth.

'What is so funny?' Mystified, Georgiana followed Sukey up the stairs. But Sukey only shook her head, refusing to say a word until they'd reached their dressing room and closed the door behind them.

'Well! Can you believe it?'

'Believe what?'

'That Lord Freckleton isn't the marrying kind,' said Sukey, twirling Georgiana round so that she could unhook her gown. 'Thank goodness Lord Ashenden dropped Mama a hint about his preferences,' she said, presenting her own back to Georgiana so she could return the favour. 'At least that saves me the exertion of attempting to fix his interest. I was wondering why I wasn't getting anywhere,' she said, then succumbed to a full fit of the giggles.

More confused than ever, Georgiana plucked her highly impractical pale pink cambric carriage dress from the peg on which it hung and stepped into it, while Sukey did the same with hers.

'When you say *not the marrying kind*, Sukey, what do you mean, exactly? Is there some special significance to that phrase?'

'You goose, Georgie,' said Sukey, taking a moment to swat her on the shoulder in between hooking up the back of the dress she'd never expected to actually get an airing. 'How can you not know? It means...' she leaned in close and whispered, though there was nobody in the room but the two of them '...that he prefers men. To women. In a romantic sense,' she finished, when Georgie turned to gaze at her, perplexed.

'What?' Oh, heavens. No wonder Edmund had been so angry when she'd used that phrase when speaking to him about marriage.

She fumbled her arms into the loose sleeves of the pelisse which went with her carriage dress in a stew of guilt.

'I have sometimes wondered if your Lord Ashenden isn't one of those,' said Sukey, making her start. It was as if she'd somehow followed her train of thought.

'Of course he isn't!'

'Oh, I know that really,' said Sukey with a sympathetic smile. 'You have no need to defend his manly honour. His mistresses do that for him,' she said, reaching for her bonnet.

'Well, then,' grumbled Georgie, jamming her own bonnet down over her curls.

'Yes, but honestly, if he doesn't want people to think he's that kind of man,' said Sukey as she adjusted the set of her bonnet with the help of the mirror, 'he really ought not to go driving about Town in a vehicle more suited to the needs of an elderly lady.'

'Ed—I mean, Lord Ashenden, does not care what people think of him,' she retorted, yanking her ribbons into some kind of bow.

'Obviously,' said Sukey and went off into another fit of giggles. 'Oh, heavens, Georgie, you are going to have to...to slap me or something, else I shall be giggling all the way to the museum.'

'I have no need to do anything so vile. You only need to consider what your mama would say if she catches you giggling in Lord Ashenden's presence.'

'Lord, yes, she would demand an explanation for my extraordinary conduct, then I would find myself confessing that we were eavesdropping.'

And so it was that Edmund conducted two very sober young ladies to his mother's barouche a few minutes later.

Sukey's face brightened when a footman in black and gold livery sprang down from his seat to open the door and hand them into the low-slung vehicle. Probably because the door he opened for them had a crest painted on it. The vehicle might not be in the slightest bit dashing, but at least now her stepsister would feel she was even with Dotty and Lotty, who were always boasting about the times their titled cousin came to take them for a drive in such a vehicle.

'Well,' said Sukey, darting Edmund one of her most winning smiles. 'I am sure I have never sat upon more comfortable seats.'

'My mother is excessively dedicated to her own comforts,' he said with a slight edge to his voice as he took the seat opposite her and Sukey. It made Georgiana wonder what his mother could possibly have done to set his back up to the extent he would make a comment that could be interpreted as a criticism.

'As you note, the hood can be drawn up so that she need never miss an opportunity to go shopping, or visiting, no matter how inclement the weather,' Edmund added with a definite hint of disapproval.

'Unless,' Georgiana pointed out mischievously, 'you purloin her means of transport.'

He dipped his head in acknowledgment of her riposte and, though his expression remained grave, there was a glint of something like appreciation in his eyes.

'I have purchased tickets for you both, for Bullock's Museum,' he said. 'So that we need not waste time gaining admittance.'

So he hadn't just been passing and thought they might like to visit the museum. He'd planned it all very carefully. Well, of course he had. He didn't have a spontaneous bone in his body.

'I am sure,' he continued, 'you must both be very eager to get inside and view one of the most remarkable collections of its kind in existence.'

'Are you?' She raised her eyebrows, wondering exactly what he was playing at.

His eyes flickered towards Sukey, briefly, telegraphing his intention to explain his motives. 'Of course,' he said, with a perfectly straight face. 'It will be a most educational experience for you. Bullock is a member of the Linnean Society, you see, and has arranged his collection according to their principles. I shall now endeavour to explain them to you both, so that you will be able to truly appreciate the specimens we are about to view.'

Sukey's appreciation of her carriage ride faded in almost inverse proportion to her own amusement as his exposition of those principles grew increasingly de-

tailed. By the time they arrived at the imposing entrance
to the museum, Sukey looked as though she was on the
verge of doing something desperate. Like leaping out
and running, screaming, for home.

'You will note,' Edmund was saying in his driest
tone, as the footman handed them out of the barouche,
'the sloping pilasters, which have been ornamented with
hieroglyphics in an attempt to replicate a temple in the
Egyptian style. Hence, the cognomen of The Egyptian
Hall.'

Sukey shot her a look of despair behind his back, as
he turned to extend his arm for Georgie to take. She
had to bite down very hard to stifle a giggle.

'You will find more touches of the East adorning
the inner rooms,' he continued as if he was completely
unaware of the effect he was having on both girls, 'although the collection itself has been gathered largely
from the South Seas and the Americas.

'I shall procure a programme for you, as a souvenir
of this visit,' he declared with a beneficent smile for
Sukey, which made her alter her facial expression into
one of gratitude so quickly that Georgie had to put her
hand to her mouth and pretend she was stifling a fit of
coughing.

'Do you need a glass of water?' He eyed her with
apparent concern.

'No, no,' she said when she could master her voice
sufficiently to speak. 'I shall be fine, presently.'

'Then let us proceed,' he said, drawing them into
the next room.

'Oh, look,' cried Sukey, brightening considerably,
though not because she'd seen an interesting specimen
in any of the glass cases arranged round the walls.
'There's Dotty and Lotty over there.' She waved fran-

tically, in a way that Stepmama would have deplored had she been there to see it. 'Oh, Georgie,' she gasped, 'whoever do you think those gentlemen can be who are escorting them?' Each girl was leaning on the arm of a rather dashing-looking young man in naval uniform, while a rather disgruntled-looking civilian was trailing along behind them. 'Oh, do pray excuse me, while I go and find out,' she said, bouncing on her toes in her eagerness to escape.

'And that, I fancy,' observed Edmund with satisfaction as Sukey practically sprinted across the room to the other party, 'will be the last we see of her until it is time to leave.'

'Which was your intention all along,' she said, rapping him over the forearm with her rolled-up programme. 'Honestly, Linnean principles indeed.'

'It is completely true,' he replied with feigned affront. And then added, with an almost boyish grin, 'As is your own deduction. I was determined to find a way to have a conversation with you in private and, when I happened to hear that the Pargetter girls intended bringing their latest victims here, I could not think of a better opportunity to do so. Therefore, I seized it.'

'And your mother's barouche.'

'That, too,' he admitted. 'Are you angry with me? For tormenting your stepsister in order to be rid of her?'

She probably ought to be. But his performance had been so funny. And she hadn't had anything to laugh about for such a long time.

'That depends,' she eventually said.

'Upon?'

'Your motives.'

'I have already told you. I wish to have a…serious conversation with you.' He paused in front of a case containing a variety of nasty-looking weapons, as though weighing his words.

'If you are thinking of asking me,' she said, when the silence had dragged on to the point where it was becoming uncomfortable, 'about the list you suggested I make, then I have to tell you, it has done me no good.'

'Oh, you actually made one, did you?'

'Yes. No. That is, I haven't actually written anything down, but I have been keeping a sort of tally in my head of the…um…potential I can see in any of the gentlemen who have paid me any marked attention, in the hopes of counterbalancing my reluctance to…er… proceed any further with any of them.'

His brows rose. 'Have there been very many such men?'

'There is no need to sound so surprised. You were the one who told me, after all, that I was bound to attract more men than just Major Gowan if I was patient.'

'But, in the space of a week? I mean…' He checked himself. 'Of course you have acquired a court. A beautiful girl like you—it was bound to happen.'

Beautiful? He thought she was beautiful? Her cheeks heated and her stomach did a funny little squeeze.

'N-not a court, exactly,' she explained. 'Though there are now two more men who are being rather obvious about their interest in me. According to Stepmama,' she added, in case he thought she was boasting.

'Tell me about them,' he said sternly.

'Well, my favourite…' she wrinkled her nose. 'Or perhaps it would be more accurate to say, my least *un*-favourite—'

'Though less grammatical,' he put in.

'Yes, well. His name is Mr Armitage.'

'Armitage?' He looked at her sharply. 'Never heard of him.'

'I don't suppose you have. He hails from the North Country where he has a lot of mills and such like. He is, according to Stepmama, obscenely wealthy.'

'And that makes him an acceptable suitor, does it?'

'I have already told you that is not the case, or I wouldn't have been seriously considering Major Gowan.'

'Point taken,' he said, with a slight nod. 'Pray, do enlighten me as to what is so tempting about this obscenely wealthy northerner.'

She bit back an objection to the scathing tone of his voice because she had an answer that was an absolute leveller.

'The thing I like *most* about him is that he prefers me to Sukey. He has come to Town to find a wife from the Quality, as he calls it, so that he can start a dynasty that nobody will be able to call vulgar. But he dislikes what he calls niminy-piminy females.'

'Niminy-piminy? He actually used that term? In your hearing?'

'No. He told Stepmama,' she said, with a smile at the memory of Stepmama's outrage at having her darling so described. 'He then went on,' she admitted in a voice that shook with suppressed laughter, 'to say that a strapping great wench like me was a much better bargain, to his way of looking at it.'

'He thinks he will get more to the pound, is that it? And for this, you will accept his suit?'

'I did not say I meant to accept his suit,' she retorted. 'It is just that I cannot help feeling, well, flattered that he prefers me to Sukey. Without betraying the slightest trace of sentimentality.' She would definitely not be able to hurt *him*, even though she was bound to disappoint him.

Edmund looked at her as though she'd lost her mind. 'Of course he is setting his sights on you, Georgie. You are of much better birth than your stepsister. I dare say he discovered that your mother came from a lesser branch of an aristocratic family, while your father was landed gentry during this interview he seems to have had with your stepmother.'

'Oh. Well, yes, he did, as it happens.' She eyed Edmund with resentment. 'You have just disposed of the one point Mr Armitage had in his favour. I really thought he was taken with *me*. But he isn't at all. It is my background he finds so appealing.'

'Very well, let us forget about Mr Armitage. Tell me of your other suitors.'

'Well, there is one I am sure you do know. Mr Eastman. Percy Eastman.'

'Eastman? Good God.'

'There is no need to say it like that. He is exactly the kind of man Papa always said I should marry, you know. A Corinthian. A connoisseur of horseflesh, with plenty of address. And yet...'

'Indeed. With Percy Eastman, there is always that qualifying *and yet*.'

'I don't know why that should be. He is always perfectly charming. And he is comfortably off, moves in the best circles and is very handsome.'

'And yet...' Edmund quoted her.

She nodded. And Edmund shepherded her to the next display case while she gathered her thoughts about Mr Eastman.

'It is something about his eyes, I think,' she said. 'There is no kindness in them. In fact, he always has this slightly mocking air, as though he regards everyone else as innately inferior and rather amusing. Though, to be fair, he is wealthier, and better connected, and better looking and more intelligent than most people I've met in London.' She sighed. 'And this is *exactly* what I mean about your idea of writing a list being so...useless.'

'In what way?'

'Well, on paper Mr Eastman would have much to recommend him. Yet whenever he bows over my hand and looks up at me from under those hooded lids...'

'Yes, quite. In Eastman's case I think you should definitely trust your instincts.'

'But then, when Mr Armitage smacks his lips and rubs his hands together as though he's just spotted a bargain, or Major Gowan spills his drink down his coat because he cannot tear his gaze from my...from the front of my gown, it puts me in mind of what they will expect of me in the marriage bed. And I just...' She shuddered.

'There is no need to get into such a taking,' he said soothingly, patting her hand.

Which incensed her so much she forgot herself.

'It's all very well for you to say that. You are not the one who has to smile politely while some horrid man practically thrusts his nose down...' She glanced down at herself, making an exasperated gesture at the mounds straining at the fabric of her pelisse. And wished, not for the first time, that she'd never grown the beastly objects.

Chapter Twelve

Edmund winced.

She wasn't surprised. She must have really shocked him, saying that.

And now he was removing his spectacles and polishing them on his handkerchief.

Today, however, the knowledge that she'd shocked him into a spectacle-polishing silence gave her no satisfaction whatever. She'd shocked herself by referring to things that ought never to be spoken of between a man and a woman.

'You know,' he said, replacing his spectacles on his nose and hooking the wires over his ears, 'there are ways of repudiating suitors...'

And, just like that, she was furious with him again.

'It's all very well being all calm and rational and supercilious, but you're not the one that...'

'That...?' He stood there regarding her calmly, his face betraying no emotion whatever.

'Oooh!' She stamped her foot. 'If it was happening to you, you'd sing a different tune, I can tell you!'

He raised one astonished eyebrow.

'Yes—just imagine if *you* had to get married and

lots of…of ugly women started…ogling you, and…and you had to put up with it all…and—' She narrowed her eyes suspiciously. 'And don't you dare smile.' He wasn't smiling, exactly, but his lips had definitely twitched in a way that hinted he was sorely tempted to do so. 'It isn't funny!'

'Not remotely.'

'And don't patronise me, either.'

'I am not doing so. I am in complete agreement, knowing far more of that sort of thing than you might imagine.'

'What? How can you possibly?'

He shrugged. 'Well, it is just that I am quite a catch myself. Why do you think I never or—to be strictly accurate—very rarely make an appearance on the social scene?'

She didn't have to think about that statement for even a second. 'At least you have a choice. Whereas I have to…' She whirled away. Walked to the next cabinet of curios.

He followed her. Stood next to her in silence. Waiting.

'Oh, very well, I beg your pardon,' she said, once she could no longer feign any interest in the display of antique weaponry. 'You don't have to tell me I am behaving very badly today. It is just that I seem to have reached the end of my tether and—'

'Yes,' he said. 'Quite.' He cleared his throat. 'Actually, having witnessed Major Gowan's behaviour I can see why you are so angry with him. I can also see that you feel trapped and observe that you appear to be struggling like any frightened creature would, when caught in a trap.'

'I am not frightened,' she said indignantly. 'But

trapped, yes, I do feel trapped. Because there isn't any way out that I can see, apart from doing the one thing I most wish to avoid.'

He gave her that look, the one he applied to a new specimen, or puzzle that he was determined to solve. And then, after a few moments' scrutiny, led her to a bench where he sat her down.

'Believe it or not, I do understand how you feel. It is something like how I felt when I was…obliged to leave Bartlesham and everything and everyone I knew. And it *was* frightening.' He gave her a stern look as though daring to argue with him. When she didn't, he continued. 'You panicked when faced with a similar exile. I know you did, because nothing else would have compelled you to propose to me.'

She blushed and hung her head.

He cleared his throat. 'The thing is, now, I can look back upon that time in the Scilly Isles and see that it was actually more in the form of…an escape,' he said, gazing off into the distance, which meant she could now look at him again and encounter nothing more challenging than his lean, closely shaven cheeks. 'An escape from a prison…a luxurious sort of prison, but a prison, none the less. I had no notion how restricted my life had been at Fontenay Court until I experienced a different life.'

'London isn't an escape from anything, for me,' she muttered mutinously.

'You have not given it a chance.' He half-turned to her. 'And nor did I, when I first arrived on St. Mary's. I was upset for a long time. Even though I knew, deep down, that I was there for my own good, I…was very, very unhappy.'

He looked uncomfortable, as though it was costing him a great deal to admit this.

Perhaps that was why he hadn't written to her, then. Perhaps he was ashamed of being so unhappy, and hadn't known how to put his feelings into words. Perhaps—

'Come,' he said, getting up and moving away from her a few paces, as though admitting that much was too embarrassing for him to be able to sit still. She followed him until he stopped abruptly by a case full of brightly coloured butterflies.

He gazed down at them, his throat working. Was he thinking about the day she'd filled his bedroom with the tiny, British cousins of these exotic specimens?

Had her gift, the time she'd spent collecting them all, meant anything to him at all?

'Do you think,' he said, thoughtfully, 'that caterpillars have any notion that one day they are going to turn into beautiful creatures like these? Do you think they have any idea what it would be like to have wings?'

'No.'

He turned to look at her, expectantly, and she knew he wasn't speaking about butterflies and caterpillars at all. 'Are…are you saying that…I am like a caterpillar? Wanting to stay on my little leaf, rather than going out into the world and becoming a butterfly?'

'Ah, not exactly. Putting it the way you have just done is to imply some sort of criticism. And I cannot fault you for thinking or feeling the way you do. I felt the same, don't forget. No, what I am saying is that you don't need to be afraid of new experiences. Of becoming the beautiful creature you are meant to be.'

'The trouble with that metaphor,' she said bitterly, 'is that I'm doomed to stay a caterpillar. No matter how hard Stepmama tries to make me into one, I simply cannot be a butterfly.'

'What do you mean?'

She sighed. 'Look, you know that I never used to fit in with the other girls in Bartlesham. But once Stepmama taught me how to behave like a lady, I did think I might be able to…pretend I was normal. But then, none of the men at the local assemblies would ask me to dance, even though they flocked round Sukey. The only way to get them to dance with me was to ask them. Which they had to do, from good manners, but it wasn't the same…' Not when she saw a flash of something like fear in their eyes. As though they were picturing her knocking them down.

'The men of Bartlesham are idiots. Take it from me. You are perfectly splendid exactly as you are.' He waved his hand at the glass case. 'There are all sorts of different butterflies. And you do not have to be like all the others to *be* a butterfly. Have you learned nothing from Miss Durant? She reminds me of you at that age, before…life, shall we say, crushed out that spark.'

He'd liked her *then*. Before Stepmama and Papa had tried to turn her into a Sukey butterfly. A task that had always been doomed to failure, because inside, she was always going to remain a grub.

But what did he think of her now?

He gazed down into her face with concern. 'Why can you not believe you are attractive? Ah—the idiot male inhabitants of Bartlesham.' His lips thinned. 'Georgiana, you believe, I hope, that I would never lie to you?'

'Ye…es.' She thought for a moment. He had actually been outspoken to the point of rudeness, on occasion, but he had never fobbed her off with anything less than the truth. 'Yes,' she then said with more conviction.

'Then let me tell you, in plain speech, speaking as a man who is most definitely not an idiot, that you are a most attractive woman. You have lovely eyes. Lovely hair. And your figure is...'

'Big,' she interjected. 'Ungainly.'

'No,' he said sternly. 'Your figure is splendid. Full, yes, but with a firmness that speaks of health and vitality,' he corrected her. 'When you couple that with your love of the outdoors and energetic pursuits, it makes men looking for a wife see that you would be a good choice to mother their children. And I am sure you could have many of them...' he seized her hands and gave them a squeeze '...with no difficulty whatever.'

'I...I...' She blinked as her eyes started stinging. She wasn't going to be a mother. Ever. Not if she couldn't overcome her revulsion at the act that was necessary to get them.

'I know your mother died in childbirth,' he said gently. 'But that need not be your fate.'

What? He thought that was why she'd asked him for a pretend marriage? He thought she was a *coward*?

'It isn't that,' she cried indignantly. 'I'm not afraid of that!'

'Then what—?'

She tore her hands and her gaze away from him, her heart beating rapidly and her stomach squirming. She couldn't tell him about...about Wilkins and Liza.

'I just...cannot, that's all.'

'Yes, you can, Georgie,' he said, walking round her until he was standing in front of her. 'You can do anything you set your mind to. I can see that your stepmother's influence has diminished your belief in yourself, but deep down, is there not still a spark of...that girl who was not afraid of what anyone said, or thought? The

Georgie I knew—' He reached out and with his forefinger lifted her chin so that she was looking into his face, rather than at his boots. 'She would have taken London by storm. She would probably have done it by flouting just about every rule governing the behaviour expected of debutantes. She'd have acquired a large following of devoted admirers. And if any of them had tried to step out of line she'd have had no trouble giving them a leveller. Probably literally,' he finished on a wry smile.

Her breath hitched in her throat. He admired all the things about her that Stepmama had told her were bad. He thought other men would find them attractive, too. That if she could just dare to be herself, they would flock round her, the way they flocked round Sukey.

For a moment, a vision of that Georgie, holding a swarm of suitors in the palm of her hand, flitted into her head.

But then she focussed on the way Edmund was smiling at her. And they all vanished. Because Edmund was the only man she wanted to smile at her like that. And find her fascinating. And look at her as a potential mother for his children.

Something happened to her insides. To her breasts. To her mouth. Something she'd never felt before.

But she knew what it was, all the same.

Oh.

It was like being slapped in the face by an enormous tree branch when galloping through a densely wooded area.

The *'right man'*, Stepmama had said, would make her feel differently. She had been speaking of some mythical Corinthian, the kind of man Papa would have liked for a son-in-law. But Georgiana was looking at the right man, right now.

It was Edmund.

And that was the moment she knew exactly why she'd proposed to him. Why she couldn't think of any other man as a husband. It wasn't because she was afraid of leaving Bartlesham, or devastated by the prospect of having to sell Whitesocks.

It was because once she married someone else, it would be over between them. Finally and irrevocably over.

She had never given up hope, she realised, that some day, somehow, he would return to her. Her Edmund.

She wanted him to love her. The way she loved him. Had always loved him.

Even as children, he'd been her favourite playmate. He'd been more intelligent, more sensible, more…*everything* than any other child in the area. It was why she'd been devastated when he'd left and apparently forgotten about her at once. Because she'd feared she hadn't meant as much to him as he had to her.

And when he'd come back, as a handsome and healthy young man, she'd started loving him in a different way. How could she have denied the way her body had leapt to attention whenever she spied him? Only to curl in on itself when he'd looked down his nose at her, reminding her that he was a lord now and not her playmate. She'd told herself she was glad to see the back of him when he'd gone away to university, after spending only a few weeks in Bartlesham. That she hated him.

But it wasn't true. Oh, it wasn't true! It had just been easier on her pride to stomp round in a fury than to curl up somewhere and weep.

And now?

As though he was in tune with her thoughts and didn't like them, he suddenly turned his head so that they were no longer gazing into each other's eyes. Let go of her hands.

Then she could hear Sukey giggling over something one of the naval officers was saying.

Her cheeks flooded with heat.

'We should join the others,' she said through a throat that was squeezing shut with the force of the emotions roiling through her and marched swiftly across the room, not daring to look back to see if he was following. Because he was so clever, he'd surely see the longing, the inappropriate and unreciprocated longing in her eyes. And he'd start avoiding her again. The way he'd done in Bartlesham. Because he'd just told her he avoided the kind of women who stalked him like some form of matrimonial prey.

So she'd have to convince him she didn't think of him that way.

At least while he thought she regarded him only as a friend, he'd feel safe keeping her company.

But if he ever guessed how she felt about him, he'd run a mile.

Chapter Thirteen

Edmund shifted from one foot to the other as he waited for his turn to hand in his ticket to Lady Chepstow's charity ball. It was no use telling himself that the cause was a good one. He didn't give a rap for indigent governesses, or whatever it was tonight's takings would fund. He just wanted to see Georgie again. Ever since the conversation they'd had at Bullock's Museum, about the way he'd felt when his mother had sent him into exile, he'd been kicking himself for not bringing up the topic of the intercepted letters.

He'd practically accused her of being too cowardly to grow up, yet he'd balked at bringing the truth out into the open. Out of concern for what the result would have been. He'd stood there, wondering if she'd be angry, or hurt, or, if she'd felt as deeply as he had about it, if she might not even have burst into tears. In the museum, of all places.

So he'd changed the focus of their conversation. Talked to her about the suitors she ought to be attracting, for heaven's sake. When there were already far too many men hanging round her for his liking. With their tongues hanging out.

He slapped his ticket into the hand of Lady Peters, the gorgon presiding over admittance to Durant House for some reason, and then stalked past, ignoring her speech about the premises tonight's profits would be used to purchase.

He needed to see Georgie for himself. To…

To do what, exactly, he wasn't sure. He stomped up the staircase that led to the ballroom, his face rigid with self-disgust. Since the day she'd made that outrageous proposal it felt as if he'd abandoned every principle by which he'd ever lived. He might have come to London with the intention of proving he was the better man, by steering her into the kind of marriage she'd said she wanted, but what had he done instead?

Deliberately sabotaged the one chance she might have had at making such a match by warning her stepmother about Lord Freckleton's proclivities, that's what. And then, when he'd seen glimpses of the old Georgiana peeping out from behind the curtain of ladylike behaviour, he'd practically dared her to come all the way out, by introducing her to that hoyden Julia Durant. And then, at the museum, telling her outright that's what he wanted her to do.

He reached the ballroom just as the orchestra was screeching its way to the conclusion of a dance and scanned the couples returning to their seats for a sight of her.

And he saw her. With Eastman. Eastman! Hadn't his warnings about the libertine been explicit enough? Clearly not, because Eastman was bending over her hand as she sat down and saying something which was making her look uncomfortable.

And her stepmother was smiling up at the scoundrel in an encouraging way, while Georgiana looked as though she was only holding a polite smile on her face with an extreme effort.

Then Eastman sauntered away, in the direction of the card room, leaving Georgiana with her lips pulled tight and shoulders so tense they were practically up by her ears.

He strode over.

'What did he say to you?'

Georgiana blinked up at him as though in confusion.

'You know who I mean. Eastman,' he said.

'Nothing,' she replied. Which was obviously untrue.

After he'd continued to glare at her for a second or two, she wilted.

'Nothing I care to repeat,' she admitted, lowering her gaze and fiddling with the struts of her fan in a distracted manner.

'I thought we had agreed you should stay away from him,' he said.

'You don't understand—'

'Then explain it to me.'

'He asked me to dance. If I had refused him…'

She didn't need to say anything else. If she had refused one partner, publicly, she would not have been able to dance with anyone else. He flicked one contemptuous glance at her stepmother. The woman whose job it was to protect her charges from just such a situation by vetoing unsuitable, or unwelcome, men.

'And he took advantage?'

'Only to say…something. He didn't *do* anything…'

He couldn't very well. Not on a dance floor. But he could guess what a man like that might have said.

'I will deal with him,' he growled. And set off in pursuit.

He caught up with his quarry just outside the card room.

'Want a word with you,' he said, just before Eastman went through the door.

'Me?' Eastman half-turned to look at Edmund over his shoulder. 'Cannot imagine what business you would have with me,' he said, with a hint of disdain.

Edmund ignored the intended insult, since he felt a reciprocal disdain for men like Eastman who frittered their lives away on a variety of trivial, and often immoral, pursuits. Then he stepped a little closer and lowered his voice before speaking again, although it was unlikely anyone could hear any conversation held at a rational level, above the general hubbub emanating from the ballroom. 'It concerns Miss Wickford.'

'Oh?' Eastman's demeanour underwent a subtle shift. It put Edmund in mind of a hound catching an elusive, yet fascinating scent on the wind. 'Wasn't aware you had an interest in the chit.'

If anything could have confirmed his suspicions about the reasons Eastman was pursuing Georgiana, it was his use of such a disrespectful word to describe her. 'And now you are,' said Edmund through gritted teeth.

'Would have thought,' said Eastman, turning to face him, 'that her stepsister was more in your style.'

He bit back the retort that immediately sprang to mind, since it was entirely his own fault everyone assumed his tastes ran to diminutive blondes, when every mistress he'd had since attending Oxford had conformed to that type.

'I have known Miss Wickford since we were children,' he therefore said, deciding to get right to the nub of the matter.

'Indeed? She hails from Bartlesham, then? I was not aware.'

'Yes. Her father was the master of the local hunt.'

'That would account for it,' said Eastman, propping himself against the panelling and folding his arms across his chest.

'Account for what?' replied Edmund against his better judgement.

'Her rollicking sort of air. Can just see her riding to hounds. A bruising rider, I'd wager. Eh?'

'I haven't come here to discuss her prowess on horseback.'

Eastman laughed. In a distinctly dirty manner.

'Ashenden, you astonish me,' he said, reaching into his waistcoat pocket for his snuffbox with a sly grin.

'I do not—that is, Miss Wickford is—'

'Makes no difference to me,' said Eastman casually flicking open the lid.

'What makes no difference?'

'Her virginity. Or lack of it,' he said with a shrug.

'I beg your pardon?' Edmund couldn't believe his ears. Even though this was what he'd suspected all along.

'No need,' said Eastman, taking a pinch of snuff between his thumb and forefinger. 'I don't mind not being the first. She clearly still has much to offer a man, being so, ah, spirited. I shall look forward to…taming her,' he finished with an evil smirk. A smirk that Edmund simply had to wipe from his face.

Before he knew it, he'd clenched his fist and lashed out.

And Eastman went down like a felled oak, snuff exploding in all directions as the enamel box went flying.

For a moment, Eastman simply lay there, looking as stunned as Edmund felt.

'Good God,' he gasped, lifting a rather shaky hand to his nose, which was bleeding. 'You knocked me down.'

'So I did,' said Edmund, reeling. And not just at the fact he'd just done something so rash, without a moment's hesitation. Nay, not even so much as a moment's *thought*. But the fact that it would mean a duel. Nobody knocked a man like Eastman down and got away with it.

Edmund would choose pistols, he decided. He'd be a fool to fence with a man whose reach was so very much longer than his own. Pistols would make the contest fairer.

Having reached that decision, Edmund felt a surge of anticipation stirring deep within him. It would give him a great deal of satisfaction to blow a hole in the smirking lecher who'd not only assumed Georgie wasn't a virgin, but admitted it made no difference to his plans.

The sound of a chorus of groans, followed by a burst of laughter wafting from the card room as someone briefly opened the door, brought both men back to their senses.

'Damn…' Eastman groaned, fumbling in his pocket for a handkerchief. 'It's going to be common knowledge in a matter of minutes that you've knocked me down.'

As if to prove him correct, Edmund heard someone exclaim, 'Good God, Ashenden is having a set-to with Eastman!'

And someone else saying, 'Ashenden? Never!'

Then the unmistakable sound of chairs scraping back and feet tumbling in their direction.

But Edmund never took his eyes off Eastman.

'Oh, lord,' Eastman said plaintively. 'When I think of

all the fellows who've challenged me to a bout and never been able to so much as to pop one in over my guard…'

'Do you require someone to act as your second?' said a voice at Edmund's side. From the corner of his eye he saw Lord Havelock, eyeing him, and then Eastman's prostrate form, with what looked suspiciously like approval.

For a moment, Eastman looked annoyed. But then his lips twitched, and he started to chuckle. 'I'm not going to fight a duel over this little…misunderstanding. It's bad enough to have been knocked down by a spindly bookworm like you,' he grumbled, dabbing at his nose. 'If it gets as far as meeting on a field of honour, they'll be selling tickets. You should consider this,' he said, gesturing to the blood streaming down his face, 'satisfaction enough. And the fact that all these gentlemen here,' he said, waving his hand at the men spilling from the card room, 'are witnesses to your triumph. Here,' he said, raising his free hand in supplication. 'Help me up, there's a good chap.'

Havelock bristled, and made a move to block him.

'Oh, for the Lord's sake, Havelock,' grumbled Eastman. 'You don't think I'm going to start a mill, right outside a ballroom, do you?'

'You had better not,' he said.

'You will apologise,' said Edmund grimly.

'Unreservedly,' said Eastman. Which left Edmund no alternative but to hold out his hand as Eastman attempted, somewhat shakily, to stand up. Eastman's eyebrows rose as Edmund hauled him unceremoniously to his feet.

'Not so spindly, after all,' he said, raising the hand that wasn't held in Edmund's grip to feel his upper arm beneath his coat. 'You may be a slender chap, but you don't spend all your time reading books, do you?'

'That is beside the point.'

'No, I don't think it is. It almost makes me...' He shook his head, and grimaced. 'No, never mind. Please accept my sincere apologies,' he said, sweeping Edmund an ironically deep bow, 'for poaching on your preserves. I shall, of course, cease pursuing your...intended bride forthwith. Shake on it?'

Intended bride? The murmur rustled among the assembled spectators like a breeze through a forest. Making Edmund wish, more than ever, to ram a couple of Eastman's shiny teeth down his throat. But if he made a production of Eastman's sly allusion to the woman over whom they were fighting, it would only increase the chances someone would guess who the woman in question was. He could not say anything, with all those others watching, without making Georgiana the subject of scurrilous gossip.

He had, in short, no choice but to take the hand Eastman was holding out to him and shake it grimly.

Eastman grinned. 'You must let me in on the secret of how you keep in such good shape, Ashenden.'

Edmund blinked at Eastman's bonhomie. But then reflected that men of his ilk often appeared to believe they'd become firm friends with someone, simply because they'd either knocked them down, or been knocked down by them.

'Rowing,' he said curtly.

'Rowing?'

'Rowing.'

'Rowing?' Eastman's incredulity increased every time he repeated the word. And Edmund saw he was going to have to offer some form of elucidation, or the idiot would be keeping him standing there all night, bat-ting the word back and forth like a shuttlecock.

'Yes. I took it up when I was sent, as a boy, to the Scilly Isles to recuperate from an illness.' At the mere mention of the word, *illness*, the men who'd abandoned their card games in the hope of witnessing a brawl began to drift away.

'It was the best way,' Edmund continued, 'to get from one island to another. And my physician encouraged me in that pursuit, hoping it would broaden my chest muscles and thus help with my breathing difficulties.'

'Continued up at Oxford, did you?'

'Well, the colleges are surrounded by water. And I found that the exercise was conducive to contempla-tive thought.'

At that Eastman burst out laughing. 'Well, I never heard of you taking part in any of the races, so it never occurred to me that—' before bursting out laughing again. 'Damn, you must be the only man there who took to the Isis as an aid to study rather than to win a wager!'

As soon as all the men but Lord Havelock had gone, the jovial expression faded from Eastman's features.

'I think,' Eastman continued, eyeing the card room, 'that this would be a good time to try my luck at the tables. Since it is not running in my favour with affairs of the heart.'

'You will need to clean yourself up a bit first,' said Havelock, then snapped his fingers to summon a foot-man who must have been hovering somewhere close by. 'Bridges here will take you to find water and a wash-cloth. And a fresh neckcloth. Cannot have you sitting down to play cards in soiled linen.'

Eastman sauntered off after the footman as though he hadn't a care in the world.

And Edmund watched him go, his fists still clenched, bitterly regretting the fact that a man could wriggle his way out of fighting a duel if he made what sounded like an honest apology.

'Come on,' said Havelock, taking him by the arm.

'What? Where are you taking me?'

'My study. Only place Mary hasn't put into use to raise money for Lady Chepstow's blessed charity school. And you look as though you could use a stiff drink. And the privacy in which to pull yourself together.'

The privacy, however, was denied him the moment they entered Havelock's study and found Lord Chepstow already in situ, nursing his own drink, in an armchair before the empty fireplace.

'Ah, Havelock,' said Chepstow, raising his glass. 'You don't mind, do you? This was the only room I could find that ain't infested by charitable types attempting to separate me from my money.'

'Not at all,' said Havelock affably, pushing Edmund in the direction of another armchair. 'We came in here for much the same reason.'

'Good God,' Chepstow suddenly exclaimed, straightening up from his slouch. 'What the devil happened to you, Ashe?'

'He had an altercation with Eastman,' said Havelock, going to the sideboard and pouring two drinks. 'Knocked him down.'

'No!' Chepstow grinned. 'Why?'

Because he'd had no choice. He'd *had* to convince Eastman that he wasn't going to let Georgie become yet another one of his conquests. He'd challenged him in the first place because everyone knew about the number of broken hearts and ruined reputations the man had casually left in his wake. It was just a pity the man's re-action had made him lash out without thinking. Which had been extremely foolish as well as being completely out of character.

But he couldn't have stood back and let Eastman add Georgie to his tally. Or hurt her in any way at all. Or even touch her, come to that. The thought of Eastman, or that bumbling cavalry Major, fixing his slobbering lips on Georgie's perfect breasts...

Insupportable.

And yet, in order to protect her, he'd given her would-be seducer the notion he was on the verge of proposing to her himself.

Which he wasn't.

But now there were at least two people who thought he might be.

And half a dozen more who suspected he had marital intentions in relation to *someone*.

Dammit!

Chapter Fourteen

'Ashe?' Havelock was pressing a drink into his hand and looking down at him with concern. And he realised he hadn't answered Chepstow's question.

'He, ah, made a remark I didn't much care for,' he said, taking the drink.

'About a lady?'

Edmund nodded in response to Chepstow's question, then swallowed almost the entire contents of his glass in one gulp.

'Want some ice?'

'What?'

'Ice,' Chepstow repeated. 'For your hand.'

Edmund glanced down to the fist he'd just clenched at the thought of any man putting his hands on Georgie, or starting rumours about her, and for the first time since he'd knocked Eastman down, noted that his knuckles were a touch sore. Not that he minded. A little discomfort was a small price to pay if it meant saving Georgie from an unscrupulous devil like Eastman.

'You should remove your coat and let one of my people sponge it down for you, too,' said Havelock, nodding in the direction of his upper arm, where Eastman had gripped him. And left a slight bloodstain.

He stood up jerkily and stripped off his coat while Havelock went to the fireplace and tugged on the bell pull.

'I wish I'd seen that,' said Chepstow. 'You, Ashe, of all men, knocking Eastman down! I mean,' he said, when Edmund glared at him, 'must be dozens of men with more compelling reasons.'

'No, there are not,' said Havelock.

'What do you mean?'

'Well, clearly, he must have insulted Miss Wickford.'

Edmund sucked in a short, shocked breath. It was almost as if Havelock possessed some kind of sixth sense.

'No need to look at me like that,' said Havelock testily. 'No secret Eastman's been dangling after her of late. And after the trouble you went to, to get her accepted into society...' he finished on a shrug.

'Miss Wickford?' Chepstow's brow puckered in confusion briefly. 'Oh, that girl from the country your sister Julia has taken such a shine to? The horsey one. The one with the brassy stepmother.'

'That's her,' said Havelock. 'And not only is she brassy, that stepmother has very little in her cockloft. She's pushing those girls of hers at any man who will look twice. It's no wonder a man like Eastman assumed she ain't particular about the kind of propositions they'll get. Not that I'm condoning him,' he added, for Edmund's benefit. 'Type of man seriously wants knocking down.'

'But,' said Chepstow, looking confused, 'she's the big strapping one, ain't she? Everyone knows Ashe here prefers his women small and blonde—like the other one. Whatshername.'

'I wish,' said Edmund irritably, flinging his coat across the back of his chair, 'everyone would stop thinking they know anything about my taste in women.'

'Look out, Chepstow,' said Havelock with a grin. 'He's clenching his fists.'

Chepstow raised both hands in the air and backed away, an expression of mock terror on his face.

'You are completely safe from me,' said Edmund witheringly, deliberately unclenching his fists, which appeared to have taken on a mind of their own tonight. 'Since you are not at present taking snuff, nor sullying the name of the woman, according to Eastman, I am about to marry.'

'What?'

'Snuff?'

Edmund had the satisfaction of getting their full attention with that cryptic remark.

'Eastman assumed incorrectly,' he informed them.

Although…if he didn't marry Georgie, what was to become of her? She'd have to marry someone else. And he'd just discovered he couldn't bear the thought of any other man touching her. Let alone subject her to the act which she'd consider an assault.

He couldn't even stomach the thought of her entering into a marriage of convenience, since no other man would have a clue how to make her happy. Or the inclination to make the attempt.

And he *wanted* her.

So perhaps he *should* marry her himself.

'At the time,' he added, thoughtfully.

'What? I say, Ashe,' Chepstow complained, 'could you not speak a bit more clearly? Because you've lost me.'

'He's decided to marry Miss Wickford after all,'

Havelock translated, testily. 'Obviously, knocking Eastman down made him realise he's in love with her.'

In love with her? He wasn't in love with her.

'Oh,' said Chepstow, breaking into a grin. 'Now I know why you cannot string three words together and get them to make sense.'

'Do you?'

'Yes. Falling in love does tend to addle a man's brains. As well as making him feel as though he wants to flatten anyone who hurts the woman he loves, then rip them to small pieces and put them through a mincer.'

'Does it?'

'Oh, yes,' said Havelock.

'But…I don't love her—'

'Oh, yes, you do,' Havelock said. 'Lord, for a man who's supposed to have brains, it's taking you the devil of a time to work out what is plain to anyone else. Ever since she arrived in Town you've been acting out of character. Getting hot under the collar, haunting balls and such just to get a glimpse of her—'

'Striding across the room to wrest her from whichever admirer happens to be with her when you do spot her,' chipped in Chepstow.

'And now coming to blows with Eastman—Eastman of all men—just because he makes a bit of a nuisance of himself.'

'That's all the hallmarks of a man in love,' said Chepstow sagely. 'Exactly how I felt about Honeysuckle when she was in trouble. Knew I had to rescue her. Look after her. Mince anyone who hurt her into tiny pieces. That sort of thing.'

That wasn't love. Love was…was…well, he didn't know exactly what it was, but it wasn't *that*. He'd read a bit of poetry. And he'd never come across a poem about turning rivals into mincemeat.

'If you ask me,' said Havelock, 'it's about time you proposed to her and put yourself out of your misery.'

'Well, I didn't ask you,' said Edmund irritably. 'Besides, she…' didn't want a normal marriage. And what kind of fool would propose to a woman, knowing the kind of terms she'd demand?

'She what? You don't mean to tell me you're afraid she won't have you, are you? You're an earl, ain't you?'

He ground his teeth. That was the trouble with letting people even just a little way into your confidence. They started assuming you would tell them everything. And there was no way he was going to betray Georgie's fears and insecurities to *anyone*.

'It isn't that simple,' he said, after they'd both been staring at him expectantly for some time. 'I…' He supposed he could give them a reason for not marrying her that they might consider valid, without making it look like Georgie's fault. He leaned forward and clasped his hands together over his knees. 'I offended her.' By turning down her proposal in such cutting terms he'd reduced her to tears. 'If I was to propose to her, now, I fear she would either think I was mocking her, or…if she took my proposal seriously, she would throw it in my teeth, just to get her own back.'

'Ah,' said Chepstow. 'That was pretty much what Honeysuckle did when I proposed. Threw it in my teeth,' he said, rubbing a hand absentmindedly down the front of his waistcoat as though attempting to remove an invisible stain.

'But you persuaded her to accept your proposal in the end,' said Edmund, whose curiosity, for some reason he didn't understand, was roused by the notion that here stood another man who'd persuaded a woman into accepting a proposal she rejected at first with some vehemence, by the sound of it.

'Well, yes, obviously,' he said as though Edmund was an idiot.

'Well, then, how?'

'Ah,' he said, turning a dull shade of red. 'Well, actually, I kissed her.'

'And that worked, did it?'

'Not to begin with,' he said, looking distinctly guilty. 'Matter of fact, had to keep on kissing her until she saw sense.'

'But that's…'

'Highly improper,' said Chepstow defiantly. 'I know, but it worked, didn't it?'

'Actually,' said Havelock, 'that's the tack I took with Mary, too. And no point saying it wasn't the proper thing to do. Time was of the essence. If I'd gone courting Mary in the regular manner, she'd probably still be keeping me dangling to this day.'

'So, both your brides were reluctant, too? And you… subdued them with, ah, masterful kisses? Do I have that correct?'

Havelock stared moodily into the distance. Chepstow tugged at his neckcloth.

'You make it sound as if we coerced them into doing something they didn't want,' Chepstow complained. 'And they did want to marry us. Deep down. Just needed to realise it. So a spot of kissing was totally justified. They're both happy now. Ain't that right, Havelock?'

'Very happy,' he said belligerently. 'You just get her alone somewhere, kiss her senseless and she'll come round, you'll see.'

Edmund snorted. 'Get her alone? How, pray, when

she is chaperoned every hour of the day and night? When she takes great care not to be alone with a man, or let any man trick her into situations where he might have a chance to take liberties.' He pressed his hands to his temples in disbelief. What was he saying? He had no intention of devising a scenario whereby he could coerce her into accepting a proposal he had no intention of making.

'Kiss her in public, then,' said Havelock. 'That's what I did, actually. Mary had no choice but to marry me after that.'

Edmund imagined walking up to Georgie in a ballroom, taking her in his arms and... He shook his head.

'She can box,' he said with impatience. 'I taught her myself. She'd flatten me if I attempted anything like that in public.'

'You'll have to kiss her in private then.'

'Yes,' Chepstow agreed. 'And even if she does draw your cork, then, you won't be obliged to desist.'

Kiss Georgie into submission? Were they mad? He certainly would be if he attempted any such thing. Even if it was for her own good.

Even if it was what she wanted, deep down.

Which some people might argue it must be, or she wouldn't have proposed to him in the first place.

'After all,' said Chepstow cheerfully, 'what's the worst that could happen?'

The worst that could happen?

For Georgie to think he was just like every other man who thought her nothing more than a lush body to grope and paw and subjugate. And he was, that was the trouble. Worse. Because he had been lusting after her whilst knowing full well that the prospect of becoming intimate with any man completely sickened her.

His own stomach promptly turned over and squeezed into a knot as he realised he was a worse scoundrel than Eastman, who'd also lusted after her without having any intention of marrying her.

He lowered his head, and almost groaned.

'No need to despair,' said Havelock. 'You'll find a way. Clever chap like you.'

'You could just try telling her you love her,' put in Chepstow. 'You'd be amazed how effective saying the words can be.'

The trouble was, they would constitute a lie. And there was no way he could lie to Georgie.

And anyway, why was he sitting here, listening to all this talk of love and marriage as though he…he…

He sat up straight. He couldn't stay here any longer, his mind going round and round in circles.

'I need to take a walk,' he said, getting to his feet. 'Think things over. Get things…straight in my mind.'

Because walking often did help his thought processes along. Though it was nowhere near as effective as rowing. Didn't build up the muscles, either, which had just come in so handy.

'Goodnight, gentlemen,' he said, making for the door.

'Wait!' Havelock hurried over, Edmund's jacket in his hand. 'Better put this on. Can't have you wandering the streets in your shirtsleeves,' he finished on a grin.

Edmund rather thought he might have growled as he took it. Before shrugging back into it, stalking from the house and heading for the nearest open space where there would be no idiots putting idiotic notions in his head.

Chapter Fifteen

Edmund strode along Jermyn Street with his head bowed, scarcely noticing the other pedestrians dodging out of his way. He couldn't bear the thought of any other man touching Georgiana. Or making her miserable. And he wanted her. It wasn't surprising Chepstow and Havelock though that meant he should marry her. But they didn't know what that would mean.

How could he bear being married to her and not really having her?

How could he bear the loveless, tepid relationship she'd painted that day, when he wanted so much more?

More? He wanted more?

Did he? Did he *really*?

The answer roared back like a toddler having tantrum. Yes, he wanted more! Everything, in fact. Everything she had. Everything she was.

He came to a standstill, a slight sweat beading his brow.

What was the point of getting so…worked up, when he knew she wouldn't listen to any proposal? The only proposal she would be happy to accept, from any man, would be the kind she'd made him. Which wasn't what he wanted.

Dammit, he was right back where he'd started.

There had to be another way out.

He took a deep breath and started walking again.

What if he were to tell Georgie that he *would* consider a marriage in name only? His stomach clenched. He took himself to task. Told himself sternly to consider it as a hypothetical situation. And found he could breathe more easily.

In that kind of marriage, the husband and wife in question would live in a state of companionship. Which meant there would be none of the jealousy, and demands and betrayals, and broken crockery that went with what usually went on behind closed doors.

There would also be no children. No heirs.

But would that really matter? He had cousins. Dozens of them scattered about the country. Fontenay Court, and all the people who relied on the Earl of Ashenden, would be secure.

He would be the only person to lose out.

Very well, that was one solution. Unpalatable, but there it was. And now that he'd come up with one possible outcome, he was ready to move on to another. One in which Georgiana accepted a proposal from some other man who would be happy with that kind of marriage. Completely happy.

No. He could not bear to see any other man taking that role. Of Georgie being grateful to any other man for living only half a life. If Georgie was going to regard any man as saviour, it would be him.

He came to a standstill again as it dawned on him that his decision was made. He was going to have to marry Georgie, no matter what it cost him. Because no matter how hard such a marriage might be for him, the alternative, seeing Georgie married to someone else, would be far worse.

So, all he had to do now was come up with a way to convince her that he had good reasons for changing his mind about what he wanted from marriage. Stating quite categorically that he was now ready to put aside his demands for heirs.

How hard could that be?

Two days later, Edmund put in his first appearance in the park on a horse he'd bought specifically to prove to Georgie that he could be the man she needed him to be. The park, he'd decided after much cogitation, would be the perfect place to have a serious conversation with her about their future, because the intrepid and headstrong Miss Durant was not likely to be much of a chaperon.

Miss Durant was not hard to locate, mounted side-saddle as she was on her famously expensive dappled grey. But she was not accompanied by Georgie and a groom at all, but by her half-brother, Lord Havelock.

'Good morning Miss Durant, Havelock,' he said, touching his riding crop to the brim of his hat as they all came abreast.

'Morning, Ashe,' said Havelock, looking distinctly amused. 'Taken up riding, have you?'

'I might ask you the same question,' he replied frostily. 'I was under the impression Miss Wickford accompanied your sister to the park, since you were not inclined to do so.'

'Georgie isn't well,' Miss Durant replied helpfully. 'Wasn't well yesterday, either, which is how Gregory managed to slip the leash this morning. Even Lady Havelock had to agree it isn't fair to make me do without my ride two days on the trot.' She giggled. 'So to speak.'

'I'll thank you not to imply I'm tied to my wife's apron strings,' Havelock snapped.

His sister made a sulky response. Edmund saw that the pair were likely to continue bickering for some time, so he made his excuses and turned for home.

'Well, that was a waste of time,' he said to the horse. 'Perhaps I should name you something like Folly. Or Pointless.' The chestnut snickered and shook her mane, reminding him that, actually, his outing had not been a total loss. He had discovered one pertinent fact. Georgie was ill. In fact, she must be really ill. Nothing but the direst circumstances would make her forgo her ride two days in a row.

If it was any other woman but Georgie, he wouldn't have been so surprised, now he came to consider it. She'd been under a great strain for a considerable period of time.

She had clearly already been in some desperation when she'd approached him and made that marriage proposal. And in the weeks since, she'd been pursued by Major Gowan and propositioned by Eastman because her hen-witted stepmother kept pushing her on to the marriage mart. And she'd endured it in a succession of outfits which made the entire ordeal ten times worse.

He dismounted in the mews with a curt nod to the groom who came running, then strode into Ashenden House, absentmindedly rapping his boot with his riding crop as he went. He'd always prided himself on being observant, in the normal run of things, but when it came to Georgie, she disturbed him so much that his intellect invariably failed him spectacularly.

Still, armed with the knowledge that she was ill and

not merely avoiding him—or, more probably, he deduced on a flare of hopeful speculation, the other suitors—he decided to act accordingly. A man who wanted a woman to look upon him as a potential suitor would call upon her and deliver flowers when she was ill. Which was exactly what he would do, as soon as he'd changed out of his riding gear and asked Poppleton if he knew where, exactly, a man could procure a suitable offering at this hour of the morning.

Later that day, armed with a posy of pink rosebuds, he took a hack as far as Bloomsbury Square. Just as he approached her front steps, the door of the house opened and a rather disgruntled-looking man emerged. Edmund had never seen him before, but the deferential way Wiggins was handing him his hat indicated that he was a regular and welcome visitor.

As the stranger clapped his hat on his head he noticed Edmund standing at the foot of the front steps, the posy of roses in his gloved hand, and his lip curled into a sneer.

'I dare say,' he said bitterly, 'they'll let *you* in to see her. What with you having a title.'

From the way he said the word 'title' as though it was some form of disease, coupled with the distinctly northern accent in which he spoke, Edmund was easily able to deduce his identity.

'Good morning, Mr Armitage,' he said and had the satisfaction of seeing surprise flit across the man's face.

'You know who I am? I wouldn't have thought—' He stopped, his mouth pressing into a grim line. Then fell silent, running his eyes over Edmund's frame as though sizing him up.

While Edmund did the same. And he didn't like what

he saw. Because there was no denying that Mr Armitage was a very handsome chap. Dark, with rather unruly hair, but exuding a kind of vitality that a girl as full of energy as Georgie must surely admire. And since Georgie had already told him that he was the least unwelcome of her suitors, he could actually see them as a matching couple.

Mr Armitage's perusal halted at the posy in Edmund's hand. Then he smiled. In a predatory fashion. 'Aye, mayhap that's the way to go,' he said. 'Good day to you.'

With that, he sauntered off, with the air of a man on a mission. Which gave Edmund a chill of foreboding. Because if Armitage started wooing Georgie with flowers and compliments, who was to say he might not persuade her...

No. Armitage was all wrong for her. He would demand his conjugal rights if he ever became her husband. Nobody but Edmund knew her well enough, or cared about her badly enough, to put her welfare above his own selfish desires.

Clutching the posy with renewed determination, he mounted the steps. Before he could knock, Wiggins, who must have been watching through the keyhole, opened the door.

'Good morning, my lord,' he said, in the way that butlers invariably had, which subtly imparted the information that he was a more favoured guest than the one who'd just departed.

'Mrs Wickford and Miss Mead are in the drawing room,' he said, motioning to the stairs. Edmund supposed he'd have to go in and endure a half-hour of their tedious conversation if he wanted to persuade everyone that he was in earnest about courting Georgie. But then that was what serious suitors did. They also informed a girl's guardian of their intentions and asked permission to pay their addresses. All of which he'd also better do.

He handed his hat to Wiggins, then stood for a moment perplexed as to how to remove his gloves whilst holding a posy.

Wiggins cleared his throat.

'The posy is for Miss Wickford, I presume?'

'Yes. I heard she was indisposed.'

The butler's face sobered. 'Indeed, my lord,' he said with a rueful shake of the head.

All Edmund's senses went on the alert. What did that mean, that grave look? The sorrowful tone in his voice? The doleful shake of the head? Just how sick was Georgie?

Terrifying visions of scarlet fever, or typhus, or smallpox claiming her before he could speak to her again leapt into his mind.

'I will have the maid take them up to her,' said Wiggins, just as a harassed-looking girl carrying a tray emerged from a door to the rear of the hall that no doubt led to the servants' hall. Or whatever passed for the offices in a house as small as this one.

She shot a mutinous look at the posy and then at the butler, then eyed the tray in her hands in a pointed fashion.

If only etiquette was not so strict, he'd save her from having to take on another duty she clearly had no time for, by taking the flowers to Georgie himself. In a more reasonable world, it would be the perfect excuse to see her. Which was what he really wanted. So that he could find out exactly how ill she was and with what. And, yes, he knew he could simply ask the stepmother those questions, but that wouldn't be the same.

And what if she died? Without ever learning the truth
about why they'd parted and how it had affected him?
Without understanding why he'd rejected her proposal
the way he had? Without hearing that now he intended
to make amends for all of it?

Why, for God's sake, were the rules governing society so rigid? Why shouldn't an unmarried man enter
the sickroom of an unmarried girl if she was at death's
door? That rule wasn't only rigid, it was downright
cruel.

Resentfully he handed over the posy to the maid,
who'd slammed the tray down on a side table, and his
gloves and coat to the butler.

Since Wiggins had long since given up trying to
make him wait in the hall while he took his outer gar-
ments to wherever it was that butlers stashed them,
Edmund began mounting the stairs only a few paces
behind the maid.

It was when he was about halfway up that it suddenly
occurred to him that if Georgie was suffering from anything contagious, and deadly, her stepmother would not
be admitting visitors to the house at all. Which was an
immense relief. In fact, he couldn't think why he'd leapt
to such dire conclusions in the first place.

But even though his fears abated, the urge to storm
into her room and tell her how he felt did not. He'd put
it off long enough as it was.

In fact...

He came to a dead halt, one foot on the landing, the
other on the last tread, as the implications of doing just
that unrolled in a series of vivid tableaux. The scandal.
The inevitability of marriage...

It would solve all his problems at a stroke. Chepstow
and Havelock had said he ought to consider kissing her,

in public, in order to compromise her. But this would be even better. In fact, it was downright brilliant. She'd be compromised all right, but he wouldn't have to do anything he had good reason to know she would hate.

Besides all that, there would be a pleasing symmetry to storming her room in order to solve all the things that had gone wrong between them. Georgie had regularly sneaked into his bedroom when he'd been sick, as a lad. And had eventually been caught by his outraged housekeeper. The events of that day had torn them apart, though neither of them had known it at the time. If he invaded her room, today, it would bring their relationship full circle.

He half-smiled at the elegance of the solution. It would mean an end to all the uncertainty, all the wild emotions that had been making him so uncomfortable of late. Once he and Georgie married, he could settle back down into a regular, ordered existence, with her at his side.

He only hoped he would have sufficient time with her, alone, before discovery, to convince her he was in earnest about wishing to marry her. Although surely sneaking into her bedroom would convince any girl a man truly wanted her, wouldn't it? It certainly wasn't a place any man who was determined to remain single would stray.

It was a great pity he hadn't thought of this in the first place, rather than wasting time buying horses and flowers. That time would have been far better spent studying this house and discovering if a handy tree happened to be growing outside her bedroom. He could have climbed it and gone in through her window. *That* was the kind of gesture Georgie would appreciate.

It was at that point that he realised that searching for a tree would have been useless without first ascertaining where, within this house, Georgie's bedroom was situated.

He swore under his breath. This was the trouble with acting on impulse, rather than taking time to make a watertight plan. The house was not all that large, but who knew what lay behind any of the doors he'd be obliged to open in order to discover her whereabouts? If he opened the wrong one, he'd have to…

But, no, actually, there would be no need to search the whole house. All he would have to do was follow the maid who was on her way to Georgie's room with that insipid posy. He'd only been mulling things over for a moment or two. She couldn't have got far. Could she?

Hastily, he took the final step that carried him up to the landing and was just in time to see his quarry turning into an alcove at the far end. Then he heard the sound of her feet, stomping up another set of stairs.

He glanced briefly to his left, to make sure that the drawing-room door was shut, before turning to his right and tiptoeing along after the maid at full pelt.

He was halfway up the second flight of stairs before he saw the flaw in this plan. The maid, having delivered the posy, was bound to return this way and she'd see him. And demand to know what he was doing.

His hand instinctively went to the pocket that held his purse. Would he be able to bribe the maid to turn a blind eye to his presence on the upper floor?

Unlikely. Even if she was of a romantic disposition and inclined to be sympathetic to his cause, her superiors would expect her to alert them at once. And, though discovery was vital, he needed time alone with Georgie first.

While he was calculating the chances of making her an ally against the odds of her losing her job, his feet were carrying him inexorably to the upper landing. He arrived just in time to see a door at the far end of the passage closing. He stood stock still, though his mind was still racing. Would ten guineas be enough to get the maid on his side? It was all he had about him at the moment, but he would give ten times that much if only he could get to Georgie. Perhaps he could offer the girl an alternative position if she was turned off. Surely she'd prefer to work in the household of an earl than one of a woman like Mrs Wickford?

Though what the hell did he know of the aspirations of housemaids?

A cold sweat broke out on his brow as the door at the far end of the corridor opened again and the maid came out. He braced himself for the inevitable confrontation, but, instead of heading his way, the maid turned to her left and disappeared into what looked like an alcove just beyond Georgie's bedroom door. He then heard the distinct sound of her feet descending another, un-carpeted staircase. And sagged into the wall in relief. She'd taken the back stairs, which must lead directly to the servant's hall. His heart pounded. So hard that it made him tremble in anticipation. This was going to work. It was really going to work. With a sense of exaltation, he strode along the corridor to what he now firmly believed to be Georgie's room, scratched briefly on the door panel, pushed open the door and went in.

At which point he blinked, wondering if this could really be her room after all. For it was tiny. More like a storage room than one in which a young lady should be sleeping. Moreover, it would have been in complete darkness if not for the light streaming in from the landing, through the door which was still open behind him.

But that light illuminated a narrow bed, in which a figure lay hunched up. A hunched-up figure that let out a moan.

Chapter Sixteen

Georgie couldn't believe that yet another person had come into her room. She'd heard the knocker going she didn't know how many times this morning, which meant the drawing room must be crowded with visitors. Surely, nobody had the leisure to come all the way up here to torment her? Couldn't they leave her in peace, for one hour? They knew she couldn't defend herself when she was laid this low. Besides, what more could she say? It wasn't her fault Edmund had chased after Mr Eastman and knocked him down. It wasn't her fault that half the people from the charity ball had taken it into their heads that Edmund must be on the verge of proposing to her.

Though, admittedly, it was her fault that he had done no such thing. There was nothing on earth that would make Edmund propose to her, not when the only reason he might ever contemplate marriage at all would be to produce heirs.

And Stepmama knew she felt guilty about something. Which was why she wouldn't listen to her protestations that Edmund merely felt protective of her, because they'd been friends as children. Why, for the first time since her thirteenth birthday, Georgie had actually welcomed the monthly event that so frequently rendered her incapable of leaving her bed.

Although, whoever had just come in apparently had no sympathy for the wretchedness of her condition. For they were marching across to the windows and…

Drawing the curtains?

'What,' she protested feebly, 'do you think you're doing?'

'I should have thought that was obvious,' said the intruder.

In a voice she recognised. But couldn't possibly. Because Edmund could not possibly be here.

Gingerly, she rolled over, and opened one eye. To see Edmund thrusting up the sash window.

'I don't know what ails you,' he said, turning to her and making as if to approach her bed, 'but you aren't going to get better in a room shut up like this. You need fresh air, Georgie.'

She held up a hand, screwing her eyes shut against the dazzling light thrusting its way into her skull.

'Shut the curtains,' she begged. 'Can't stand the light.' Even saying as little as that made her feel nauseous. With a whimper, she dragged a pillow over her head and gave a series of rapid, desperate swallows.

From the sound of curtain rings rattling along the rail, and the subsequent dimming of the light, she knew he'd done as she'd asked.

'Sorry,' he said. And then approached the bed. 'Can't abide the smell of a sickroom, you know.'

By the creak of the webbing she could tell he was sitting down on the chair beside it.

'Comes of having been shut up so often as a lad,'

he said. 'And I know how you love the outdoors. I thought…'

She felt a tug at the edge of the pillow. Presumably, he was trying to see her face. If she'd had the energy she would have snatched the pillow out of his inquisitive fingers and thwacked him with it.

'Actually, no, I didn't think,' he said, his voice full of concern. 'What is the matter with you, Georgie? Do you have a fever?' He reached under the pillow and touched her forehead. His strong, yet gentle fingers felt wonderfully soothing. They'd probably feel even better if he would only stroke her there, where the pain in her head was so intense. 'Sore throat? Is that why you aren't yelling at me to get out?'

She shook her head. And winced.

'Hurts my head to speak,' she said.

'And you cannot stand the light.' He paused. 'If you were a man I'd say you were suffering from a hangover.'

If she were a man, she reflected bitterly, she wouldn't be going through this.

He shifted in his chair and leaned forward until his face was almost next to hers.

'You shouldn't be in here,' she whispered, because at least, now that his face was only inches from hers, she didn't need to speak at a volume that set her head ringing.

'Of course I should,' he murmured. 'You are ill. And whenever I was ill, you used to sneak into my bedroom to try to cheer me up. And you never feared catching anything that I had, either.'

'But we were children then, so it didn't matter. This, now…it isn't proper.'

'Mrs Bulstrode didn't think it was proper back then, either. Don't you remember how shocked she was when she came in and caught us on my bed with the curtains drawn closed?'

The word *trollop* screamed at Georgie down through the years, making her shudder. 'As if I could ever forget.'

'I thought it was funny, at the time, but looking back, it must have been most unpleasant for you,' he said, reaching out his hand to stroke her hair.

She flinched. She couldn't help it. His gesture was so unexpected, but more than that, she craved his touch so much she was afraid if she didn't retreat, she'd somehow give herself away.

He drew his hand back.

'I'm sorry,' he said. 'I did not mean to make you uncomfortable.'

'You mean, more uncomfortable than I already am at having a man invade my bedroom?'

'If you were really uncomfortable, you would be demanding I leave. Or screaming for help.'

'I cannot scream,' she retorted. 'My head hurts far too much. The sound of my voice is like someone banging a mallet inside my skull.'

'Poor Georgie,' he said. 'Is there anything I can do to help? Some medicine I can administer?' He glanced at the bedside table, upon which lay the water bottle she'd discarded once it had cooled, and the posy of roses Betsy had just slapped down, spraying her pillow with a shower of pink petals.

'Nothing helps. I just need peace and quiet and darkness. Until it passes.'

'You get these headaches regularly, then?'

Not every month, fortunately. But even when her head didn't feel as if it was about to split open, she could never go riding, sometimes not even out walking. And she always felt so unclean, so diminished at this time of the month. Not even Sukey could understand why she couldn't manage her monthly indisposition with more grace. But then Sukey floated through it all so daintily. She hardly ever complained about experiencing anything more than the occasional twinge. Because she was far better at the business of being a woman.

She dragged the pillow from her face and scowled up at him.

'Yes,' was all she said.

'I'm so sorry. I always thought…I mean, you always seem so healthy.'

She made an effort to peer at him more intently and saw that he was not as calm as she'd at first thought. But then, how could he be calm when the chances were he was going to be discovered, in her bedroom, at any moment?

'Edmund, I don't know why you came in here, but really, you shouldn't have done.'

'Yes, I should,' he said with a glint of defiance in his eyes. 'When I was ill, you always came to visit me. Nothing could keep you away.'

'That was different. I didn't know any better.'

'Do you mean,' he said slowly, 'that you regret befriending me and offering me comfort?'

She sighed. 'Sometimes, yes, I do,' she admitted. She was sick of hiding the truth from Edmund. Sick of having to put on a brave face when he was about. Of having to pretend that she only thought of him as a friend. Only pride, stubborn pride had kept her going, through so much, for so long. But he was seeing her at her absolute worst today. And somehow, now he'd seen her reduced to this, there didn't seem any point in hiding *all* her feelings from him, any longer.

'It wouldn't have been so awful when you went away, if we hadn't grown so close. Or at least, if *I* hadn't thought of *you* as my best friend. But what I meant about not knowing any better was that I honestly had no notion that it was wrong to make friends with a boy, or to be alone with a boy, or to go and play in a boy's bedroom.'

'Ah.' He lowered his gaze to where she'd curled her fingers into the edge of her sheet. 'Well, now there are two points that need addressing there. Firstly, your approach to your own gender. Which is understandable, since your father treated you as though you were a son. No concession was made to the fact that you were, in actuality, a girl. Which meant that it was perfectly natural for you to look for companionship from a boy of about your own age, rather than any of the local girls, whose habits and interests were limited to a strictly feminine sphere.'

'That's true.' The other girls in the area had always seemed such silly, empty-headed little things. All too easily shocked at the notion of climbing trees, or wading through a pond to see how deep it was, or saddling their ponies and staying out all day, eating whatever they could find in the hedgerows.

Which had made it come as a terrible blow when her body began to demonstrate that it was capable of conceiving a child. She felt as if it had betrayed her. Along with Edmund and her father. Her whole life had undergone a series of drastic changes in such a short period of time that she'd sometimes thought she knew what it must be like to live through an earthquake. There had been no solid ground on which to stand. Nowhere to run, to escape from the huge great boulders that were raining down on her, threatening to crush the life out of her.

'So you need not feel any guilt, whatsoever,' he said firmly. 'You acted in complete innocence.'

She felt a great rush of affection for him, so strong it was all she could do not to reach for his hand and clasp it. It was a good job she was hanging on to the sheet so hard, to preserve her modesty, or who knew how foolishly she might have behaved?

'And now to move on to the second point,' he said, his jaw firming, as though it was something he felt very strongly about. 'From the emphasis you placed on the personal pronoun, I take it you were implying that *I* did not consider *you* my best friend.'

Golly. She wouldn't have thought he would want to take issue over that.

'But you didn't, did you? I didn't realise at the time, because I was such a silly little goose. But later on I realised you simply tolerated me, because you were bored and your parents wouldn't let you have anything to do with any other child—'

His hand shot out, but the touch of his finger to her lips to silence her was very gentle.

'That was not how it was,' he said sternly. 'You *were* my best friend, Georgie. My only friend.'

He seemed to mean it. But it couldn't be true.

'You soon forgot me, though, didn't you?'

'No. Far from it.'

'Oh, come on—'

'The memory of that last day we spent together, the day you brought me the butterflies—' He shook his head and blinked, as though attempting to rearrange his thoughts. 'No, that was not the last time I saw you, in point of fact. It was the day they sent me away. I caught a glimpse of you, through the carriage window. You were waving.'

'You didn't wave back.'

'I did. But clearly you didn't see.'

'No.'

'You looked as though you were crying. But then I thought, no, not Georgie. Nothing makes her cry. She's too brave. But funnily enough, it helped me to think you might almost be on the verge of tears. Because it meant that you were going to miss me as much as I was going to miss you.'

She shook her head in disbelief. 'But you didn't miss me. You forgot all about me the moment you left Bartlesham.'

'You are wrong. I missed you very much indeed. And I was hurt, very hurt, when you appeared to break your promise to me.'

'What promise?'

'To write to me.'

'What? But I did! That is, I didn't!' She groaned inwardly at her clumsiness of speech. 'Why are you trying to twist everything round?' she hissed furiously. 'I kept my promise. You were the one who didn't write to me.'

'Oh, I wrote to you,' he said. 'Every week. Even when I received no reply I kept on, in the hope that your letters were delayed by…bad weather, or something.'

'What?'

He carried on speaking though his mouth twisted with bitterness. 'Then I began to think you must just be too busy out riding, or swimming, or fishing, to want to sit down and write. I struggled to forgive you. I reminded myself you'd never been much of a one for sitting down and applying yourself to anything of the sort. Surely, I kept telling myself, she will at least send me greetings for Christmas. But Christmas came and went, and there was nothing from you, and I ate my solitary Christmas dinner, far from everything I'd known, wondering how you could be so...' he drew in a sharp, pained breath '...so cruel.'

'But I wasn't. Edmund, I *did* write.'

'And then it was my birthday.' He carried on as though she hadn't spoken. 'And still no word from you. And I was halfway through my weekly letter to you, when I saw that it was more or less an inventory of the wildlife I was discovering on the island and it struck me that it was probably so boring, that all my letters had been so boring, that it was no wonder you hadn't written back. That you probably didn't know how to reply without revealing what a bore I was. Not when you'd never had it in you to dissemble.'

'No,' she grated, horror struck. 'I would never have found any letter from you boring, Edmund. And I had never found you a bore. Surely you must have known that? Why, you were so clever. Noticing things that nobody else did. Like the differences between all the beetles we found in the woods, which everyone else just...crushed, if they bothered to think about them at all. And I did write. More than once a week. At first...'

He nodded, grimly. 'Yes. I expect you did. At first. But then you gave up, didn't you?'

'Well, yes, because I thought you'd forgotten all about me. And I started thinking that perhaps, before, you'd only tolerated me hanging around you when you'd been so ill, because you were so bored.'

'No,' he said vehemently. 'That was not how it was between us.'

'But then what—?' It felt as though she was experiencing yet another earthquake. 'If you wrote to me—'

When his face tensed up, she hastily amended her statement. 'I mean, where did your letters go? And what of mine to you? If you didn't receive them…oh! I gave my letters to my father to post. Are you trying to tell me he…he didn't send them? Any of them?' It felt as if someone had just punched her in the stomach, to think Papa might have started betraying her as far back as that.

'That I cannot say. What I do know is that my tutor used to collect all the mail that arrived at St Mary's. To begin with. And I gave my letters to him to post.'

'So it was *him*. It must have been him.' She heaved a sigh of relief. It had been bad enough that Papa had married a woman who'd imposed such a strict new regime upon their household. When he'd turned a blind eye every time his new wife had beaten her. For things that had never been crimes before.

'But…why would he have done it?'

'Obviously because he had instructions to that effect.'

'What? Why? Why would anyone want to make you so miserable? And me? It doesn't make sense.'

'Yes, it does, Georgie, think about it.' He leaned forward. 'Don't you recall Mrs Bulstrode's reaction that day she found us in my bed with the hangings closed?'

Georgie winced. 'She called me a trollop. I didn't even know what a trollop was. Not until much later.' When Wilkins had got Liza into trouble. And then, from the names flung about during Liza's dismissal, she had worked out that a trollop was a girl who spread her legs in the stables so that a man could use her like a brute beast.

'I heard her berating you all the way downstairs. I've already told you that, at the time, I just found it amusing. But recently, I discovered,' he said, looking uncomfortable, 'that she carried tales of that escapade to my mother. And that my mother subsequently took action to…separate us from one another.'

'But why? Why go to the lengths of…sending you so far away and stopping us from keeping in touch at all?' She pressed her hand to her head, which was throbbing at the struggle to make sense of what Edmund was telling her. 'Why didn't someone just explain to us that it was improper? And why it was improper?'

'Because Mrs Bulstrode believed that we were past the stage of needing explanations.'

'What? What do you mean?'

'Georgie, think about it. She drew back the curtains to see your skirts hitched up round your waist, while you have to admit I was wearing only my nightshirt.'

'But I only drew the bed hangings round because I wanted to fill the air with colour for you. Like…like putting flowers in a vase, rather than strewing them all over your room. Which would have happened if I'd just let the butterflies out to fly where they wanted.'

'I suspect they would all have headed for the window, and arranged themselves decoratively across the panes,' he said pedantically. 'Not that it wasn't a splendid idea of yours,' he added, reaching out his hand to pat hers. 'I never forgot it. Even when I had persuaded myself I hated you, I remembered the joy you brought me that day and couldn't turn my back on you entirely.'

'You hated me?' Her stomach lurched. 'What had I ever done to make you hate me?'

'You broke my heart,' he said.

'I…what?'

'You weren't just my friend, Georgie. You were my sunshine. My joy. You were too young, probably, to feel the same about me, but…the truth is, I loved you. When you didn't write—or to be more precise, when they made me believe you hadn't written—I was devastated.'

'Oh, Edmund. Oh, no!' She turned her hand over and gripped his as hard as she could. He returned the pressure, his face working.

'The only way to survive the devastation,' he grated, 'was to twist what I felt for you and turn it around into hatred. When I returned to Bartlesham, for that short spell before I went up to Oxford, all I wanted to do was hurt you. So when you tried to greet me as though nothing was wrong, I…'

'Looked down your nose at me. I thought it was because you'd become the Earl. I thought that you were ashamed of letting me dog your heels when you were just a boy and were doing your utmost to put me in my place, the way your mother puts people she considers encroaching in their place.'

He shook his head. 'There was an element of that, in my behaviour, I dare say. But it was because I couldn't bear to look at you, thinking you'd forgotten all about me, that you hadn't cared how badly you'd hurt me. It was like a nest of snakes writhing inside me every time I caught a glimpse of you.'

Oh, how cleverly he described things. That was exactly how she'd felt. All those emotions, swirling through her, making her want to strike out, the way snakes struck out and spat venom.

'I acted as badly, when you came back. Because, even though I never received any letters from you all that time you were away, I went to the gatepost, hoping…' She couldn't say more.

'You looked for a message from me? Even after what you believed I'd done?'

She nodded. 'I sneaked out and went to the trout stream, too, hoping you might go there, the way you used to. I thought if I could catch you there, I could make you tell me why we couldn't be friends any more. But—'

'Georgie,' he gasped. 'Even after everything you thought I'd done, you still hoped… God.' He bowed his head over their clasped hands. 'You had more faith in me than I had in you. I believed,' he said, raising his head and looking into her eyes, 'I really believed that you thought so little of what we had that you found it easy to toss aside the promises we'd made.'

'Oh, Edmund. All these years…' She felt her lower lip quiver. And her vision blurred.

'Don't cry Georgie. Just be glad we've found each other again,' he said. And then leaned forward to press his lips gently to her forehead.

She sucked in a short, shocked breath.

Just as the air was rent by the sound of a scream of outrage.

Chapter Seventeen

Georgiana made a desperate attempt to free her hand from Edmund's clasp. Somehow, it wouldn't seem so bad, Stepmama finding him in here, if only they weren't holding hands.

Or if he hadn't just been kissing her.

But Edmund had a very firm grip and was refusing to let go. What was more, before Stepmama had a chance to draw breath, he was saying, with marked irritation, 'Do you have to make so much noise? Have you no consideration for Georgie?'

'Do *I* have no consideration? Do I…? You…' She pulled herself together, stepped into the room and bore down on Georgie's bed. 'Just what do you think you are doing in here?' she hissed into Edmund's face.

'I should have thought that was obvious,' Edmund calmly replied. 'I was kissing Georgie.'

'How dare you?' Stepmama uttered in an outraged shriek.

Georgie experienced a strong urge to pull the quilt up over her face. And not only to drown out the screeching. The sound of footsteps thundering up the stairs meant that any second now, even more people were going to burst in on her.

Not that it appeared to bother Edmund in the slightest.

'I dare,' he said, 'because it was essential that I persuade Georgiana that I am determined to marry her.'

Marriage? He hadn't said anything about marriage before.

'Only a gesture as dramatic as invading her bedroom and kissing her was going to convince her that I am in earnest, given the rift that had developed between us.'

'Marriage?' Stepmama shook her head. 'But Georgiana swore it was no such thing. That you were merely friends.'

'Nevertheless—'

'No! You cannot marry her. Otherwise...'

She shut her mouth with a snap. Georgie looked over her shoulder to see Betsy and Wiggins jostling each other in the doorway to get a glimpse of what could possibly have occurred to make Stepmama shriek so.

'Otherwise?' Edmund was eyeing Stepmama coldly.

'I only meant to say, I'm sure you cannot really wish to marry a girl like Georgiana.'

'Not only do I wish it, but, should you attempt to oppose me in this, you will regret it.'

'I...' Stepmama swallowed. Wrung her hands. Turned to look over her shoulder at the servants.

'Precisely,' said Edmund, rather grimly. 'There will be no way to keep my presence in Georgie's room a secret.'

He was right. These were London servants. Hired along with the house. They had no particular loyalty to the tenants. And she could hardly expect them to keep such a juicy morsel of gossip to themselves. Oh, no—poor Edmund.

At this point, he let go of her hand, rose to his feet and went to the door.

'You may be the first to congratulate me,' he said to the servants in a determined voice. 'Miss Wickford has just done me the honour of accepting my proposal of marriage.'

Wiggins's left eyebrow rose in patent disbelief. But Betsy clasped her hands together and beamed at him.

'Congratulations, your lordship,' she said, bouncing on the tips of her toes.

'Just so,' said Edmund, reaching into his pocket and producing some coins, which he pressed into the hands of both servants.

Judging from the maid's gasp, and the way the butler's eyebrow immediately resumed its correct position, the bribe had been sufficiently generous to remove any malicious inference from the way they would relate the incident to anyone willing to listen. Which would probably be half of London.

Having ensured the servants' goodwill, if not their silence, Edmund closed the door firmly on them and turned to Stepmama, his expression set.

'Have you come to your senses yet?' Edmund gave Stepmama one of those looks. The kind that put her in mind of his mother when she was depressing someone's pretensions. Though Stepmama didn't look as though she was about to meekly surrender. There was a martial light in her eyes that made Georgie suspect a battle royal was about to commence.

'And do not attempt to hamper me by reminding me that Georgie is technically your ward and refusing to grant your permission for the match—'

'Technically? There is no technically about it!'

'Because,' he continued as though she hadn't interrupted, 'if you should do anything so foolish you will find yourself presiding over a scandal that is bound to reflect very badly upon your guardianship. And that will not only adversely affect Georgie, in the short term, but also hamper your own daughter's chances of *ever* making a good match.'

Stepmama's eyes flashed fury. She clenched her fists.

'Very well,' she said, tossing her head. 'Why not? Why shouldn't you marry her? It isn't as if *she* kept her word to me, is it? All that talk of advancement and doing Sukey whatever favours she could, it never came to anything, did it?'

'Ah,' said Edmund as though he understood perfectly what Stepmama was talking about, when Georgie felt as though she'd dozed off in the middle of a play and had woken up again only at the end to discover she'd missed too much of the plot to be able to make sense of anything anyone was doing. 'Is that how you became her puppet?'

Puppet? Why was Edmund calling Stepmama a puppet? Just whose puppet Stepmama was supposed to be, Georgie couldn't tell.

Stepmama flung up her chin. 'For all the good it did either of us,' she said bitterly. 'Sukey never met anyone higher ranking than tradesmen's sons in Bartlesham, for all that her stepfather was the local squire. I waited and waited, but she did nothing.'

She? What she?

'Not until we had no choice but to leave Bartlesham,' Stepmama was continuing, without appearing to draw breath, 'and I reminded her of the bargain we'd struck, did she finally agree to arrange a court presentation for both girls. And how did she *arrange* it? Not by presenting them herself—oh, no! She just sent me an introduction to Lady Ackroyd, who is so deep under the hatches she'll do just about anything legal for cash. And not only did that bit of business cost me the best part of her inheritance,' she said, waving in Georgie's direction, 'but it didn't do any good. It was vouchers for Almack's I should have got, if my girls were going to be accepted, not an expensive day out at the palace which everyone knew was a put-up job the minute they heard Lady Ackroyd's name in connection with it. Which they always do, somehow. And the end result was that not one of those stuffy patronesses was willing to give vouchers to girls whose mother had to *pay* to have them presented at court.'

'As my wife,' Edmund pointed out, 'Georgie will most certainly obtain vouchers. As will her stepsister. I will make sure of it.'

Stepmama sat down, rather suddenly. It was fortunate that she happened to be sideways on to Georgie's bedside chair as she'd squared up to Edmund, otherwise she would have ended on the floor.

'I will also make sure Sukey has a respectable dowry,' he said. 'As my stepsister by marriage, it will be my duty to provide for her.'

Stepmama's mouth opened and shut a few times. For which Georgie was immensely grateful. The volume of the bargaining—for that, she saw, was what had been going on between these two even if she hadn't fully understood the nuances—had been drilling holes in her skull.

'Edmund,' she whispered, since there was a lull into which she could at last interject her own opinion, 'you don't have to marry me.'

'Nonsense!'

'Of course I do,' said Edmund, and Stepmama, at the same moment. And as Stepmama got to her feet, Edmund nudged her aside and took her place on the chair.

'But there must be a way out,' said Georgie plaintively. She couldn't bear to think of Edmund trapped into a marriage he'd been so determined to avoid. Just because he'd come in here, in a spirit of friendship. Oh, he'd come up with a wonderful reason to explain his presence, and swiftly, but then he had a brilliant mind. Of course he was going to say the only thing that would make everything appear acceptable to everyone.

The only trouble was she knew it wasn't really acceptable to him.

'Don't be so stupid,' hissed Stepmama from over Edmund's shoulder. 'There is no keeping the two of you apart. There never has been and she should just have made the best of it. And then none of this would have happened.'

'None of what?' If Georgie hadn't already had a headache, this conversation would have been enough to give her one.

'Yes, Mrs Wickford,' said Edmund, taking hold of Georgie's hand again and patting it soothingly. 'Why don't you explain just how you came into it? I should love to hear how my mother persuaded you to do her dirty work.'

His mother?

'Come, come,' said Edmund firmly. 'There is no point in prevarication at this stage. I have worked out much of what has happened. All that has so far eluded me is your motive. Though your statement just now leads me to suppose it was to benefit your own daughter?'

Stepmama tossed her head again. 'I am a mother. A

mother will do whatever she can for her children. Even to the extent of—' She stopped. Glanced at Georgie. Flushed. 'Well, I am sorry, dear, but though I grew fond of your father by the end, you have to admit he was not exactly the stuff of a maiden's dreams.'

Georgie gasped. 'Do you mean to say, you married Papa to…that you were…put up to it?'

'Well, I'm sorry if you don't like it, but you have no notion of how hard it is, trying to maintain standards when you are a widow and your husband has left you with nothing but debts. I was at my wits' end when Lady Ashenden approached me with what sounded like a wonderful opportunity. A chance to give Sukey every advantage she should have had, what with her being so pretty. Her ladyship told me she knew of a widower, a man of substance, who had a daughter in dire need of feminine guidance. That she'd arrange a match between us and see Sukey had the chance to rise in the world.' She reached for a handkerchief to dab at her nose, which had grown pink with distress. 'Well, of course, I agreed on the spot. And married your father.'

Georgiana was suddenly aware she'd been clutching Edmund's hand so tightly his fingers were going white. She made a determined effort to relax her grip, even though it felt as though he was the only solid thing left in a world that was splintering apart.

'Had my mother,' he said, flexing his hand as his fingers flushed pink once more, 'by any chance, had a word with him, too?'

Stepmama nodded vigorously. 'At our first meeting, he told me that Lady Ashenden had felt obliged to warn him that his daughter was on the verge of creating a scandal that was entirely his own fault for bringing her up in such a lax manner. And that if he didn't do something soon, she—you—would become the talk of the county. Very upset, he was. Admitted he'd made a mull of things. Said he should have seen he needed a woman about the place to teach you how to go on,' she said, turning to Georgiana.

Lady Ashenden had told Papa he'd been a bad parent? When he'd been so utterly wonderful?

'Lady Ashenden had told him how well behaved Sukey was and what a good influence she'd be, just by living alongside of you. And said that if I'd brought up one girl so nicely, she was sure I could achieve the same with you. Well, he only had to meet Sukey the once to see the difference.'

When Edmund winced, she realised her grip on his hand had reached painful proportions once more. But her own pain was so great it was a wonder she wasn't howling.

'Begged me, he did, to steer you back to the straight and narrow. As well as explaining all…' she waved her hand at the bed in which Georgie lay '…this sort of thing.'

Now, *that* Georgie could understand. Her father would never have been able to cope with explaining what was happening to her body, when she started maturing. She'd always, instinctively, tried to keep all *this sort of thing* hidden from him.

'He said he hadn't the heart to discipline you for the faults you'd acquired, when he was the one who deserved a beating for not teaching you right from wrong.'

Georgie let go of Edmund's hand to press her hands to her own mouth to stifle a sob. Because she finally understood why Papa had seemed to suddenly turn against her. Knew what lay behind those looks he'd given her—as though he was disappointed in her. It hadn't been any such thing. It had been guilt. He had been trying to correct a fault for which he felt responsible…

No wonder he had turned away whenever Stepmama got out the cane. No wonder he had been unable to look her in the eye.

He hadn't been ashamed of her. Disappointed in her. He'd been ashamed of himself.

Edmund slid his arm round her shoulder as though he knew how hard she was struggling not to weep. She turned her face gratefully into his shoulder. For all these years, she'd thought first Edmund, and then her father, had turned against her. But it hadn't been the case at all.

It had all been Lady Ashenden's work.

'Why did she do it?' Once she'd regained control of herself, she lifted her face to Edmund's and looked beseechingly into his eyes. 'Why go to such lengths to make us hate each other?'

'She wanted to make sure the split was permanent.'

Georgie frowned, her confusion only growing. 'But…why?'

He sighed. 'She didn't want me to have to marry you.'

Her confusion only grew. 'Marry you? Then? But… we were children. Far too young to be thinking of marriage.'

'Juliet was only fourteen when she conceived her fatal passion for Romeo, I believe,' he said. 'When Mrs Bulstrode told her how she'd found us together, I dare say she thought you were more precocious than that hot-blooded Italian. And took steps to prevent me from succumbing to your charms.'

'My charms? Succumbing? You?'

'Well, I think that is quite enough of that,' said Stepmama, who had clearly regained control of her equilibrium. 'Put Lord Ashenden down, Georgie, there's a good girl,' she said firmly.

And because she was in the habit of obeying her stepmother, Georgie, who'd been clinging to him like a limpet, forced herself to do so.

'And now, my lord,' she said, going to the door and opening it, 'if you would care to take tea before you leave, while we discuss the legalities?'

It was framed as a question only out of deference to his rank. What Stepmama was really doing was ordering him out of her room.

'Leave? No, Edmund…' She reached for his hand. He couldn't leave, not as things were. It was all very well to have cleared up the misunderstandings that had blighted their childhood friendship, but if he left it like this, they would end up married. When it was the last thing he wanted.

But Edmund evaded her questing fingers and stood up. 'Your stepmother is correct. The mode of our betrothal has been unorthodox enough to cause gossip. I shall not subject you to more by doing anything likely to tarnish your reputation further.'

Unorthodox? What an understatement. If Stepmama hadn't blundered in, or if she hadn't set up such a screech that it had brought the servants running, there wouldn't *be* a betrothal.

But now that Edmund had pointed out the advantages such a marriage would mean for Sukey, Stepmama wouldn't rest until she'd seen the notice in the *Morning Post*.

'No, Edmund, there must be some other way to straighten out this mess.'

He turned to her, his face grim. 'You regard being betrothed to me in the light of a misfortune?'

'Of course it is!' He'd turned her down when she'd all but begged him to save her from having to come to London and go through a Season. Since then, he'd done all he could to teach her how to handle suitors, including getting her to itemise the things that would make some other man bearable as a husband.

Some *other* man.

'You know it is!'

He gave an elegant shrug of his shoulders. 'Nevertheless, we will marry. We have been caught in a compromising position and this is the only way to salvage your reputation, and ensure that Sukey's remains untarnished. You had better,' he said, striding to the door, 'accustom yourself.'

And with that Parthian shot, he stalked out, Stepmama hard on his heels.

Chapter Eighteen

Edmund waited until the notice of his forthcoming marriage to Miss Georgiana Wickford appeared in print before calling upon her again. He wasn't going to give her any opportunity to wriggle free now he'd got her hooked.

Besides which, it turned out that arranging a wedding at short notice required a great many hours of work.

However, he did want to speak to Georgie before the ceremony. He didn't want her walking up the aisle fearing he had the slightest reluctance to marry her. She had such an expressive face that every member of the congregation would wonder what was amiss. And would start inventing stories that bore no relation to the truth, but would be accepted as gospel simply because the inventor had attended the wedding.

It was a great pity, he mused as he mounted the front steps of her house, three days after he'd invaded her bedroom, that eloping was regarded as being scandalous behaviour. He'd much rather whisk Georgie away and marry her in private.

But on that point both his mother and her stepmother

were in accord. Nothing would do for either of them
but the biggest, most extravagant wedding that could be
arranged in the short time he'd agreed to wait to make
Georgie his wife.

'Good morning, my lord,' said Wiggins with an
avuncular smile as he opened the door. 'The ladies are
all in the drawing room this morning,' he continued,
taking Edmund's coat, hat, and gloves. 'I take it you do
not require my escort upstairs?' And then, to his astonishment, the fellow winked.

'No,' he said tersely. 'There is no need.' He might
have imagined it, but he could have sworn the fellow was chuckling as he sauntered off with Edmund's
things.

He mounted the stairs, cursing over-familiar servants
under his breath. And was still frowning when he entered the drawing room.

Georgie's stepmother and stepsister both leaped to
their feet and greeted him effusively. Predictably, Georgie sent him a troubled, guilty look before lowering her
gaze to a tangle of needlework that lay in her lap.

'I was hoping,' he said, once the initial hubbub occa-
sioned by his arrival had died down, 'that Miss Wickford would be well enough to take the air with me today.
I have—'

'Of course she is!' Mrs Wickford cut him short. 'Run
along and put on your coat and bonnet, dear,' she said
to Georgie, who rose to her feet with reluctance.

'I do hope you will not mind, my lord,' Mrs Wickford added, archly, as Georgie trailed to the door, 'but
Sukey and I will not be coming with you. We are expecting visitors we do not wish to offend by putting off.'

Georgie's face flushed.

'I am sure,' said her stepmother, when it looked as

though Georgie meant to voice some sort of objection, 'that there can be no impropriety in you driving in the park with your betrothed. You will have a groom and footman with you and will be in public view at all times.'

Mrs Wickford must have been looking out of the window and seen the carriage in which he'd driven up to be able to say that. Though she was correct. He'd borrowed his mother's barouche, again.

'No impropriety at all,' he said. Was impropriety even possible, in a barouche? 'I am glad you understand the necessity for us to appear in public as a betrothed couple, Mrs Wickford, now that the announcement has been made. We do not wish anyone to suspect there is anything irregular about our forthcoming union, do we?'

Georgie shot him an anguished look before, shoulders slumped in defeat, she went off to get ready for their outing.

He sank on to a sofa to wait for her, the inane chatter of her female relatives washing over him as he struggled to maintain an appearance of calm. Though his heart had plunged somewhere below the region of his boots at her hangdog expression. Or even lower perhaps. Downstairs somewhere. Possibly even in the servants' hall, if it was in that little area whose windows he'd spied when mounting the front steps. Anyway, wherever it had gone, the fact that his heart had done so was extremely annoying.

But then this was the way he'd been ever since managing to clinch the deal with Georgie's stepmother. Fluctuating wildly from one extreme to the other. One minute he'd be elated at the ease with which he'd managed to snatch her out from under the noses of all her other suitors. The next he'd be ashamed for resorting to such ruthless methods that had left her no choice. But then he'd remind himself that he'd saved her from a fate she'd been dreading. And now nobody would have the right to 'paw at her'.

Except him.

At which point he'd have a vision of a future in which they slept in separate beds. Or at least she would sleep. He would lie there thinking about her, down the corridor. In her nightgown. With her hair streaming across the pillows…

In fact, over the last few days he'd come to understand why some men drank so much they rendered themselves insensible. It was going to be unbearable having her yoked to him, passively, when he yearned for so much more.

And then the door opened once more and there she was, looking utterly captivating in the carriage dress she'd worn when he'd taken her to Bullock's Museum, the pink one with all the white fluffy trimming down the front and round the edges of the loose sleeves.

He rose to his feet automatically. Which was just as well. His brain seemed to be taking a holiday.

'You do have your parasol with you, Georgie, don't you?'

Mrs Wickford was fussing round Georgie, who was staring back at him across the room as though she, too, was in a daze.

'You must take more care to protect your complexion, what with the wedding taking place so soon and the sun deciding to shine today. And you will be in an open carriage, don't forget.'

Her lips compressed at the mention of the vehicle. And he suddenly wondered if he ought to have made time to go and buy himself a phaeton, so that he could have driven her himself.

His heart beat erratically as he led her downstairs and out on to the street as his mind frantically seized upon, and then rejected, excuse after excuse. But in the end, only honesty would suffice.

'I know,' he said, his cheeks heating as he handed her into the low-slung vehicle, 'that we are not exactly going to cut a dash, driving about in this carriage, but you have to admit it does make it easy to sit and converse. Which was my intention.'

Georgie gave him a quick frown as she took her seat and arranged her skirts. 'There is no need to apologise for being who you are. I know you have never wanted to *cut a dash*, as you put it. In fact, I would have thought you despised the kind of young men who thought of nothing else.'

His spirits sank. 'In short, you find yourself about to be shackled to a very dull dog.'

Her eyes widened in surprise. 'You are not dull. At least,' she amended, 'I have never found you so.'

'Thank you,' he said glumly, since he didn't believe her. For, after all, wasn't it his very dullness that had made her propose to him in the first place? If he only had ink running through his veins, rather than red-hot blood, then she didn't need to fear he would ravish her, did she?

'It has never bothered me before,' he said as they set off, 'what anyone thinks of me. But I do not want you to find me…lacking, in any way.' A sweat broke out on his upper lip when he realised he'd almost admitted that he didn't like the image she carried of him, or the hopes she cherished for a bloodless union, in which she probably saw him taking a kind of brotherly role.

Fortunately, he'd stopped himself in the nick of time. He must absolutely not alarm her by telling her exactly how hot his blood ran, sometimes, when his thoughts turned in her direction. Or his eyes did.

'Edmund?' She looked at him with concern. 'Surely you know that I would much rather you carry on being yourself than trying to ape the antics of any of those idiots who think they are *dashing*. Though, actually,' she said with a curl of contempt to her lips that made them look even more kissable than usual, 'dashing is a good word to describe them, for they do tend to go dashing about in their high-perch phaetons, don't they, terrifying innocent pedestrians and drivers of market carts? Or racing down to Brighton, to win a stupid wager. Or prancing about in the park on a showy piece of rubbish Papa would never have permitted in his stables. Or dressing themselves up like peacocks and strutting round with smug looks on their faces, expecting every female in the vicinity to swoon in admiration.' She was breathing rather fast by the time she'd finished unburdening herself of her view of the male of the species.

And he was feeling even more diminished than he had when he'd handed her into his mother's barouche.

'Yes,' he said in a hollow voice. 'I would regard acting in any such way as completely frivolous.'

'Exactly,' she said with an approving smile. 'You don't strew your conversation with fatuous, insincere compliments, either, about the lustrous sheen of my hair, or the sparkle in my eyes, without once taking your own gaze higher than my...' She made a gesture to the front of her coat.

What had she made, then, of the compliments he had paid her? How had she felt when he'd told her she looked magnificent in that gown which had been practically falling off her shoulders?

And hadn't he told her she had lovely hair and eyes himself? In Bullock's Museum? 'Would you prefer it if I didn't pay you any more compliments, then? I would not wish to make you…uncomfortable.'

She gave him a strange look, then turned her head to regard the shop windows that edged the street through which they were driving.

After a short pause during which he held his breath, she turned back to him. 'You would not make me uncomfortable, Edmund. Because I know you would never say anything you did not mean.'

'Never,' he vowed on a rush of exhaled breath.

She smiled at him. In a way that made his heart turn over, as well as making him long to crush her to his chest and kiss her in such a way that she would know exactly how dashing he could be.

'Because,' she continued, 'we are…friends again, aren't we?'

'Friends,' he echoed.

'Yes. I…I missed that. This. Very much when we… weren't. Having someone to talk to.'

'Talk to.' Well, that neatly summed up exactly what was wrong between them. While she was thinking of their marriage in terms of having a friend to talk to, he was longing to get his hands on her bare flesh. To sink into that bare flesh. Over and over and over.

'Yes. The only times that I haven't been utterly miserable, since I came to London, were the times I spent with you.'

'But we hardly had a polite word to say to one another.'

'I know.' She grinned up at him. 'You cannot imagine how wonderful it was to just…let go of all the etiquette and be myself.'

'Hmmm.' Well, that was something.

'And you always manage to make me see the funny side of things.'

So now he not only had ink running through his veins, but he was also some sort of clown?

Georgie certainly knew how to cut a man down to size.

'At least you appear to be reconciled to the notion of marrying me,' he said.

'Ye…es…'

'What is it?' He turned to study her pensive face, ignoring the lady who was hailing him from a landau bowling along in the opposite direction. Because if Georgie had any doubts, now was the time to quash them. 'Come now, Georgie, this was the whole point of bringing you out for a drive. So that we could talk to each other. We never had time, did we, before your stepmother burst in upon us, to settle things.'

'Well, no, and I'm sure you didn't want to settle things that way, did you? I mean, you had to tell her you were in the process of proposing. It was the only thing to say, wasn't it? But, um…'

He seized her hand. At last, she'd given him the opening he needed to explain what he'd been planning. 'Georgie, you cannot imagine I came up to your room with any other motive except to propose?'

'What? But—'

'Your stepmother did not coerce me into making a proposal. I simply decided—' He drew in a short, sharp breath. She'd just made it clear, yet again, what she wanted from marriage. He couldn't scare her by telling her that her vision of marriage sounded to him like a form of torture. That he didn't want to be just her friend, he wanted to be her lover.

'I decided I had to make amends,' he temporised. 'For the way I let you down, when you needed me to get you out of having to endure a Season at all. It didn't take me long to see that your suitors were all making you wretched. That you would be even more miserable if you had to marry any one of them. And I couldn't bear watching you suffer a moment longer.'

'So, you decided to…mount a rescue?'

'Exactly so.' She still looked confused, so he hastened to explain, 'I had meant to tell you, at some stage, that should you not find a suitable husband by the end of the Season, that I would agree to enter into the kind of marriage you proposed to me. That day. Your stepmother's intervention has just brought that, um, event forward.' He patted her hand.

'But—'

'I promised I would always be your friend. And what sort of a friend would I be if I were to stand back and watch you embark on a life of misery?'

'I…I d-don't know,' she said, looking stunned.

'By then, as well, I had pretty much worked out what happened when I was sent away to St Mary's. I could see that you were still the same person, basically, as you had always been. Loyal and loving. You could not have broken your word to a lonely boy, sent so far away from home.'

'No. I didn't,' she said indignantly. 'And I don't think Stepmama realised just how dreadful it must have been for you. She explained it to me, the other night. The Countess stressed, you see, that she had to turn me into a proper lady. And gave her a whole list of errors into which I'd fallen. She dropped the fact that I should learn that it wasn't appropriate for a girl to write secretly to a gentleman into the list.'

'But...my tutor...'

'Oh, I'm sure he prevented our letters reaching each other at first. Stepmama was a second line of defence. If you had ever managed to smuggle a letter past your guard dog, then she would have intercepted it at the other end.'

'She is nothing if not efficient.'

'Which brings me to something I really wanted to ask you about.'

'What is it?'

'Your mother's reaction to the discovery that she has not been able to keep us apart, after all. She must be furious to learn that all her plans came to nothing in the end. Is she? Very angry?' Georgie shook her head, making the feathers on her bonnet bob wildly. 'Of course she's angry. She must be livid.'

'Not as angry as you might suppose. At least, not by the time I finished with her.'

'Oh, Edmund,' she said, her face lighting up. 'What did you do? What did you say?'

It did something to soothe his wounded sensitivity that she looked up at him with complete trust that he had, in fact, done something.

'I simply pointed out to her that I was finally doing what she had been urging me to do ever since I came down from Oxford. She has not ceased to remind me of my duty to ensure the continuance of the line. She wastes no opportunity to thrust some eligible female or other under my nose.'

'Yes, I can understand that she wishes you to marry somebody. But not me. I mean, else why would she go to all that trouble to separate us?'

'Ah,' he said, removing his spectacles and reaching for a handkerchief as he considered how best to word the next part of his confession. 'It turns out,' he said, polishing his lenses with painstaking care, 'that her worries on that score were more in the nature of us creating a scandal due to our, or at least your, extreme youth. She did not, in short, want the family name tarnished by an illegitimate child, conceived when you would have been far too young for anyone to credit you knew what you were doing.'

'What? She really thought that you could…'

He could see her waving her arms about. Fortunately, without his spectacles, he was unable to see the look of disgust on her face. For disgust she must surely feel, at discovering that people had suspected his feelings for her, back then, had been far from pure.

He cleared his throat. 'I have convinced her that you will make me a suitable wife. She has agreed to vacate the London house, and Fontenay Court, and base herself in the dower house.'

'Oh, but I couldn't turn her out of her own home. She will hate me!'

'Georgie, it is well past time my mother stepped down from the role she has played virtually all my life. This is the perfect opportunity for me to take the reins from her grasping fingers, without her losing face. An opportunity I have sought for some time. I need you to stand with me in this. Staunchly.'

'Well, if you say so, Edmund, then of course I will do so, only…'

He replaced his spectacles to see her chewing on her lower lip. 'Out with it. What is troubling you?'

'Well, only that I haven't been brought up to run a household, the way she has done. Stepmama has taught me how to behave like a lady, as far as she is able, but she isn't a…a lady of Quality, is she?' Her cheeks flushed prettily. 'And obviously, she has no experience herself of the way things are done in grand houses, so—'

'To quote you a little earlier, all you have to be is yourself. Although—' his mind worked swiftly '—I believe it may help my mother to accept her diminished role if you were to ask her advice, from time to time.'

'Would she give it? I mean, I've always thought she hated me.'

'She may have, possibly, hated your being the catalyst that forced her to send me away,' he conceded. 'But…' he cleared his throat, which suddenly felt very tight as he launched an oblique approach to the most awkward issue that lay between them '…she is now of the opinion that, actually, you are a practical choice for me, in at least one respect. You are so full of energy, as a rule, that she is convinced your health will go a long way to counteracting the lack of vigour she claims has dogged the last two generations of earls. She foresees you presenting her with half-a-dozen healthy grandsons.'

'How silly of her.'

He flinched. 'Yes, but—' He was about to explain that he had been trying to spare Georgiana any unpleasantness by not telling his mother that their marriage was to be in name only. In that way, when no children appeared, she would blame him for being unable to father them. His shoulders were broad enough to take the blame.

But while he was collating the appropriate words to explain this, Georgiana had half-turned to him, her eyes sparkling with indignation.

'No, Edmund. It simply isn't true, is it? I mean, when you were a boy, you never had any ailments that every other child in the village didn't have, did you? And… you were never as ill as the rumours would have it, either. When I got in to see you, I was always surprised that you weren't at death's door, after what I'd heard. I never saw you delirious with fever, or gasping for breath, or anything like that.'

He blinked. For some reason she now saw him as being full of health and vigour, of being capable of siring half a dozen sons, did she? When she wasn't prepared to give him the opportunity to do so? When, to begin with, she'd practically accused him of not being a Real Man at all.

'Which is why I put it the way I did.'

'Put what how?'

'When I mentioned the lack of vigour she *claims* has dogged the last two generations of earls.'

'Well, your father certainly wasn't lacking in vigour, either, was he?'

Either? So it was true. She did see him differently, now.

Was that a good thing, or another obstacle he'd have to overcome?

'My father,' he said drily, since he couldn't very well speak about the questions she was raising in his mind, 'as you seem to be aware, simply preferred being vigorous in any woman's bed but my mother's. Which contributed to her almost obsessive devotion to my health.'

'A case of having all her eggs in one basket?'

'Very perceptively put.' But then Georgie always was quick on the uptake. 'I also discovered, recently, that my father had been urging her to send me to school. I always assumed he took no interest in my welfare, but now I wonder if the reason he made no objection to my eventual removal from Fontenay Court was that he saw my exile to a more moderate climate as a chance for me to escape her…smothering, and experience something more regular, for a youth of my age.'

'But…surely, as your father, it was his right to decide whether you should go to school, or not?'

'Ah.' He wished he hadn't already polished his spectacles now. He had nothing to do with his hands. 'As I said, I always assumed he took no interest in my welfare. However, it turns out that my parents struck a sort of bargain. Which was, in short, that so long as I lived, he would leave her alone. She in turn would make no attempt to interfere with his hedonistic lifestyle.'

'Golly,' she said, her hold on her parasol slackening to the extent that it almost went overboard. She rescued it just before it struck a horseman heading in the opposite direction. Turned in her seat to make her apologies as the gentleman in question brought his startled mount back under control.

'It cost her dearly, to send me away,' he said, once Georgie was paying attention again. 'For all her faults, I truly believe she was attempting to do her best. For my health. And for your reputation. She was so afraid I was going to turn out like my father. I look so very like him, you see…'

'Oh, Edmund, no! You are nothing like that.' She reached out and took his hand. If only they hadn't been in an open carriage, bowling along in a public park, he'd have seized it and carried it to his lips.

'The point is,' he forced himself to say instead, 'you need have no fear of her reception. When next you meet, she will greet you with open arms. So to speak. The only thing is…'

'Yes? What?' She clutched his hand a little tighter.

'She may well speak to you in terms of…bringing new blood to the line. She is still more than a little obsessed with the lineage. Which is why I thought it only fair to warn you. Because I do not want you to think that *I* regard you in the light of a—'

'A brood mare?'

'Exactly. I mean, nothing of the kind! Georgie, I am not going to demand my conjugal rights immediately, you need have no fear of that.'

She removed her hand from his and placed it, curled up, in her lap. 'No,' she said in a small, defeated voice. 'I don't fear that.'

Though, for once, he wasn't at all convinced she was telling the truth.

Chapter Nineteen

Georgie's spirits, which had just started to revive, took a steep dive. Poor Edmund. In spite of all the things he'd just said, he couldn't really want to marry her, or he wouldn't have said that about not demanding his conjugal rights, when she knew how much he wanted children.

He was just being kind. Trying to make her feel better about a situation they couldn't escape. He'd even had what sounded like an excruciatingly difficult conversation with his mother, in order to clear the air and make things easier for her.

She sighed. She wished she could be as stoical as him, that she could just accept that there was no getting out of the marriage, not now Edmund had put that notice in the paper. Though if only she'd been able to see him before he'd done that, she might have…

Actually, no, to be honest, there had never been any stopping it. Not once Stepmama had discovered him in her bedroom.

Oh, but he was being so noble about it. Even going so far as to declaring that it was what he wanted.

When she knew full well it wasn't.

He cleared his throat.

'Is something troubling you?'

Oh, so many things. But she couldn't burden him with any of them, not when he was trying so hard to make the best of things. So she shook her head.

'Then I shall take you home,' he said and gave the order to his driver.

'Actually,' she said, as the carriage rolled inexorably closer to the exit at Cumberland Gate, 'there is just one thing I wanted to say. Something I should have said at once, only I was too…' She waved her free hand in a vague manner to indicate the complexity of what she'd been feeling the day he'd invaded her room.

'What is it?'

She took a deep breath. 'I wanted to thank you for giving me back Papa. Oh, that didn't sound right. I wish I was more eloquent. But, to be honest, that is what it has felt like.'

'How so?'

'Well, when he married again and handed me over to Stepmama so entirely, it felt as if he'd washed his hands of me. I thought I must have displeased him in some way for him to want me to change so much. Or that he loved his new wife more than he loved me. It was…awful. Just awful.'

Edmund's hand found hers and gripped it, though he never took his eyes from her face.

'But now, now that you've dug into all that happened, I know that it wasn't like that at all. He only married Stepmama because he thought it was best for me. He did it because he thought *he'd* failed *me*, not the other way round. Knowing that he never stopped loving me, the way he had when I was little is…'

Once again words failed her.

'I am glad that I have been able to undo some of the damage done to us back then,' he said gruffly, then studied their hands, linked in her lap. 'That time of our lives has blighted everything that has happened since. For me, at least. It has been as though how I was made to feel, then, kept on seething through my whole being, no matter how hard I tried to prevent it. It was as pointless as attempting to prevent mist rising from the river, first thing in the morning. Sometimes, when the sun is hot, it obscures everything else from view. That mist is all you can see. You feel totally alone in it. Even when it isn't there, you know the slightest little thing will set tendrils unfurling and wreathing themselves round the landscape.'

'Oh, Edmund, that is so beautifully put. And so exactly right, too.'

He nodded curtly and said no more. Not that it was possible, once the carriage got out into the bustling streets. Not that she could very well have put what she was feeling into words. She ought to be feeling far happier that Edmund was content to offer her exactly the kind of marriage she'd asked of him in the first place. But her first reaction had not been joy. It had been... dismay. Because ever since he'd taken her to Bullock's Museum and he'd given her that talk about caterpillars growing into butterflies, she'd wanted him to kiss her. She wanted to have his children, too, even if it meant doing what Liza and Wilkins had been doing to each other in the stables.

Each other? Oh. Yes, now that she came to think of it, Liza had been running her hands up and down the groom's back, and even, briefly, squeezing that revoltingly hairy bottom. As though she was urging him on.

Why had she never recalled that aspect of it before?

Because she'd been remembering it through the eyes of a child, that was why. All tinged with her memories of betrayal, and her body maturing, and Liza's tears, and the groom's indifference, and the unfairness of it all.

She shut her eyes and tried to recall the event without prejudice. Without recalling the subsequent events which had made the whole scene so very sordid and unsettling. Without the…the *mist* that Edmund had spoken of obscuring everything.

But for some reason, instead of seeing Liza flat on her back in the straw, with her legs spread, she pictured herself in that position. With Edmund on top of her. With no breeches on. Her eyes flew open in shock at the funny illicit sort of thrill that speared through her.

And then they were home and she was inviting him to come in and take tea. Which he declined to do. And she was trying not to reveal her disappointment. After all, he'd already given a huge portion of his day over to soothing her fears and attempting to make her believe he was perfectly happy to marry her, when he must have a hundred more important things to do.

She sighed as she tugged off her gloves and began to trudge upstairs. Poor Edmund. Marrying her because he felt as though he had to make amends…what rot! Edmund had nothing to make amends for. Though if he felt he did, that would explain why he'd been so good to her, well, to them all, actually, ever since he'd run across them in London.

She sighed again as she dragged off her bonnet, letting it dangle haphazardly from her fingers. How could their marriage be a happy one when it was all obligation on one side and a thwarted, stunted sort of love on the other?

'What is the matter?' Sukey was in their dressing

room, where Georgiana had gone to put her bonnet and pelisse away. 'Didn't you enjoy your outing?' Sukey pulled a face. 'Silly thing to say. How could you? Lord Ashenden must have bored you silly.'

'Indeed he did not,' replied Georgiana indignantly.

Sukey shrugged. 'If you say so.'

'I do,' said Georgie, taking down the hatbox in which her bonnet was to reside.

'Well then, why do you look so glum?'

Georgiana sighed again. One of the plumes on her bonnet was looking distinctly bedraggled. She'd have to pull it out and replace it before she could wear this hat again. Why was it always *her* clothes that fell apart like that when Sukey's never needed anything more than laundering?

'It's just that…well, you know, the way this betrothal came about.' She shoved the hat in its box. Perhaps she need not confess that, yet again, one of her outfits was in need of repair. With any luck Stepmama would be too busy buying new bridal clothes to bother very much about her old ones.

'I cannot help worrying that marrying me isn't what he really wants.' She shut the lid and put the box back on the shelf.

Sukey grinned. 'Oh, is that all? Georgiana, you goose! He must have known what would happen if he got caught up here. And yet he still came up. So he must have been prepared to take the risk.'

'Yes, that's what he said, but that still isn't the same as actually deciding he wanted to marry me and proposing in the regular way, is it?' She dropped on to a stool by the full-length mirror.

Sukey made a dismissive motion with her hand. 'Who cares what he thought, or why he acted how he did? You are going to be a countess. And I'm going to have a whopping great dowry. Which means clothes galore!' She whisked off her shawl and twirled round with it over her head, almost knocking the candlesticks from the mantel.

'There's more to life than clothes,' said Georgie, flinching out of the way as one corner of Sukey's shawl whizzed past her nose.

'Such as?' Sukey stopped twirling and draped the shawl over her head, letting it droop over her eyes like a veil.

'Such as being a good wife,' said Georgiana wistfully.

'I don't know why you are worrying about that. It's easy.'

'Is it?'

'Oh, yes,' said Sukey blithely, settling the shawl round her shoulders with an effortless flick and a shrug. 'Mama says all you have to do is ask your husband, at the outset, what he wants of a wife and then pretend you are trying to be that.'

Georgie rested her chin on her fist. 'He's already told me what he wants. He wants children. Heirs,' she said despondently as she cast her mind back to the reason he'd refused her proposal in the first place. 'But—'

Sukey shuddered. 'Oh. I see what you mean. You are picturing having to *do your duty* in the bedroom. With *him.*'

'I don't know why you should pull a face like that. I am sure it won't be...' She struggled to find a suitable word.

'Nasty,' supplied Sukey.

'No. It most definitely won't be nasty.'

'How can you tell?'

Because of Liza and Wilkins. It had been a miracle for her to have imagined that scene in the stable without shuddering. For her to have experienced a shaft of wicked excitement when she'd replaced herself and Edmund in those positions told her a lot.

Not that she could admit as much to Sukey.

'Well, because whenever most men take my hand, or even look at me in a certain way, I feel…contaminated,' she finished on a shudder. 'But when Edmund does so, it is quite the opposite. I get a sort of fluttery feeling, here.' She pressed her hand to her stomach. 'And when he kissed me—'

Sukey shrieked. 'He kissed you? When?' She dropped to the floor at Georgiana's feet.

'When he came to my room,' she said. And paused, reliving the wonderful moment when he'd leaned forward and pressed his lips to her forehead.

'What was it like?'

A warm tingle swirled through her middle as she recalled how close his face had been to hers. She'd been able to smell his soap and his clothes, and his skin. She'd wanted to turn to him and press her lips against that smoothly shaven cheek.

'It was lovely, actually. It made me want to—' Her lips had actually parted, now she came to think of it. If Stepmama had not burst in she might very well have kissed him back.

'Yes?' Sukey leaned forward eagerly.

'Well, it made me feel…' She shrugged her shoulders. 'I cannot describe it. It has just made me realise—' although not until this afternoon '—that nothing he does, no way he could touch me, could ever possibly disgust me. Not even…the ultimate intimacy.'

'There, you see? Did not Mama tell you that it was

all a question of finding the right man? Now you have found him, you feel differently, don't you? Oh, it is all going to be wonderful. I am so happy for you.'

'No, it isn't,' she said. 'Edmund wants…or rather, he doesn't want…or doesn't seem in any hurry to—' She broke off, blushing, and started fiddling with the trimming on her sleeve.

Now it was Sukey's turn to gasp.

'Did he actually tell you that? Today?'

Georgiana nodded.

'Why do you think that could be? Do you think—? No, there isn't anything wrong with him. He's had several mistresses, hasn't he?'

'Yes. But none of them have looked anything like me, have they? Not according to gossip. They've all been dainty, extremely feminine little things. I'm just not his type, Sukey. And…well—' She broke off in consternation as a big chunk of tulle came away in her agitated fingers. At which point Sukey urged her to her feet and began undoing the buttons.

'See? I'm not feminine, or graceful,' she moaned as Sukey pulled off the damaged pelisse and strode across the room to hang it up. 'I'm not pretty, or clever. I don't have a title. Or a dowry. The only thing I could give him is an heir and, if he isn't even interested in me in that way…'

'You really do want to be a proper wife to him, don't you?'

'Yes. And if I can't make him…you know,' she said, with a blush. 'I'm afraid he might go on taking mistresses. And that would kill me, Sukey. I can't bear to think I'm so lacking that he would need to take his pleasure elsewhere.' Especially as it would be her own fault. She'd told him she couldn't face that aspect of matrimony.

'He won't.'

'How can you say that? Oh. It's because you are trying to make me feel better, aren't you?'

'No,' said Sukey, taking both her hands and giving them a squeeze. 'Georgie, are you blind? You are the one in whose bedroom he was found. You are the one he has followed into routs and balls he generally avoids like the plague. You are the one he introduced to his friends and their wives, and their sisters. And it was on your account that he set everyone in a bustle by knocking Mr Eastman down. Which could only have been because he was jealous.'

'Jealous? Edmund?' No, she couldn't believe it. She could see him being protective. He'd seen how uncomfortable Mr Eastman had made her and correctly guessed it was because he'd made a lewd proposition.

Or perhaps he'd seen her clenching her fists and had decided to knock the man down before she could do so herself and ruin herself for ever in the eyes of society.

'Oh, it's so romantic,' Sukey chirped. 'Everyone says so. In fact, the only person who is surprised you are getting married seems to be you.' Sukey giggled. 'Come on, Georgiana, don't dwell on all your imperfections. Just enjoy the prospect of marrying an earl and becoming a countess. I do not know of any other girl who wouldn't be crowing in triumph at achieving such a coup! For there have been dozens of women who have tried with Lord Ashenden and failed, you know. The rumour is that he hasn't even noticed them, not even when they've practically flung themselves at his feet.'

'Well, no, he wouldn't, not if he was thinking of something else.' Like the discovery of a new species of moth, for example, or some other advance in the field of the natural sciences. 'But, how do you know all this?'

'Oh, Lotty and Dotty can find out just about anything that goes on in society, now that their cousin has married Lord Havelock. And everyone is convinced he is in love with you.'

'In love with me?' She shook her head. 'He just feels an obligation to me, that's all. He told me so.'

'Hmm…' Sukey pondered for a moment. And then her face lit up. 'He might say that. But actions speak louder than words. And he has behaved like a man who is head over heels in love.'

'Has he?'

'Yes. So even if you do feel as if you've bagged him in an underhanded way—'

'I didn't bag him at all!'

'But you have definitely triumphed where many prettier, richer, better-bred girls have failed. Doesn't that tell you something?'

'Only that he couldn't see anything improper about coming to my room. Because he doesn't think of me as particularly female at all. If anything, he probably still thinks of me in a kind of brotherly way.' With his vision blinkered by that mist of past perceptions he'd mentioned. 'Or as the rather grubby little playmate who dogged his every footstep,' she finished glumly.

'And you want him to see you as a woman.'

'Well, of course I do!'

Because he was the right man for her.

'Well, then, all you have to do is show him you are not his childhood playmate. Show him you are a woman now.'

'But how?'

'Goodness, Georgie, I should have thought that was

obvious,' said Sukey, gesturing to the front of her gown. 'You don't get more womanly than those.'

Georgiana blushed. Was Sukey suggesting she...? Her mind skittered away from what she thought Sukey might be suggesting. Surely only...*trollops* bared themselves to a man in order to...*entice* him. And she didn't want Edmund to think she was like that. To disgust him. Because then she might even lose the friendship which was all he seemed willing to offer her. And she would have nothing left.

Not even her self-respect.

Oh, lord. What was she to do?

She didn't know.

She was too busy over the next few days to come up with an answer, what with fittings for gowns and expeditions to purchase accessories, and lists to make, not to mention feeding and entertaining all the people who suddenly crowded their drawing room when they were at home.

And on the few occasions she saw Edmund, Stepmama made sure they were never alone, so that she couldn't have broached the topic with him, even if she had known what to say. Besides which, whenever he did walk into the drawing room, everyone else would fade away and she would feel all dreamy. And she'd look at his mouth and wonder what it would feel like if he ever kissed her properly. Or his hands, and imagine them stroking her arms, or even cupping her breasts. And she'd go hot all over and have to avert her gaze, and could only stammer a stilted reply when he spoke.

And he would study her with concern, or remove his spectacles and polish them for far longer than necessary.

And she would shrink. Because she just couldn't see how it was ever going to work between them.

Then she was walking into church, on the arm of Lord Havelock, who'd agreed to give her away. And then she was promising to love, honour and obey Edmund. Then they were walking out of the church, into a dazzlingly bright day, and his mother was standing before her with a determined smile on her face.

'Welcome to the family,' she said, leaning forward as though she was about to kiss her cheek and missing it by several inches. 'You do my son credit in that gown. It is lovely. Quite lovely.'

Since Stepmama was responsible for the choice of her gown, the compliment managed to avoid saying anything to credit Georgie for anything at all. Still, at least his mother had given the appearance of approving of her son's choice of wife, which was more than she'd expected.

There was the wedding breakfast, with a witty speech from Lord Havelock about Edmund's propensity for making lists and planning everything down to the last detail, then being surprised when love got hold of him by the scruff of the neck and made him throw all his lists out of the window. Which everyone else thought hilarious, but only made her more conscious of her unsuitability to become his wife.

But she *was* his wife. They were toasting the bride, which was her. And then she was standing at the doorway, bidding her guests farewell. And he was handing her over to a tall, thin woman who he said was his housekeeper, who was going to show her to her room, and bidding her goodnight.

And she couldn't breathe properly.

For how could she tell him that she *did* want to consummate their marriage right away, without sounding like a…*trollop*?

Why didn't she have the skills to…to indicate to him, somehow, that she wanted to be his wife, right now?

She'd wager Sukey wouldn't have problems like this on her wedding night. She would instinctively know how to arouse and inflame her husband until he had reached a state where he'd dismiss all the servants and drag her off somewhere private, not send her off to her bedroom while he strolled off to his own.

But she'd spent so long disliking her body that she now had no idea how to wield it the way a normal, natural woman would. Because of being called a trollop, and fearing that she might actually be one, she'd ruthlessly suppressed all that side of her nature, so that now she actually wanted to give it free rein, she had no idea where to start.

How did a bride seduce a reluctant groom on their wedding night? Without losing all her self-respect? For that was what would happen if she were to leave her bedroom and go searching this massive mansion for his.

So she allowed Mavis—the maid who was waiting for her in the sumptuous and enormous room allotted to her—to prepare her for bed. And resigned herself to spending her wedding night alone.

But a few minutes after she'd climbed into her richly decorated, lavender-scented tester bed, and the maid had departed with her wedding finery draped over her arm, there was a knock on the door.

Her heart leaped. She clutched the sheet to her chest, in sheer surprise. Could that be Edmund?

'Come in,' she said, in a voice that sounded, to her own ears, full of all the insecurities that had been bubbling up inside her all day. Longer. Ever since they'd become betrothed. No, longer than that. Ever since Papa had married Stepmama and they'd made her believe she was a failure as a female.

It was Edmund.

He was still fully dressed.

And he was frowning.

'Is something amiss?' He was looking at the way she was clutching the sheet to her chest. 'I have already told you, you need not fear that I will pounce on you and demand my marital rights. I only came in to—'

'But that's just it,' she cut in. Because she was never going to get a better chance to tell him how she felt than the one he'd just handed her.

'I would *like* you to pounce,' she said, flinging the sheet aside and scrambling out of bed. 'I mean, not pounce, exactly. But for you to…start…um…'

'Georgie, you don't need to say that,' he said, going to her dressing table, and setting down the large box he was carrying. 'I could see how nervous you were all day. And if it is a case of wanting to get it over with, then—'

'No! I am not nervous. Well, that isn't completely true. I am terribly nervous. But not frightened any longer. Or…revolted by the idea of…' She glanced in the direction of the bed.

He noticed that sideways glance and frowned.

'Georgie, I only came in here to bring you a…a small wedding gift.'

Her heart sank.

Because it wasn't her feelings about…*it* that were the issue here, was it? It was his. And he definitely didn't look the least bit like an eager bridegroom.

It was all very well Sukey suggesting she tempt him

with her…best assets. But he'd never given any indication he was the slightest bit impressed by them. While other men had addressed all their remarks to the front of her gown, Edmund had nearly always looked her straight in the eye.

As he was doing now. With a touch of impatience as he fiddled with the handle on the walnut box he'd just put down.

As though he wanted to get the gift-giving over with and retreat to the safety of his own room.

'Oh, I see,' she said, as calmly as she could, considering it felt as though her courage was leaking out of her like water through a sieve. 'Well, thank you then.'

If Edmund really didn't want her, the way a groom should want a bride, then somehow she would just have to learn to live with it.

And learning to deal with the kind of marriage he wanted might as well start right now.

She crossed the room to where he was still fiddling with the handle of the walnut box, a rather forbidding expression on his face.

'May I open it now?'

'Of course. In fact, I particularly wanted to be here when you opened it,' he said, taking a step back as she reached out a hand to remove the lid.

'It occurred to me,' he said, 'that if we'd had a conventional courtship, I would have given you many gifts already. So this, my first one to you, had to be extra special. But remember, Georgie,' he said, putting out his hand to stop her just as she was about to remove the lid, 'that I'm a man of science, not some damn fop.'

She looked up into his face, startled by the defensive note she could hear in his voice.

'My first wedding gift to you is…at least, some people may consider it a touch…' He frowned down at the box. 'Actually, a lot of people would say it was downright eccentric. But not you.' He glanced down at her, a hint of uncertainty in his eyes.

'I'm sure I won't,' she said, sensing that whatever he was about to give her was not only a gift, but also a test of some sort. A test she was determined to pass.

Chapter Twenty

'May I see?'

'Oh. Yes, of course,' he said and pulled his hand away.

Really intrigued now, by his uncharacteristic display of uncertainty, she finally pulled off the lid and peeped inside.

Inside the sleek walnut case was a glass box with a wooden lid, filled with what looked like a selection of leafy twigs. Only when she peered really closely did she see that there were also about a dozen different sorts of caterpillars, wriggling about amongst the foliage. Some of them were really ugly-looking things. At least, a lot of people would find them so. Especially if their groom handed them a box full on their wedding night rather than a diamond necklace, say, or a book of poetry. But Edmund was setting so much store by it that she knew it had to have a special message.

Not that she had to think for long before seeing exactly what it was.

'Are they going to end up the same as all the varieties of butterflies I brought you, that last day we had together, before you were sent away?'

The tension he'd been carrying across his shoulders eased at once.

'That's right. All the ones I could find, that is. This one,' he said, pointing to a pale green grub with black spots, 'is going to become a large white butterfly. The little brown ones feeding on the hops will become commas and these black ones, amongst the nettles, will become, believe it or not, peacocks.'

Their heads were so close together as they examined the box of caterpillars that she could feel the warmth of his breath on her cheek. Which made her feel warm all the way down to her toes. Until she remembered that he didn't seem to feel the same way.

'This is really…sweet of you,' she managed to say, though her voice wavered. 'It would have been well-nigh impossible for you to find the butterflies, in London, at this time of year, so you couldn't give me back, exactly, what I gave you, as a boy. But you are saying that you want me to look upon you as a friend. A friend who will always come to my side, no matter how hard it might be, or what obstacles you have to climb.'

'That's it,' he said, in approval. 'We were good friends when we were children, weren't we? And I see no reason why we cannot base our marriage on friendship. And caring. And mutual respect. I know you only proposed to me at the start because you were scared of leaving Bartlesham, but now we are married you can go back there as often as you like. And stay as long as you like. Fontenay Court is your home now. You need never fear someone will take it from you. You are safe now you are married to me. Secure.'

A great depression seized her. Because he was giving her everything she'd asked him for when she proposed. Oh, how stupid had she been that day at the stream?

'But more than that, I hope you will be happy, too. And to that end, I will fill the stable with horses for you. Actually, I've already started negotiations to buy Whitesocks back for you.'

'Oh, thank you,' she whispered through the lump in her throat. At one time, hearing she was about to be reunited with Whitesocks would have filled her with untrammelled joy. But not any longer.

'It's nothing.' He cleared his throat. 'Furthermore, I will never put pressure on you to join me in London, if you don't wish to come. You don't seem to care for all the social frippery that most women come here for and I'm quite sure you wouldn't want to attend lectures or dissections with me. Well…' he gave a hollow laugh '…what wife would?'

'But, when I proposed, you said you didn't want that kind of marriage,' she pointed out.

'I said that because…largely because…that was the kind of marriage my parents had. My father with his life and my mother with hers. But I have realised that we don't need to be like them. Because I will respect you and treat you with courtesy. You won't be staying at Fontenay Court because you are too embarrassed by my behaviour to face the gossip, but simply because you prefer life in the country. When I come down to Bartlesham, or you come up to London, it won't be to have furious arguments, but because we actually want to spend time together.'

He smiled at her then and regarded her expectantly. 'Well?'

She thought for a bit. And could only draw one conclusion.

'You have decided you want to keep on having mistresses, then. And you don't want me…at all!'

'Not want you? Are you mad?' He checked himself. 'That is, of course I find you very attractive, but I know how you feel about that sort of thing and I care for you too much to distress you by—'

She came to the end of her tether. 'What rot!'

'What?'

'Rot,' she repeated. 'If you cared for me at all, you would want to…' She waved her hand in the vague direction of the bed, since she wasn't too sure of the correct term to describe what a man and woman did there.

'It is *because* I care for you that I won't—'

'Don't give me that,' she said, tears welling in her eyes. 'All your mistresses have been tiny, wispy little blonde women. Practically the opposite of me in every way.'

'Well, doesn't that tell you something?'

'Yes,' she sniffed. 'It tells me that I am not your type.'

'That is not it at all,' he said irritably. 'It is…' He took a pace away from her and ran his fingers through his hair. Turned back to her, a rather sheepish expression on his face. 'When I first began to…um…experiment with that particular pastime—' he rolled his eyes bedwards '—I deliberately avoided involvement with females who could remind me, in any way, of you.'

'And why, pray,' she said sarcastically, 'could that possibly be?'

'Because there is nothing more pathetic,' he blurted out, 'than a man who selects his bed partners because they remind him of the one woman he cannot have.'

'Oh.' The world rocked. At least that was what it felt like. As though the very floorboards under her feet were shifting and settling into a different pattern. His admission that the women he'd selected for his liaisons did not truly reflect a preference for dainty blondes sounded such a typically Edmundish thing for him to do, in order to prevent anyone knowing how he really felt, that it gave her hope for the first time in days. 'You mean...'

'Yes. Forgive me, Georgie, but even that day you brought me the butterflies, my feelings for you were not completely brotherly.' He swallowed and lowered his head. 'My mother could see it, even before I had acknowledged the way my feelings for you were changing, myself.'

'Oh,' she said again. 'You mean, you *do* want me?'

'I've *always* wanted you. Even during those days when I thought I hated you, it infuriated me to see how very beautiful I still found you.'

'Oh.'

'But you need not worry that I shall behave like Major Gowan, or his ilk. I can control myself...'

'But perhaps I don't want you to.'

'What? No.' He shook his head. 'You don't need to say that...'

'I know I don't. You have made it very clear that should I wish it, we can live out the remainder of our lives like...like a brother and sister. But, Edmund, I don't wish it.'

'You don't?' An expression that could have been the precursor to panic flitted across his face. But this time, she didn't let it stop her. She was going to be utterly miserable in the kind of marriage she'd asked for, the kind that Edmund was so determined to give her. And if she didn't speak up now, before they set out, then how far along that road would they go before she got another chance to get him to change direction?

'No. Because I am not a caterpillar any longer.'

'Caterpillar?'

'I meant to say, a child,' she said, just barely suppressing the urge to stamp her foot at her lack of eloquence. 'When I proposed to you, I was still thinking like a…well, not like a grown woman. But when you spoke to me about caterpillars not being able to imagine being butterflies, or what it would be like to fly, it really struck a chord. I need more, to be blunt, than a roof over my head, and someone to keep me company. I need…I need…' She ran out of words. Until inspiration suddenly supplied the perfect one.

'I need love, Edmund. Not the love a boy and a girl can feel for each other. But real, adult love.'

He flinched. Shook his head.

'That is the one thing I cannot give you.'

'You…cannot love me?' The ground beneath her feet shifted yet again. 'But…from the way you were talking, I thought…' She reached out blindly for something on which to sit as her legs almost gave way. And found herself landing on the dressing-table stool.

'Georgie, I'm sorry.' He knelt at her feet, and took her hands between his. 'I am just not capable of it. I… after I thought you betrayed me, I…made myself hard. Swore I would never give anyone the power to hurt me like that again. I…am no longer capable of that sort of sentiment.'

'So why did you hit Mr Eastman then, if it wasn't in a fit of jealousy?'

He frowned. As though confused.

'And why did you go to all those balls, and d-dance with me?' A single tear finally broke free and slid down her cheek. 'And cut out other men? And drag me into the refreshment room? And sneak up to my room?'

'Don't cry, Georgie,' he said, aghast as a second tear slid from her other eye and ran down her face. 'I cannot bear to think I have made you cry. On our wedding night, too, when I thought my offer would make you so happy.'

'It isn't your fault. You can't help not being able to l-love me. I'm just not very l-lovable.' She hiccuped.

'Of course you are lovable. In fact—' a wild look came to his eye '—Havelock and Chepstow told me I loved you. They said my actions bore all the hallmarks of a man in love, but I—'

All of a sudden he got to his feet and began pacing back and forth. 'Do you think it is possible that…that they could be right?'

She held her breath.

'I couldn't bear the thought of any other man touching you,' he muttered, pacing away from her. 'Or making you unhappy,' he said, pacing back. 'Or making you happy, either.' He ran his fingers through his hair. 'It was seeing Armitage outside your house and wondering if he might be able to persuade you that he could that made me determined to get you to listen to a proposal from me. And then, when I thought you might actually be dying, I panicked. That was why I came up to your room, Georgie, because I panicked.' He whirled round on the spot, to stare down at her with a touch of belligerence in his stance.

'The thought of never seeing you again, of never being able to tell you about the letters, was so dreadful that suddenly, enduring only half a marriage, if that was all you were capable of giving me, was as nothing. Do you think…am I describing the actions of a man in love?'

He looked so distressed at the prospect that Georgie's heart went out to him. What good was it demanding words he wasn't sure he could define with absolute precision, when his actions described his true feelings so very much better?

'It sounds as if you might be,' she said. 'But,' she added, getting to her feet, 'never mind that, for now.' Because when a caterpillar emerged from its cocoon it was bound to be a bit confused by the discovery it had wings. And Edmund had confessed to having wrapped a hard, defensive shell round his heart a very long time ago. And just as a newly emerging butterfly needed the warmth of the sun to be able to unfurl its wings, so Edmund needed the right conditions to be able to start trusting in his feelings for her.

'I...' She took a deep breath and a step towards him. 'I love you, Edmund. I always have, I think. First I loved you as a grubby little girl. And then our love for each other seemed to die, when they tried to separate us. We both went through a stage of...being in a sort of cocoon. We had to wrap ourselves up in pride, and denial, to survive. But now we are emerging into something new. Something I think could be wonderful, for us both, if only we can find the courage...'

And with that, she reached for the ribbon at her throat, which tied her nightgown closed. And tugged at it, defiantly.

His breath hitched in his throat as her nightgown parted. But he kept his eyes glued very firmly to hers. 'You do not need to do this, Georgie.'

'I want to do this,' she countered, undoing a second ribbon tie.

Edmund clenched his fists. 'Georgie, if you undo any more of your gown—'

She undid another ribbon.

His breathing grew ragged. 'I'm just a man, dammit. With the same base needs as fellows like Major

Gowan.' He took a step back. 'I'm sorry. I couldn't bear it if I repulsed you, the way he does, which was why I swore, my dearest, dearest friend, that I would never do anything you don't like.'

'You could never repulse me, Edmund,' she said, staying exactly where she was. She wanted to follow after him, but her legs were shaking so much she wasn't sure if she could. 'It is true that I couldn't face…love with any other man. But you aren't any other man. You are…' She shrugged. 'Edmund. My Edmund.'

He looked as though he was trembling slightly as well. Which was a comfort because standing here, with her nightgown open, practically daring him to look at her partially exposed breasts, was just about the hardest, scariest thing she'd ever done.

'If anyone can help get me over this hurdle, it is you. I realise that I'm going to need a lot of help. More than most women, probably. Because I have no idea what to do. I am aware that I am painfully lacking as a woman, on account of avoiding the issue of…attraction between the sexes, all these years. And I know you deserve someone better than me. But I don't think you will ever find anyone who wants to try harder to please you. I…I really do want to be the best wife I can be. If only you will tell me what to do, and show me how to do it, I swear—'

'Georgie, no,' he said. 'You don't need to do anything but be yourself. And you don't need to strive to please me. You do please me.'

'Do I?'

'Very much.'

'Well, then, why are you still over there then, when I have…' She gestured to the front of her open nightgown.

'Because I would rather die than give you a disgust

of me. I know you find all…this sort of thing a bit repulsive—'

'With any other man, I would. And when I said all those things to you, I meant them. But…you bringing me these caterpillars has opened my eyes to certain things.'

'Has it?'

'Yes, Edmund. It's time I learned to be a proper woman. I don't want to stay stuck in this state of…' She shook her head. 'Being in a female body but not being at home in it, if you know what I mean? Always at war with what I am. It's…it's miserable, Edmund.'

'I don't want you to be miserable.'

'Then teach me how to be a butterfly,' she said, spreading her arms wide. 'I need to spread my wings to the sun. To your love, Edmund.'

'I need…' he gasped '…I need…oh, God,' he groaned and closed the distance between them, wrapping his arms tightly round her and burying his face in her neck.

And then he let go, rather abruptly, and stepped back.

'You have bared yourself to me,' he said, shrugging off his jacket with a very determined look on his face. 'It is only fair that I do the same.' He ripped off his neckcloth and tugged off his shirt.

'There,' he said, stepping close to her again. Within touching distance.

And she so wanted to touch. Because his chest was so beautiful. So powerful-looking. So she reached out and swept her palm over the sculpted surface, her fingers lingering in the fine dusting of hair in the centre.

He sucked in a sharp, shocked-sounding breath. But when she instinctively snatched her hand back, he took hold of it and placed it back over his heart. And then stood perfectly still as she explored him, though he shuddered when she stroked down along the line of hair that led directly to the buttons that held his breeches closed.

And grabbed her hand before it got there.

'No more of that, for now.'

'Was it wrong?' She'd thought he'd been encouraging her to explore him. 'Shouldn't I have done that?'

'No, it wasn't wrong. And I am glad you did it. Glad you don't find my body repulsive, or frightening.'

'Nothing about you is repulsive or frightening. Because it is all you, Edmund.'

He swallowed. And his eyes glistened. Then slowly, almost tentatively, he reached out and slid his hand inside the gaping front of her nightgown.

And now it was her turn to gasp, as he began to stroke and then fondle her. It felt so good that she half-closed her eyes with the pleasure of it. At which point he stopped gazing directly into her eyes and stared, as though transfixed, at his long, supple fingers curling round her breast.

They were both breathing raggedly now. She could have stayed like this, with one of his arms round her waist, his free hand caressing her, for ever.

But then he lowered his head and began to place tiny, gentle kisses on the upper slope of her breasts. And for some reason she took hold of his head, spearing her fingers into his hair as though urging him on.

And it was all the encouragement he needed. He suckled her and squeezed her, and even nipped at her with his teeth for several utterly blissful moments. Until she groaned with the sheer pleasure of the feelings that were flooding her.

He glanced up. 'Are you sure about this?'

'Yes, yes,' she responded, halfway between a whimper and a plea.

He swept her up into his arms and carried her over to the bed, where he laid her down gently. Stood back and just looked at her for a moment or two.

'I don't think I have ever seen a more beautiful sight,' he said thickly. 'You, Georgie, lying there, waiting for me. Wanting me.' He knelt on the bed beside her. Took her left hand, upon which she wore his ring, and kissed her knuckles, one by one. And then her wrist and then the skin of her inner forearm.

'So soft,' he breathed against her skin, sending hot shivers racing through her veins.

He knelt down on the floor by the bed, and, still keeping hold of her hand, leaned forward to kiss the toes that were peeping out from under the hem of her nightgown, on top of the counterpane.

'Your feet are so dainty,' he said and kissed one ankle. Pushed her nightgown a little higher up her leg. 'You have such shapely legs,' he breathed, smoothing his hand over her calf as he gazed at it. And he bared her knees. Kissed one, then pushed her legs slightly apart so that he could kiss the inside of the other. His mouth felt so hot. His hair so soft as it brushed her inner thigh.

'You are not so soft here,' he said, looking up at her with a grin as his hands slid up the outside of her thighs. 'You have strong muscles from all your horse riding.'

He got up off the floor, to sit next to her on the bed again.

'Is that…a bad thing?'

'No. It is a good thing.'

So why had he stopped touching her legs, just when she'd started to feel as though she could let him touch her *there?* No, more than that, when she'd started *wanting* him to touch her there?

'You know,' he said, reaching out to part her nightgown that last little bit, 'that I find these as intriguing as any other man does, don't you?' He looked an enquiry at her as he slowly pushed the fabric down and away from her shoulders. As though giving her the chance to object.

'But they are not all you see when you look at me, are they, Edmund?'

He smiled at her. 'No. They are only a part of you. A very beautiful part, but not all that I...' His breath hitched. He darted her a troubled glance.

So she reached out and took his hand, and carried it to her heart. And as he began to caress her again, she sighed with pleasure as warm feelings whooshed to that place between her legs she'd been expecting him to touch before, making her feel as if she was melting from the inside.

'How does that feel?'

'I don't know how to explain it,' she panted. 'But my heart is hammering so fast you must be able to feel it.'

'Yes, I can feel it.'

Oh, and so could she.

'How would you feel if I were to explore a little further?'

I'd probably explode with excitement, was what she wanted to say. But all that came out of her mouth was an indeterminate little mew. But he must have understood her, because he gave a low, throaty chuckle, then lowered his head so that he could kiss her there. Gentle, butterfly kisses at first, and then, when she began to gasp at the pleasure of it, deeper kisses. Kisses that tugged at the flesh.

When he grew bolder, nibbling at her nipples and licking them, she moaned and drove her fingers into his hair.

'Oh, my goodness, Edmund,' she panted, 'I never dreamed I could feel like this.'

'How do you feel?'

He wanted her to put it into words? Of course he did. This was Edmund.

'Hot. Alive. Expectant. As if this is only the beginning.'

'It is only the beginning. You are going to break free from the cocoon in which circumstances and your own fears have bound you. And fly.'

Edmund stood up and, with an expertise that impressed her immensely, removed her nightdress and gently encouraged her to lie back on the bed, easing her arms and legs wide, as though she really was a butterfly, spreading its wings to the sun.

She closed her eyes, embarrassed at being spread out before him like that. Utterly naked. And rather shocked by how excited she felt, too.

There was a rustling noise and the sound of clothing landing on the floor. Which meant that Edmund was naked, too.

The mattress dipped and she could feel that he was, because he was kneeling between her legs, and it was hair-roughened flesh, not fabric brushing her skin.

She felt him crouch over her, then he was kissing her breasts again. And then her belly. And then, shockingly, lower. Right where she'd wanted him to touch her before. Only she'd never imagined him fastening his mouth there.

He started stroking at her breasts after a while, though he kept on kissing her between her legs. Kneading at them. Weaving a new cocoon, this one spun out of hazy sensuality. She found she couldn't keep still. It was as if her limbs had developed minds of their own. She discovered that she wasn't a failure as a woman after all. The moment she stopped trying to rein it back, her body knew exactly what to do. With the right man. As his lips caressed,and his teeth nibbled, and his tongue delved and his hands caressed, she started actually writhing under him. And her heart was pounding faster and faster, as though she was galloping flat out to some unseen destination. Then something happened that was like diving into the lake at Fontenay Court on a hot summer's day, only more so. Something that both soothed her, yet brought her to a boiling point, all at the same time. In her confusion, and helplessness, she cried out, clutching at his hair.

'I'm sorry,' she panted, as soon as she could. 'Did I hurt you?'

He gave a bark of laughter. 'Did *you* hurt *me*? The question is usually asked by the groom, not the bride.'

'I beg your pardon. I didn't know. I don't know how I'm supposed to feel or what to say.'

'You are doing splendidly,' he said, sliding up her body and dropping a kiss on the tip of her nose. 'Better than I could ever have hoped. You really let go, just then, didn't you?'

'I couldn't help it. You are…' She stroked his shoulder, letting her fingers trail down the beautifully sculpted contours of his upper arm. 'You make me feel…'

He made a sound that could only be described as a growl. 'I fear this next bit might actually hurt you. But after, directly after, I will make you feel what you just felt, all over again, I promise.'

He gazed into her eyes as though waiting for her response.

'I know you will, Edmund. I trust you. You are a man of your word.'

He made that strange growly sound again, then came over her, pushing her legs apart with his own and spearing into her.

There was the slightest stinging sensation, but then a wonderful feeling of togetherness replaced it and all coherent thinking ceased. She let her body do as it wanted. It writhed. Her hands swept up and down the intriguing muscles in Edmund's back, as they bunched and flexed. She pressed kisses to his shoulder and neck, and opened her mouth wide when his own kisses became blatantly intrusive.

And it was all wonderful. Especially the fact that he was clearly enjoying taking possession of her. When he cried out and shuddered over and into her, she clasped him tightly and a huge wave of emotion so powerful surged through her that tears began rolling down her cheeks.

He suddenly reared back.

'Georgie! Did I hurt you?'

'No,' she gulped. 'It w-was l-lovely.'

'Then why are you crying?'

'I d-don't know. Maybe it is b-because I have b-been so silly for so long. K-keeping all my feelings b-bottled up.'

'It was perfectly understandable,' he said gently. He propped himself up on his elbows, his hands cupping her cheeks. 'Your father let you run wild until my mother stepped in and told him he'd been negligent. And then he married a woman who tried to turn you into something you could never be. It's no wonder you became…discouraged. Confused. That you even began to…to despise your very self.'

'Yes. Yes, that is just what I did. Because no matter how hard I tried, I was really, really useless at being a girl.'

'No. No, you are not useless. You never have been. You are a good woman, who will be a wonderful mother.'

'What? Me? How can you think that?'

'Because you were the only one in Bartlesham to have compassion on a lonely, socially inept boy. And the courage to visit him when nobody else spared him a second thought. That is the kind of mother I want for my children. A woman who will go through fire and flood—or climb a tree and break through locked windows—to make sure that child is properly cared for. Who won't care about convention, or worry what people might say or think. You will be the most splendid, fiercely protective, nurturing mother there has ever been.'

'Edmund,' she whispered in amazement. 'You almost make me believe it.'

'You should believe it. And believe this, too,' he said sternly. 'You will be the most perfect wife for me, while we are waiting for those children to arrive. You won't…' he toyed with a curl of her hair '…you won't really leave me in London and stay down at Fontenay Court, now you know I won't be having any mistresses, will you?'

He said it like a plea.

'Not if you don't want me to.'

'I *don't* want you to.'

'Edmund, I've already told you I will be whatever kind of wife you want me to be.'

Something flared in his eyes. 'I want you to stand

at my side. To support me as loyally as you did when we were children. When I am in London, I want you here with me. Even if you cannot stomach attending the lectures I wish to attend, I want to come home to you every night. I want you here in my bed.'

She didn't point out that, technically, this was her bed. Because he wouldn't have made such an error if he'd been in a rational frame of mind. Which meant that what he was saying came from his heart.

'I want,' he said, 'to wake up with you every morning.'

'Oh, I would love that, too' she said and heaved a sigh of utter contentment. 'It sounds perfect.'

'Even though I haven't said that I love you?'

'Yes, you have,' she said, looping his arms round his neck.

'What? When?'

'When you chose to have half a marriage, rather than see another man take care of me. When you gave up the hope of having those heirs you told me are so important to you. When you knocked Mr Eastman down. When you…' She half-smiled at the frown forming between his brows. 'When you came storming down to our stream, determined to put me in my place.'

'I was vile to you that day. How can you regard that as a proof that I love you?'

'Because if you didn't love me, you wouldn't have been so angry. You would have been able to ignore my note, and my presence in the village, or in London, with scarcely more than a raised eyebrow. Instead of which…'

'I couldn't leave you alone. Couldn't bear the thought of any other man doing…this,' he said, flexing his hips.

Which set off a delightful ripple that went all the way up her spine and made her flex right back.

And then he kissed her. Hungrily. And something flared between them that meant there was no more talking for quite some time.

After that interlude, Edmund rolled to her side, where they lay, hand in hand, breathless.

'I feel ridiculously happy,' he said, once he'd got his breath back. 'If only I'd admitted sooner how I feel about you, and wooed you properly, we could have been together ages ago. Neither of us needed to go through any of the agony we've endured…'

She rolled to her side and lay one finger over his lips.

'Don't forget the caterpillars, Edmund.'

'The what?'

'You know full well they have to go through a stage of…what is it called? When they are in their cocoon or they will never become butterflies. If you had just stayed in Bartlesham and nobody had tried to part us…'

He rolled on to his side to face her. 'I would have been content to let you trot after me, like a shadow. I would have taken you completely for granted. Had we drifted into marriage I would never have appreciated the treasure that you are. But we *were* forced to part. And our friendship seemed to die. And when I saw you again, after the years I spent on St. Mary's, the emotions I felt were all violent. I boiled with hatred, and hurt, and yearning. Nothing tepid, unformed and spineless like the feelings I'd had for you as a youth, that I would have continued having for you as a man.'

'Yes, Edmund. That time in our lives, terrible though it was to live through, will only make our future richer.

Because we have glimpsed what life would be like without the other in it.'

He shuddered. 'Hellish. Cold. Lonely.'

She cupped his cheek with her hand.

'You are right, you know,' he added, looking deep into her eyes. 'I do love you.'

'I know,' she said. And smiled.

Because she finally believed it.

* * * * *

*If you enjoyed this story, you won't want to miss these
other great reads from Annie Burrows*

*PORTRAIT OF A SCANDAL
LORD HAVELOCK'S LIST
A MISTRESS FOR MAJOR BARTLETT
THE CAPTAIN'S CHRISTMAS BRIDE
IN BED WITH THE DUKE*

*And make sure you look for
Annie Burrows's short story*
'CINDERELLA'S PERFECT CHRISTMAS'
in our
ONCE UPON A REGENCY CHRISTMAS
anthology!

Name	(PLEASE PRINT)	
Address		Apt. #
City	State/Prov.	Zip/Postal Code

Signature (if under 18, a parent or guardian must sign)

Mail to the **Reader Service:**

IN U.S.A.: P.O. Box 1867, Buffalo, NY. 14240-1867
IN CANADA: P.O. Box 609, Fort Erie, Ontario L2A 5X3

Get 2 Free Books,
Plus 2 Free Gifts—
just for trying the Reader Service!

❖HARLEQUIN®
Western Romance

Get 2 Free Books,
Plus 2 Free Gifts—

just for trying the Reader Service!

Get 2 Free Books,
Plus 2 Free Gifts—
just for trying the Reader Service!

Get 2 Free Books,
Plus 2 Free Gifts —
just for trying the Reader Service!

HARLEQUIN
ROMANTIC suspense